PRAISE FOR *BLOOD SONG*

'A truly European thriller … Assured telling of a complex story'
Sunday Times Crime Club

'I don't think there's a crime writer who writes with such
intelligence, darkness and deep sadness as Johana Gustawsson. This
was extraordinary' Louise Beech

'This book has managed to fascinate and haunt my head in equal
measure, it is a truly magnificent book' The Quiet Knitter

'Johana Gustawsson wields a seriously eloquent pen, she creates an
acutely vivid picture while tackling the most difficult of subjects
with a beautiful balance … *Blood Song* caught and has held on to
my thoughts; it is clever, provocative, and a seriously good read'
LoveReading

'It's this unpredictability that makes *Blood Song* so good … an
intricate plot and a mind-boggling ending' Crime Fiction Lover

'A gripping plot, moments of heartbreak, vivid scenes, and
characters that will remain with you long after you've reached the
final pages' The Book Review Café

'A well-plotted, intelligent thriller … tragic and heartbreaking – a
book of love, loss and hope, and a book to make you cry and make
you think' Off-the-Shelf Books

'A sobering book all round but an excellently told story' Blue Book
Balloon

'Sharp writing, the unfolding of a gripping plot, dark subjects
dealt with with care and attention yet never shying away from the
horrific truth' The Book Trail

'A beautiful but haunting tale that has its roots firmly embedded in the truth. The author writes with such intensity that she paints a picture that will forever be captured in your heart and in your mind' Chapter in My Life

'Dark and twisted – a brilliantly complex plot that has twists and turns throughout' Have Books Will Read

'It's difficult to explain how such a grotesque plot line can be so beautifully written. The author has a delicate touch with words, and then, out of nowhere, her writing becomes darker and vicious as she brings the horrific scenes to the reader' Random Things through My Letterbox

BY THE SAME AUTHOR

Block 46
Keeper

ABOUT THE AUTHOR

Born in Marseille, France, and with a degree in Political Science, Johana Gustawsson has worked as a journalist for the French and Spanish press and television. Her critically acclaimed Roy & Castells series, including *Block 46*, *Keeper* and *Blood Song*, has won the Plume d'Argent, Balai de la découverte, Balai d'Or and Prix Marseillais du Polar awards, and is now published in twenty countries. A TV adaptation is currently under way in a French, Swedish and UK co-production. Johana lives in London with her Swedish husband and their three sons.

Follow Johana on Twitter *@JoGustawsson* and Facebook, *www.facebook.com/johana.gustawsson*.

ABOUT THE TRANSLATOR

David Warriner translates from French and nurtures a healthy passion for Franco, Nordic and British crime fiction. Growing up in deepest Yorkshire, he developed incurable Francophilia at an early age. Emerging from Oxford with a modern languages degree, he narrowly escaped the graduate rat race by hopping on a plane to Canada – and never looked back. More than a decade into a high-powered commercial translation career, he listened to his heart and turned his hand again to the delicate art of literary translation. He translated Roxanne Bouchard's *We Were the Salt of the Sea* for Orenda Books. David has lived in France and Quebec, and now calls beautiful British Columbia home.

Follow David on Twitter *@givemeawave* and on his website: *wtranslation.ca*.

BLOOD SONG

A Roy & Castells Thriller

JOHANA GUSTAWSSON

translated by David Warriner

**ORENDA
BOOKS**

Orenda Books
16 Carson Road
West Dulwich
London SE21 8HU
www.orendabooks.co.uk

This edition published by Orenda Books, 2019
Published in French as *Sång* by Bragelonne, 2019
Copyright © Johana Gustawsson, 2019
English language translation copyright © David Warriner, 2019

A catalogue record for this book is available from the British Library.

ISBN 978-1-912374-81-6
eISBN 978-1-912374-82-3

Typeset in Garamond by MacGuru Ltd
Printed and bound by CPI Group (UK) Ltd, Croydon CRO 4YY

For sales and distribution, please contact *info@orendabooks.co.uk*

For Elsa,
My little sister, my kindred spirit.

'Is the sea beautiful?'

'Yes, it is very beautiful.'

'That's what people who have seen it say. I would
like it to be true – that it's very beautiful.'

'Why?'

'Because my sons lie in the sea.'

—Dulce Chacón, *The Sleeping Voice*.
Quotation translated by Johana Gustawsson.

Author's Note

PARTS OF THE BOOK you are about to read take place in Spain, during the Civil War and under the Franco regime.

During the Spanish Civil War, Republicans and Nationalists battled for nearly three years. The Nationalists, led by General Francisco Franco, emerged victorious in 1939. Franco went on to tyrannise Spain for thirty-six years, until his death in 1975.

Every dictatorship brings its share of atrocities. The Franco regime was no exception and under it Spain suffered one of Europe's highest death tolls of the twentieth century, second only to Germany. Here are some numbers that may convey some sense of the sheer scale of Franco's repression:

- During the Spanish Civil War, between 1936 and 1939, 150,000 people were executed by Franco's army – not counting the many more who died in combat.
- From 1939 to 1940, Franco's regime imprisoned close to a million people.
- More than 500,000 prisoners of war were deported to around 200 concentration camps.
- 300,000 women and men were incarcerated in prisons that were only made to hold 20,000 inmates.
- In March 1939, nearly 500,000 people fled Spain and crossed the border into France.
- Between 1944 and 1954, more than 30,000 children disappeared without a trace.

- After Franco's death, some 800 mass graves were discovered all around Spain, containing the remains of an estimated 40,000 to 60,000 people who had been arbitrarily executed.

During the same era, Vichy France and Fascist Italy, respectively, imprisoned 60,000 and 15,000 people. For Franco, war was just the first stage in what he – with the Spanish Catholic Church's blessing – saw as a crusade: the complete eradication of undesirable 'Reds' from the country. These included Communists, freemasons, socialists and Republicans – in other words, anyone who did not share the dictator's ideology. Hence, even the slightest word uttered against the regime or the state, against the Church, the police or the army, would be considered a personal insult to *El Caudillo* and constitute grounds for immediate arrest.

As an assertion of his power, Franco perpetuated the state of war he had declared in 1936 for twelve years, only lifting it in 1948. For these twelve years he imposed on the people of Spain his state of terror, barbarity, killing, moral repression, Church-sanctioned morality, media censorship and obscurantism. Once his people were enslaved by fear and the Republicans were silenced, Franco used the Church to maintain his grip on the country.

While the victims of execution, deportation and imprisonment were mainly men, women were certainly not spared. If they did not fall victim themselves to arbitrary execution for simply adhering to the Republican ideology, or because they were close to a 'Red' loyalist, the killing or imprisonment of their husbands would leave many women socially isolated or struggling in extreme poverty. It is practically impossible to determine exactly how many women were imprisoned for political reasons. The Franco regime did not confer this label on women: as such, their prisons were filled with prostitutes and delinquents. However, according to numbers from Spain's national institute of statistics, in 1942 there were 7,275 female political prisoners.

Madrid's Las Ventas prison alone housed close to 11,000 women between 1939 and the end of the Second World War in 1945. It was designed to hold 500 inmates. Those who were mothers were allowed to keep their children until they turned three years old. However, many did not live to that age due to overpopulation, famine, lack of care and hygiene and disease. Meanwhile, their mothers often vegetated for years in these death camps, living in fear that they might be hauled before the firing squad at any time.

The nature of the conflict was what made this dark time in Spain's past particularly terrifying. This intense and bloody episode of Spanish history saw some of the worst human atrocities imaginable: one people with two political ideologies opposing one another, first with arms, before the 'victors' subjected the 'victims' to their fierce repression – giving thousands of torturers and executioners the power of life or death over strangers, neighbours, friends, fathers and brothers.

The acts of violence depicted in the historical chapters of this novel were inspired by actual events that have been recognised and confirmed. While these acts are certainly cruel and some may find the images hard to stomach, there has been some softening to spare sensitive readers the most brutal details and avoid these pages sinking too deeply into the misery of those times.

Although the characters who live and die in these pages are the figment of my writerly imagination, the experiences they endure are rooted in the terrible truth of a dark, dark chapter in Spanish history.

—Johana Gustawsson, *2019*

KERSTIN WISHED SHE COULD have stopped the hands of time ticking. Cling on for just a few more seconds, so she could hold back the monster. Hide it. Tame it, somehow. But she had no longer had a choice. It had been now or never. So she had taken Göran by the hand, thrown open the gates of hell and released her inner demons.

Now Göran was asleep, face down in the well of his pillow. None of the words exchanged after their dinner had stopped sleep from coming and his anger had ebbed away into the night. Set free from the day and numbed by fatigue, his whole body now rested soundly, in childlike surrender.

Kerstin took off her dressing gown and slipped into bed beside him. Placing a hand on her husband's greying chest, she kissed his shoulder, where it curved to meet his armpit, the sweet spot where she loved to lay her head. She wished she could slide her thigh across Göran's legs and quiver at the touch of the soft hairs and hard muscles. She longed to hold him until the grief fought its way to the surface and flooded over her. She was waiting for the tears to come. For them to trickle timidly, one held-back drip at a time, then suddenly well into a raging torrent that would sweep her away. She wanted to cough up all the sadness caught in her throat and spit it out. Feel the panic set in as she struggled to breathe. She wanted the sorrow to sweep her away. She wanted to drown in it.

Kerstin shivered and pulled the duvet up to her shoulders. She hated this never-ending darkness. Some days, the sun seemed to never rise at all, and only snow would break up the clouds. Without it the moon could never part the heavy blanket of the night. Their bedroom was above the living room, overlooking the sea. Every night, Kerstin savoured the moment when she would lie in bed, gazing out at the water. But the sea was never more resplendent than when it shimmered in the summertime. Now, on the cusp of winter, it shivered with goosebumps as the wind whipped the surface into whitecaps. Perhaps the snow wasn't far away, after all.

Earlier, as Kerstin had stepped out of the shower, Göran had asked her to sleep in the guest room; nowhere near him. He had then taken the cushions off the bed, folded the fur throw and placed them all on the chaise longue with the same calm, calculated movements as every other night, but this time avoiding her gaze. Kerstin had left the bedroom in her dressing gown, her damp hair dripping splotches onto the floorboards. She had closed the door behind her and waited as obediently as a dog told to sit outside. With her nose pressed to the door frame she had listened to the silence, and waited for stillness, before opening the door again and getting into bed beside her husband. She didn't know how to sleep any other way.

Suddenly, she felt a weight descend on her lower abdomen, as if a heavy rock were crushing her pelvis. That was where all her repressed anger tended to build up. According to her acupuncturist, it was a boundary thing – something to do with how she related to others. Whatever. Although perhaps there was some truth to that. She had to admit, she hadn't really known whether she'd been coming or going that evening. Kerstin massaged her belly in a circular motion, pressing with the tips of her fingers to smooth the edge off the pain.

The mattress heaved as Göran stirred and turned onto his side, staring out to sea, at anything but his wife. Kerstin reached for her husband's hand, intertwining their fingers, pressing her moist palm to his. Trying to catch his eye. She wanted to draw him closer, put in words what had happened. But Göran twisted out of her embrace as if she were a stranger he couldn't bear to be around. He threw off the duvet, sprang out of bed and left the room.

Kerstin opened her mouth and drew a deep breath of air; the atmosphere in their bedroom was stifling. Fire flared in her chest, and flames of rage and desperation licked their way up her throat. She clamped her hands over her mouth and screamed. Creases ravaged her face, but the tears never came, only dry sobs. Always the same arid anguish. Except this time, she warmed to it, snuggling up to it as if it were Göran's arms and she were finding solace in his embrace, taking refuge in his shadow. She let the grief wash over her.

Suddenly, hands grabbed her ankles, yanking her naked body off the bed. Her head cracked against the floorboards, and the pain felt like it was crushing her skull, shooting all the way down to her fingertips. She clawed desperately at the floorboards, but only succeeded in tearing her nails to shreds.

The panic felt like it was tearing her chest apart. As the blows pummelled her body from left to right, all she could do was stare wide-eyed at the ceiling as the searing pain gave way to sheer terror, which paralysed her lungs and her throat.

Louise, Louise, Louise, Louise.

Her sleeping daughter in the bedroom down the hall.

JENNIFER MARSDEN'S FATHER had contacted the police at eight that night. Detective Chief Superintendent Jack Pearce's first reflex was to turn to Emily Roy. The profiler had interviewed the girl's parents, then her grandparents, who lived a few doors down the street, before moving on to the neighbours.

Emily looked to Aliénor Lindbergh for the go-ahead. Aliénor nodded. Emily rang the bell and retreated a few steps.

The door was opened almost right away by a thirty-something woman bundled up in a dressing gown, black hair pulled into a messy bun on top of her head.

'Martine Partridge?'

The young woman scratched at her cheek with blue false nails. 'Yeah…'

Aliénor registered Emily's smile. Took a mental picture of it. Tight-lipped, mouth turned up at the corners. Narrowed eyes, too.

'I'm Emily Roy. I work with the Metropolitan Police. This is my colleague, Aliénor Lindbergh.'

The woman looked down her nose at Aliénor, giving her the once-over. 'You recruitin' in primary schools these days then, are yer? This about young Jennifer, innit?'

Emily squinted at her. 'Sorry to bother you so late, Martine,' she continued. 'Is it all right if I call you Martine?'

'I prefer Marty.'

'Marty.'

'What's 'er name again – your colleague I mean? I didn't catch it.'

'Her name's Aliénor.'

'Alien-or? Well that don't exactly 'elp a girl get ahead in life, does it! They must've 'ad a field day wiv you at school, innit?'

Emily frowned.

Aliénor bit her tongue. That was the hardest thing, really: knowing when to say something and when to keep her mouth shut, even when the other person was expecting a reply. So much behaviour to decode all the time. To understand and integrate. A whole other language to learn.

'That's not from 'round 'ere, is it? *Alien-or,*' Marty went on. 'Where's that from, then?'

Emily gave a discreet nod.

Aliénor replicated Emily's smile: mouth turned up at the corners, narrowed eyes. 'It's French,' she said, trying not to let her smile falter.

'French? *Ooh la la!* You don't have a French accent, though. I'd never 'ave pegged you as a frog.'

'I'm not French; I'm Swedish.'

'Swedish? Why make fings easy, I s'pose…'

'When was the last time you saw Jennifer, Marty?' Emily interjected.

'This morning. She walks past 'ere to catch the 182 on 'er way to the 'igh school.' Marty slowly opened and closed her eyes like a lizard lazing in the sun.

Emily let the silence percolate between them for a moment. 'Would you mind if we continued our conversation inside?' she suddenly ventured.

Marty's eyes zeroed in on her sharp nails. She traced an index finger around the edges. 'Jones … My Jones needs 'is rest…'

'Jones? Is he your husband, Marty?'

'Yes,' she whispered, as if suddenly afraid she would wake him up.

'I'll be careful,' Emily replied, striding forwards.

Marty had no choice but to step aside and let her pass.

The profiler made her way through to the kitchen and took a

seat at the small, square table. The dirty dishes from what looked like dinner had not been cleared away. Marty stood on the other side of the table, as if she were waiting to be told what to do. Emily motioned for her to sit down.

Aliénor was still standing in the doorway, watching Marty fidget with the belt of her dressing gown.

'You didn't see her come home again this afternoon?' Emily prompted.

'What?'

'Jennifer. You didn't see her coming home from school this afternoon?'

'No.'

'Do you know the Marsden family well, Marty?'

'Not really … Just as a neighbour, y'know,' she replied, with shifty eyes.

'Jennifer never stopped in here on her way home from school, for a chat?'

The corners of Marty's mouth turned downwards. She smoothed her dressing gown with the back of her hand. 'Do you really fink I'd let a tramp like that set foot in 'ere? In my 'ouse? Under my bleedin' roof?'

Emily gave Aliénor a subtle glance. 'Do you mean Jennifer, Marty?' she replied, as Aliénor disappeared down the hallway.

'Yeah, Jen … Miss Marsden, yeah,' she spat, with a pout of disgust.

'Marty, could we have a word with Jones?'

The young woman shook her head like a stubborn child.

'Why not, Marty?'

'I don't want you to see 'im like that,' she replied, twisting the belt of her dressing gown around her index finger.

'What do you mean, *like that*?'

'The way 'e is … naked … not a stitch on 'im…'

'That's not a big deal, Marty. We can cover him up. So no one sees him.'

'Yeah … I s'pose…' Marty tilted her head to one side.

'Your colleague … I don't want 'er to come upstairs wiv us.'

'No, don't worry, Marty. We'll go upstairs just the two of us. My colleague will stay down here. Is that all right, Marty?'

'Yeah, 's all right … I s'pose that's all right.'

Two armed police officers suddenly burst into the kitchen, barking orders. Marty looked up at them in a daze. Then she did what she was told and got on her knees and lay face down on the kitchen floor with her arms and legs spread apart.

Emily went upstairs to join the two other officers, who were waiting for her in the bathroom doorway. There were half a dozen overturned candles wallowing in red puddles on the bathroom floor. A man was lying in the bathtub, his body immersed in the bloody water, right arm hanging over the side, head slumped over his chest. Jennifer also lay in the bath facing him, her throat slit.

Emily walked downstairs and out of the Partridge house. DCS Jack Pearce was waiting for her by a marked police car. Aliénor was crouched beside the car, hugging her knees into her chest, rocking back and forth.

'What's happened?' Emily asked Pearce.

Her superior gulped and moistened his lips. Hesitated for a second or two. Emily stiffened. In that short silence, she sensed the pain. The urgency. And the fear.

El Palomar, Spain
Tuesday, 21 December 1937, 10.00 pm

SOLE WAS ABOUT TO GET UP, but Teresa placed her hand on her shoulder. 'Please, just sit for a while, Sole. You're going to make me dizzy. You've been on your feet all evening!'

'Well, I'm not exactly going to let you do everything, am I?' Sole protested.

'I don't want to see you move out of that chair,' Teresa insisted.

'Your dinner was delicious, *mi Sole*,' said Paco, stretching his long arms above his head. '*Gracias, mi amor*, you've made it such a wonderful birthday.'

Sole smiled at him as she rubbed the big round belly stretching her woollen dress.

'I feel like there are two of them in here,' she wheezed, running the tips of her fingers around the contour.

'I think it's just the one, but a hefty one at that,' Teresa replied as she cleared the table. 'Just like his father. Have you seen the size of Paco?'

'You see, *mi Sole*, she agrees with me,' Paco said, draining his glass of Montitxelvo. The smooth dessert wine enveloped his mouth with its gentle sweetness as he clicked his tongue against his palate to savour every last drop.

Teresa piled the cutlery, plates and glasses into a big metal bowl.

'Are you sure you want to go to the *font* and do the dishes right now?' Sole asked her.

'*Sí*. Concha should be down there as well. We'll have a little gossip.'

'The river must be as cold as ice, Tere. You won't feel your fingers! Why don't you wait until tomorrow?'

Teresa and her brother exchanged a knowing glance. It couldn't wait until tomorrow.

'I'll be done in no time, you'll see,' she argued as she hoisted the bowl up and balanced it on the top of her head. The dishes shifted and clanged against the sides, echoing the first knocks at the door, which were soon followed by a louder, more insistent banging.

Paco drew himself up to the full height and breadth of his stocky frame as he opened the door – and froze.

A group of Blueshirts, three of them, stood in the doorway.

Teresa gripped the handles on the bowl so she wouldn't lose her balance.

'Paco Morales Ramos, come with us!' the one in the middle barked, adjusting his hat before hooking his fingers over his belt, where the Astra 400 was waiting in its holster.

Sole stood and placed one hand on her belly and the other on her chair. A film of cold sweat was spreading across her neck and upper lip. She clenched her jaw so she wouldn't gnash her teeth.

Paco turned his palms upwards, spread his arms wide and forced a smile. 'What's all this about, *señores*?'

The man on the left reached out and clamped a hand around Paco's wrist.

'All right, all right,' Paco said.

'Soledad Melilla Santiago,' the one in the middle barked at Sole.

Not daring to say a word, Sole gripped the chair more tightly, as her belly began to contract intermittently.

'No, *I'm* Sole,' Teresa interjected.

'Is that so? *You're* Sole?' the militiaman smirked. He took a step forwards, leaned his face down towards hers and brushed his lips against her ear. 'Don't you dare insult *El Caudillo*, you dirty little *puta*,' he hissed. 'You think we don't do our homework, eh, before we come and round up the traitors of Spain? Think we don't know who's red, like your brother, and who's blue, like us? Do you think we don't know that bastard of a Republican brother of yours knocked up his wife? And that your husband, *Teresa Morales Campos*, is with the Resistance?'

Teresa swallowed. 'My husband died six months ago, *señor*.'

'Are you sure about that, Tere? That your Tomeo's been dead for six months?'

She shivered. '*Sí, señor*.'

The man nodded and straightened himself up, but kept his eyes trained on her. He tugged at his sleeves to adjust his jacket, then stepped back to join his colleagues. 'Round up all three of them,' he calmly instructed.

THE PACKET OF GROUND COFFEE *next to the box of English Breakfast tea. The jasmine green tea, on top of the plain green tea. Then the thyme honey. The jar of Demerara sugar. And the four boxes of Anna's* pepparkakor, *one on top of the other.*

Aliénor Lindbergh breathed a deep sigh of relief. Everything was organised properly in Emily's kitchen cupboard. She watched as the profiler put three mugs out on the worktop.

Emily filled the stainless-steel basket with black tea leaves and put it back in the teapot. Then she poured a splash of milk into one of the mugs, forgetting again that Jack preferred to add it afterwards. One hand on the handle, she was waiting for the kettle to finish boiling. Next, the three of them would sit down at the table. The conversation would take a while to get going. Jack would be the one to say the first word. The first sentence. And she and Aliénor would listen as they drank their tea.

Aliénor wondered whether her parents' cellar had been reorganised while she had been away. Was the O'boy chocolate drink powder still in its place between the coffee and the peppermint tea? Had her mother arranged the books on the family shelves by colour, like she had always wanted, rather than by topic and then alphabetical order, the way they were when she left?

That's what she should be doing when she went back to Sweden. Before she saw her parents. Before she kissed them. And pressed her cheek against her sister's. She should check that everything was in its place. The chocolate powder and the books. And the dogs' baskets, in the cubbyhole at the back of the kitchen. Even though they'd been dead a while, the dogs.

Aliénor tried to focus by running her fingers along the grooves of the vintage solid oak table. Seven months. Seven months since she had left her parents' home. Seven months since she had started as an intern with the Metropolitan Police alongside Emily and Jack. Emily was training her to be a BIA like her. A Behavioural Investigative Adviser. Or, as most people would say, a profiler. Jack Pearce didn't approve. But he didn't know how to say no to Emily. Maybe because they were sleeping together.

Emily had suspected Marty Partridge from the start. Her intuition had been right. She had solved the disappearance and murder of Jennifer Marsden in a matter of hours. While her own family – of sorts – was being torn apart.

The packet of ground coffee next to the box of English breakfast tea. The jasmine green tea, on top of the plain green tea. Then the…

Aliénor knew they wouldn't let her kiss her parents, though. Or press her cheek against her sister's. The three of them must be on the autopsy table right now. Or perhaps they were still in body bags? Were they naked or clothed? She had no idea.

'Aliénor?'

Emily's voice. Her posture mirrored Jack's, their hands cupped tightly around their mugs, which were no longer steaming. They were watching her. With a stern look in their eyes. Or concerned, perhaps. Yes, it was a look of concern. She recognised the crease above the nose, between the eyes.

'Yes?'

'Is nine in the morning all right?' Emily repeated.

'What are you talking about? I wasn't listening.'

'The flight at nine in the morning to go back to Falkenberg.'

'Yes, that's fine.' Aliénor pressed her index finger into the groove in the wood. 'Are you coming with me?'

'Yes, of course. Of course I'm coming with you.'

Falkenberg, Strandbaden Hotel
Saturday, 3 December 2016, 12.00 pm

ALEXIS CASTELLS FILLED HER GLASS, and her mother's, with Christmas beer.

'*Mon Dieu*, that saucisson is good! What's it made with?' Mado Castells asked, licking her lips as she wolfed down her third slice.

'Are you sure you want to know, Maman?'

'Listen, I used to make you fritters with sheep brains when you were little, and we eat rabbit, don't we? So I'm not afraid of eating Bambi and friends. Go on, tell me what's in there.'

'Elk.'

'Ha! I knew it, *Madame* Eklund.'

In two weeks' time, Alexis was going to become '*Madame* Stellan Eklund', as her family liked to tease. Even though they were actually doing the opposite, with Stellan taking Alexis's last name. That was all the rage in Sweden, apparently. *Mr Stellan Castells* was going to be a true poster boy for multiculturalism. Alexis's father Norbert was over the moon that his son-in-law to be was embracing their family's Catalan heritage to the point of carving it into his family tree.

Mado polished off her plate and went back for seconds to the *julbord*, the traditional Christmas buffet Swedish restaurants served during the festive season.

They had enjoyed their relaxing mum-and-daughter date that morning at the market in Halmstad, where they had sampled some local *glögg*, the traditional mulled wine sprinkled with raisins and slivered almonds. Mado had splashed out on lots of candles and

Christmas decorations, gleefully anticipating her husband's protests when the time came for them to pack their suitcases for the trip home. She figured they would have plenty of room, considering the kilos of Sassenage and Morbier cheese they had brought over from France for Alexis and her in-laws.

'It's actually quite a sweet little tradition, isn't it?' Mado conceded, dipping a chunk of sausage into a dollop of Västervik mustard. 'A bit like Christmas tapas, don't you think? I mean, it's not as classy as the food *chez nous*, but it's not bad, I suppose.'

'Maman, can't you give the poor Swedes a proper compliment for once? Don't you think it's a bit snobby to criticise their food all the time?'

'Me, a snob? That's a bit rich, isn't it? I used to put up posters for the Communist party, I'll have you know!'

An icy gust of wind whipped the bay window. Mado flinched. The wind was toying with the sea, stirring up frothy waves that teetered their way in to the shore before crashing against the jetty.

'You're going to end up settling down here, I know it…' Mado sounded like she was trying to come to terms with the tragedy of such a conclusion.

Alexis stiffened. *Keep calm*, she told herself. 'Maman … you know it's easier for me to move to Sweden. I can write my books from any-where. But Stellan's business is so Scandinavian, it'd be impossible for him to work from London. The company he runs with Lena is here, not there, you know that.' She stroked her mother's face, and Mado nuzzled her cheek into her daughter's palm.

'I get that it's more complicated for you to travel to Falken-berg,' Alexis carried on, 'but you *have* always said London was too sprawling and intimidating for you. Falkenberg is much more of a human-sized town.'

Mado wriggled free of her daughter's embrace. 'Well, yes, I suppose it is, but still, it's going to be a shock for you to go from a city of millions to a town of a few thousand people. It'd be one thing if you were moving to Stockholm … but Falkenberg? Good heavens!

They might as well bury you alive. And you know I never have the chance to get used to you living somewhere before you pack up and move again!'

'Oh, come on, Maman, give it a rest. I've been in London more than ten years!'

Alexis's patience was already wearing thin. Mentally, she was drumming her fingers on the table.

'All right, then, spit it out. Tell me what's really ruffling your feathers. Is there something about Stellan that's bothering you?'

'No, no, not at all, it's not that,' Mado mumbled into her plate.

Alexis suddenly had the feeling the roles were reversed. Or maybe not. Surely mothers sometimes felt the need and were within their rights to seek reassurance from their grown children.

'It's the Scandinavian culture, Alexis. It's … such a world away from our own. It's … full of little quirks. It's … They're unemotional, indifferent, stuck up, almost, while we Mediterraneans, we're spontaneous and expressive, if not a bit over the top. Every time I open my mouth, they jump out of their skin. As if I were some kind of alien! I know I'm larger than life, but they're so lukewarm they make me want to slap them sometimes. Seriously, though, these people are bizarre. Take that cartoon with the duck, for instance, what do they call it?'

'Donald.'

'No, the name of the cartoon, not the character. What's it called again?'

'*Kalle Anka.*'

'That's the one. Every Christmas Eve, they show the same cartoon on TV at exactly same time, and they've been doing that for the last fifty years or more! Seriously? Not to mention that dried-out bread they put on the table that you have to slather with butter and load up with cheese to give it half a chance of tasting like anything. It's like eating a straw mat! Back home, we wouldn't even feed that to the chickens. And what's with their obsession about golf…? Well, it's your choice, I suppose…'

'Here I was, thinking you were enjoying yourself…'

'Now, if you were to tell me you're doing all this because you're planning to start a family, then I'd understand, you know,' her mother carried on, oblivious.

There it was. Mado had finally spat it out. Now they were getting to the heart of the matter. Alexis was childless and fast approaching forty. For Mado Castells, nothing was worse than letting the sacrosanct uterus go fallow. If you asked her, women flourished and proved themselves through motherhood. Above all else, women were mothers. Mothers – and she-wolves too. So, ladies, show us your wombs, then bare your teeth!

Alexis spread some butter on a piece of crisp *knäckebröd*, which promptly broke in her hand.

'You see. What did I tell you? Just like straw, that stuff is!'

'Oh come on, Maman! Don't tell me you're going to get on your high horse about the almighty French baguette now, are you?'

'I don't even have to,' Mado argued, as she swept the crumbs of unleavened crispbread away with the tips of her fingers.

Alexis sighed. It was going to be a long afternoon. *Like a day without bread*, as her mother would say.

El Palomar, Spain
Tuesday, 21 December 1937, 10.30 pm

THE SHORTEST OF THE THREE FALANGISTS, the thin one who had grabbed Paco by the wrist, shoved them into the back of the van. There were two bench seats, one facing the other, down the sides. He barked at Paco to sit on the right, and Sole and Teresa on the left. Then he slammed the rear doors shut and the van pulled away.

Teresa wrapped an arm around Sole's shoulders and placed a hand on her sister-in-law's belly. She could feel her nephew rippling around like a little sardine, and caught Paco's eye when she looked up. She wished she could snuggle up to her brother now, clasp his fingers in hers and give him a kiss for their mother. For herself too. And for the *Yaya*. He was the man of the family now. The only one left. Apart from the little one in Sole's belly. Teresa was sure they had been blessed with a baby boy.

Paco looked back at his sister with eyes full of resignation. Teresa tried to swallow her fears, but they lodged in her throat.

The van slowed down and came to a halt. Teresa heard the front doors open and slam shut, then the dull thudding of boots on the ground. Slow, shuffling steps that kicked up the dust beneath their soles as they went. They were taking their time, as if they were enjoying the anticipation.

Suddenly, Teresa felt a wetness spreading under her buttocks. Sole shot her a look of panic and started to tremble, right as the rear doors were flung open.

'Outside! Now!' one of the Falangists barked.

Teresa helped Sole out of the van. Paco offered his arm for his wife to lean on, but the thin man shouted for him to keep his hands off her. Paco did what he was told and retreated behind Sole.

'She's pissed herself!' the thin man cried, when he saw the big stain seeping through Sole's dress.

Sole opened her mouth. But Teresa opened her eyes wider, imploring her to stay quiet. If the men caught on that her water had broken, they wouldn't hesitate to kill them all. The last thing they wanted was a woman in labour getting under their feet.

Sole and her baby had to survive.

The thin man punched Paco in the shoulder, herding him towards the front of the van, where the headlights were still blazing.

Teresa felt her legs buckling under her.

'Not feeling tired, are we, my pretty? Get a move on! Sit down there, next to your brother! You too, pissy pants, come on! Right there, with your husband!'

He gave Teresa a kick in the back. She lurched forwards and got a mouthful of dirt. Struggling to straighten her wobbly legs, she managed to get back to her feet. Sole followed her in a daze, folding her arms to protect her belly.

They lined them up in the middle of the road, in the glare of the headlights.

All Teresa could see were two, huge, yellow pools of light floating in front of her eyes. She heard Sole weeping. She heard her brother cry '*No pasarán!*' Followed by an explosion, then a dull thud and a crunching sound as Paco's body crumpled to the ground in a cloud of dust and dirt.

Teresa's arms flew in front of her face, as if a gust of wind had caught hold of them.

Her cries were smothered by a second gunshot.

Then a third shot rang out in the night.

Skrea Strand, Falkenberg
Saturday, 3 December 2016, 2.00 pm

THE SILENCE IN THE CAR was deafening. Because those who whisper in the darkness swallow up every other sound around. Consumed by the anticipation of what awaited them, Kommissionär Lennart Bergström and Emily Roy had not said a word since they left the police station.

Bergström parked in the driveway, in front of the double garage. Emily got out of the car first. The icy air burned its way down to her lungs.

'Snow's on the way,' the commissioner said as he extricated himself from the vehicle.

The Lindberghs' property sprawled over nearly six thousand square metres. In the middle of this barren landscape, their land seemed to go on forever. The luxurious property was visible all the way from the main road that ran parallel to the shore. A charming, traditional-style wooden house with a pale-green façade and white trim, it exuded the sweet, carefree days of childhood.

Emily followed a string of stepping stones to a patio overlooking a huge garden and a thin strip of sand that snaked a path to the Skrea Strand beach. A copse of apple trees was the only thing obscuring the panoramic view of the sea.

'The house used to belong to a Norwegian film director,' Bergström explained, standing behind her. 'Aliénor's parents bought it in the eighties.'

Still taking in the surroundings, the profiler didn't turn around.

She stayed there a few moments, watching, listening, before joining the commissioner on the doorstep.

Bergström said hello to the young female police officer posted at the door and signed the register. Emily strode into the house without looking at the officer. Bergström glanced at the new recruit in apology, but she shook her head and waved her hand with a smile. Emily Roy had worked with the commissioner and his team twice already, so no one raised an eyebrow anymore at her quirks.

Bergström followed Emily inside and closed the door behind him. He had been the first on the scene the night before. *It was only last night,* he thought. Barely a few hours had elapsed since they had combed the scene where Aliénor's family had been massacred. The expansive Lindbergh residence had been invaded by a colony of white protective suits, all buzzing around, doing their jobs in an apparent sense of chaos that belied a meticulously organised operation. A hive of activity. Run by Björn Holm, the head of the SKL, the crime-scene unit. His worker bees had just left with three bodies in tow.

Bergström remembered the silence that reigned over operations like these. A silence just as laden with fear as the one that had hung over him and Emily in the car earlier. Death commanded deference, however often it crossed your path. He glanced over to Emily. She seemed not to feel the presence of the Grim Reaper. Either that, or she had learned to live with it. Emily's petite frame projected an intimidating aura of toughness and strength. She had pulled her hair into a ponytail and was standing, sure of herself, in the middle of the hallway. Scoping out the territory, like a cat eyeing up its prey. To her right was a double living room that opened onto the patio. To her left, a dining room led through to a vast North American-style kitchen. Straight ahead, she saw a giant bow window with a sweeping view of the sea. To the right of the window was a steep staircase leading to the first floor.

Emily turned to look at Bergström. He answered her silent question with a nod of his chin towards the living room.

They traversed the first room, which was furnished with two sofas and a coffee table, and Emily stopped under the arch of a double sliding door. In front of another bow window, facing the beach, sat a huge U-shaped sectional sofa. Traces of black and white powder lingered on every surface – furniture, windows and light switches alike.

'That's where Göran Lindbergh was lying, with wireless headphones over his ears,' Bergström explained as Emily approached the sectional.

The blood had soaked deep into the dark leather of the seat and armrest, as well as the carpet. Emily pointed to the spatters she could see on part of the backrest. 'His head was propped up on a cushion, I presume?' she asked.

'Two of them,' the commissioner clarified.

'Was he wearing anything?'

'Pyjamas.'

'With a blanket over him?'

Bergström nodded. 'He was stabbed through the blanket,' he added.

'Where's the stereo?'

'The stereo?'

'What were the headphones connected to?' Emily rephrased her question.

'Spotify.'

The profiler shook her head, none the wiser.

'He was listening to music on his iPad,' Bergström translated with a smile.

'Were the double doors closed?'

'Yes.'

And the bow window?'

'Also closed.'

'Locked?'

'No.'

Emily's gaze lingered on the sofa before scanning the rest of the living room. 'Upstairs?' she ventured as she retraced her steps to the hall.

Bergström had forgotten how abrupt Emily could be. She gave everything a sense of harshness, making things feel like a rough wool sweater you're itching to take off.

'Upstairs,' he nodded, with a forced casualness.

She let him lead the way. He strode quickly up the stairs and turned down the hallway, then entered the room at the very end. When he was here the night before, the air had been saturated with a rancid, metallic smell, mixed with a whiff of something softer, sweeter, which had taken him a while to put his finger on: coconut. The tropical scent had since faded away. All that remained now was the pungent stench of death and urine.

Emily ran her eyes around the master bedroom, then moved closer to a large brown stain on the oak parquet floor at the foot of the bed. She kneeled gently, as if Kerstin Lindbergh's body was still lying there. Her gaze shifted from the blood-crusted floorboards to the spattered bed frame.

'Duvet? Blankets, sheets?' she asked, rising to her feet with her eyes still glued to the floor.

'A duvet. Scrunched up at her feet.'

'Completely naked?'

'Yes.'

Emily stood contemplating the bed for a long time, then left the room.

'Down the other end, last door on the right,' Bergström said.

Emily made her way down the hallway.

Bergström kept his distance while she took in the blood-soaked mattress, the bare walls, the objects neatly lined up on the desk and the books on the two shelf units, all organised by topic and alphabetical order.

The profiler turned to look at him, her mouth agape.

Bergström nodded.

Louise Lindbergh had been killed in Aliénor's bedroom.

KRISTIAN OLOFSSON DOWNED HIS ESPRESSO in one mouthful and strode across the open-plan office. He hadn't slept the night before. He had showered, thank goodness, in the changing room at the station no one ever used. He had never set foot in there before, much to his regret, as the place was smart, stylishly decorated and clean as a whistle.

The previous night, Kommissionär Bergström's call had torn him from Mona's arms ... so to speak. When his mobile vibrated in his jeans pocket, she was lying in bed, waiting for him, with a glint in her eye, twirling her thong in one hand as her firm breasts spilled out of the seams of her bra. There had been no time, not even for the tiniest little taste of her, before Olofsson had had to pull himself away, quaking in his boxers at the sight of her.

But as soon as he had arrived at the Lindberghs', all visions of the sublime Mona evaporated from his mind. Aliénor had lived here, of all places. 'Google', as he liked to call her, even if it was just to get her innocent little back up.

He knew the place. He drove past it every week on his way to hockey practice, and he always noticed it from the road. Never would he have imagined that Google had grown up there.

Now, Olofsson entered the interview room. A woman who must have been in her fifties, with long legs and a haughty air, sat waiting at the steel table with her large handbag on her lap, as if anywhere else was far too dirty for her to put it.

'Gerda Vankard?' the detective asked.

'Yes.'

Bloody hell, Olofsson thought. *Rich people's housekeepers – well, housekeepers, full stop – really do end up looking like their employers. Just like dogs take after their owners.*

'Hello, Gerda. Detective Olofsson.'

She nodded in greeting.

'I'd like to go over the timeline of the evening with you,' he explained, taking a seat.

'Yes. Of course. I…'

'I'll ask the questions, OK? It's simpler that way. You don't mind if I record our conversation, do you?'

'Not at all, no.'

'Right.' Olofsson pressed a button on the built-in tape recorder on the table. 'What time did you get back to the Lindberghs' last night, Gerda?'

She swallowed audibly. 'Shortly after midnight.'

'What happened when you arrived?'

Gerda Vankard swept a lock of hair behind her ear with a trembling hand. 'The front door was wide open. I thought that was strange and … I started to worry. All the lights were on in the living room. Anyway, I went in, and I closed the door behind me, and when I went into the living room to turn the lights off … that's when … Göran … my God…'

Gerda closed her eyes and bit her lower lip in an attempt to calm her shaking.

'Take your time,' Olofsson coaxed. 'Would you like a glass of water?'

She shook her head and wiped tears from her eyes with the back of her hand. 'I ran upstairs … to Louise's old bedroom – she was home for the weekend, but her bed was still made, so I ran over to Kerstin and Göran's bedroom and…'

The rest of her sentence tailed off and gave way to her sobbing. Her body was shaking like a leaf. She bowed her head and gave up fighting the tears. Her handbag slipped off her knee; she picked it straight up again, laid it flat on her lap and started to fiddle distractedly with the leather flap.

Olofsson stared at the embossed double G logo.

'I went straight back downstairs and called the police,' she continued. 'The inspector was there ten minutes later.'

'Do you mean Kommissionär Bergström?'

'Yes, I do apologise. Kommissionär Bergström.'

'Nothing else jumped out at you? Nothing was missing, or in the wrong place? Nothing out of the ordinary?'

'I don't know … I didn't really pay much attention, what with…' Gerda looked at Olofsson as if she had finished her sentence.

The detective waited a few seconds before leading with a new question. 'How long have you been working for the Lindberghs?'

'Twenty-six years.'

Olofsson tried to hide his surprise. Twenty-six years cleaning up other people's shit. Jeez, the stuff that floated some people's boats. That said, she could obviously afford to buy a bag that must have cost thirty thousand kronor, so maybe that was motivation enough.

'I saw their three children grow up.' Her lips started to quiver.

'Where is your room?' Olofsson asked, changing the subject to avert another wave of tears.

'On the second floor,' she sniffled. 'I live in the attic.'

'I see. There's a separate entrance so you can come and go without going through the house isn't there? Via a spiral staircase, if I'm not mistaken?'

'Yes.'

'Did you lock the door to your room?'

'Obviously. The door to the inside of the house too. I always lock them both. Especially as the outside door is hard to close properly. Believe me, I'm not likely to forget it.'

'What are your usual working hours?'

'Since Aliénor went to live in England, I've been doing a few hours less. Now I work about five hours a day, Monday to Friday, depending on the Lindberghs' commitments and my partner, Nicole's schedule.'

Her partner, Nicole. She was full of surprises, this housekeeper.

'And I spend weekends at Nicole's place, in Varberg.'

'What happened last night, then? Why weren't you with your ... partner?' he struggled to ask, as the image of Mona floated through his mind. All this lesbian stuff with Nicole had thrown him completely off his train of thought.

'Her daughter gave birth to her first baby three weeks early, so Nicole went off to the maternity ward and ... I wasn't welcome, so, I went home to my place.'

My place. Olofsson felt like reminding her it wasn't her place: it was the Lindberghs' home.

'What time did you leave the Lindberghs' on Friday?'

'At one in the afternoon.'

'Were the Lindberghs home?'

'No. They came home just before five. I know because Kerstin called and asked me if I was still there, because she had forgotten her keys. She had to wait until Göran got home from the supermarket with the groceries.'

'Did Louise make a habit of sleeping in Aliénor's room?'

Gerda frowned. 'Louise, in ... no, no, not at all ... Louise was in Aliénor's room? Oh, my God...' The words were painful for her to swallow.

'Do you know anyone who might have had a falling-out with the Lindberghs?'

Gerda shook her head vigorously.

'Even if it might seem a bit blown out of proportion, perhaps a disagreement between neighbours? A family feud? Any infidelity?'

'Nothing that could ever explain ... all that...' Gerda lowered her eyes to the scaly skin on her fingers. Clasping her hands, she played with her thumbs, crossing them back and forth.

'But Carina Isaksson would know,' she blurted suddenly, just as Olofsson was about to ask if he could join in her game of rock-paper-scissors. 'Carina is our neighbour and a great family friend of the Lindberghs. I go over to hers twice a week to do housework, ever since her housekeeper dislocated her shoulder. I'm sure she'll be able to help you, detective.'

THE FIRST BULLET KILLED PACO. The second blew Sole's face off. The third finished off their son.

Teresa stuffed her fist into her mouth, and bit until it bled.

'You can sit down now, Teresa,' she heard someone say.

She let herself crumple to the ground, where her body shook with waves of deep, uncontrollable tears. She didn't dare reach out and touch the lifeless leg of her brother by her side, nor the curly hair that cascaded over Sole's dead shoulders and across the gravel.

'See what we do to the wives of traitors, eh, Tere?' the thin Falangist mocked as he kneeled beside Sole's body, lifted her flowered dress over her pregnant belly and pulled a knife from his belt.

Teresa screamed and buried her face in her hands.

'Hey-ho! Look over here, *chiquita!*' The thin man brandished the knife and pressed it to her temple, forcing her to watch what he was about to do to her sister-in-law.

Teresa blinked away the tears and did what she was told.

The thin man planted the knife deep into the flesh above Sole's hip bone, then slowly drew the blade in a semicircle, below her belly button, all the way across to the other hip bone.

Teresa squeezed her eyes closed. But she could still hear; she tried not to think about what the sticky, squelching sounds – followed by the dull thud of something hitting the ground – surely meant. She tried to think about her Tomeo's voice and the touch of his calloused hands on her skin.

'Hey-ho, *chiquita*! It ain't siesta time yet,' the man growled, pulling out his gun and tapping the barrel against her cheek.

She opened her eyes. And saw him stuffing fistfuls of grass and brush into the gaping hole in Sole's belly, before wiping his hands on her dress.

Then he took the knife and ripped the bloody garment in half, from the waist up to the neck. He tore Sole's dress off her, yanked her to one side and unhooked her bra. Then he shoved her over onto her front, skin crunching on gravel, her right arm now crushing her bare breasts against her.

He turned to the other Falangists and knotted Sole's bra around his head like a trophy. Then he stuck his tongue out and started panting like a dog as he bounded over and around the bodies on the ground. The bodies of Sole ... Paco ... and their baby.

Teresa prayed to the God she had never believed in. For this nightmare to stop. For the clock to turn back to her being in the kitchen with Paco and Sole. But God did not grace her with a reply. She heard the voice of the thin man instead. 'Right then, what should we do with you, now, my pretty Teresa?'

IT'S LIKE WE'RE ALL sitting down to dinner, Aliénor thought. Subconsciously, she was trying to break the ice and rationalise her trauma. *Well, Bergström, Olofsson and Emily were all seated around the interview table*, she thought.

The commissioner had suggested the conference room, but Aliénor had refused. Interviews should take place in the interview room, she very matter-of-factly insisted. Bergström had seen no reason to argue.

Aliénor looked at each of them in turn with the impatient, hopeful air of a child waiting to see if she could come out of the naughty corner.

'We're going to need you to paint a portrait of your family for us,' Bergström ventured with some hesitation.

Aliénor stared at him blankly.

'Lennart would like … *we* would like you to tell us about any tension or conflict there might have been between the members of your family, or with anyone else,' Emily explained. She shifted forwards in her chair and put her hands on the table, close to Aliénor's. 'Are you sure you feel up to this?' she asked.

'Who should I start with?'

'Whoever you like.'

'I'll start with myself, then. I caused a lot of problems for my family before I was diagnosed with autism. My parents didn't understand why I always reacted differently. I wasn't like my brother or my sister, and I wasn't like my classmates or the children of the neighbours or my parents' friends.' As Aliénor tilted her head to one side, her gaze drifted back in time. 'My father used to tell me off a lot when I was a child, because I didn't understand what he was asking me to do. Or what I was doing wrong. Mum found me difficult to be around. If she was still here, she'd tell you I was lying. But it's true. Louise helped me to see that. My sister would always stick up for me. She tolerated me. She liked that I was different. And loved me in spite of it. When I was twelve years old, my history teacher, Owe Edwardson, suspected I had Asperger's syndrome, and the doctors confirmed the diagnosis. Then my parents were much more patient with me. It was like they finally had a dictionary to help them speak my language, Louise told me. It was a lot easier for them after that. But still, my autism created a lot of tension and caused a lot of arguments in our family.'

Bergström had to suppress an urge to give Aliénor a hug. She was in her late twenties, but looked like she was only going on sixteen, with her virginal face devoid of makeup, eyes full of questions and sensible half-ponytail.

'And Léopold?' Emily asked.

'My brother was always reading science and sci-fi magazines and he used to watch *Star Wars* on repeat. I don't really know what he thought about me. Louise and I have always been closer. I mean, we were…' Aliénor left the words hanging. Her eyes darted around the room like butterflies caught out in the rain.

'No, Louise and I *have* always been closer. I can still use the present tense.'

Bergström reached out and clasped her hand in his. He regretted the gesture as Aliénor wriggled her fingers free from his broad palm. He should have resisted his paternal instinct. Aliénor used to be his intern and had been a valuable colleague. But he knew the rules.

'How did your parents get on?' Emily pressed.

'Very well. They were still in love with each other and were very close. And they often excluded us children from their relationship.

One day, Louise got mad and told our mother she didn't understand why they had children. She said that it was obvious there was only room for the two of them in our family and that they treated the three of us like intruders. I think she was right.'

'How did your mother react to that?'

'She walked slowly over to her office and closed the door behind her.'

'Charming!' Olofsson whistled through his teeth.

Bergström glared at him. Olofsson glued his eyes to the table in contrition.

'Was their work very demanding?' Emily continued.

'Extremely. Louise thought so too. She said the clinic was their baby. Or rather, their babies. It was all about the image, I think. Their job was to run the clinic, and that was a huge stress for my father. He only used to sleep two or three hours a night. I never saw him go to bed or fall asleep before three in the morning. He just used to sit in the living room and listen to music or watch films or documentaries on his iPad.'

'Clinic? What kind of clinic?' Emily asked.

'A medically assisted reproduction clinic. They started it themselves, years ago.'

'Are you aware of any problems related to the clinic?'

'I haven't finished talking about my parents and their relationship.'

'All right. Carry on.'

'I don't think they were ever unfaithful to each other. I can't guarantee that, but they didn't argue a lot, they worked well together and often laughed. They were happiest when it was just the two of them, without us.'

Aliénor's observation met with an awkward silence.

'Going back to the clinic: no, I'm not aware of any problems. I just know that they earned a tremendous amount of money and that my father hoped Léopold would take over and manage the business someday. But Léopold was only interested in the scientific side of the clinic, not the administration, so my father wasn't very happy.'

'And your mother?'

'She would listen. And she would always end these conversations with the same words: "Try to put yourself in your father's shoes." She used to say the same thing to me too, when he shouted at me for curling up to sleep in the dogs' baskets in the kitchen. He didn't like it when I did that. Especially when we had guests over.'

Aliénor opened her mouth and closed it again.

She placed her hands on her thighs and interlaced her fingers. 'I … I need to get out of here. Now.'

He's wearing his father's christening dress. White, with an embroidered hem and little green rosettes all around the waist.

My little man. My little grandson.

God, how handsome he is, with those cheeks still rosy from sleep and all the joy of the world in those blue, blue eyes. The three of them are standing at the altar in their Sunday best, and the little one is nuzzling his cheek to his mother's breast. He sees us with Nino and waves his chubby arm. My heart melts with joy. I squeeze Nino's hand. God, how happy this tiny little man has made us. I had always heard about the joy of becoming a grandmother. About a different, detached kind of love, free from duties and obligations. A love that was all about the simple pleasures. I used to think it was just another one of those stories, like those singing the praises of the first year of motherhood. One of those lies. But this little human being fills me with happiness. He really does.

Our little bundle of joy stuffs his chubby little hand in his mouth and sucks on it greedily, then spits it out with a grimace. He wants his dummy. He starts crying and my daughter rocks him, all in a fluster like any first-time parent. A chorus of embarrassed shushing ensues. Then our little cherub notices the priest. He's walking down the centre aisle, followed by two choirboys and waving the thurible in front of him, bathing their path in solemnity. My little cherub squirms and wriggles his way out of his mother's arms, trying to grab at the smoke that's billowing from the holy incense burner.

But it's the priest's stole he latches on to. He tugs at it, burbling a monologue that resembles a language all its own as a serious, concerned crease spreads across his face. The priest waves his fingers in front of our little one's eyes to distract him, so he can straighten his stole.

Nino chuckles beside me. All I can feel is his elbow against my ribs. But I can't hear him. My ears are buzzing. Or rather, they're whistling. An urgent, relentless sound that drowns out whatever the priest is asking, and whatever my daughter and my son-in-law are answering. My heart is pounding in my chest and echoing in my temples. Beads of sweat pearl across my forehead and the back of my neck. My tongue swells in my mouth. It feels like it's getting thicker. It's parching my throat. I feel like I'm suffocating.

Am I suffocating?

All of a sudden, my chest caves in. It feels like there's no place for my heart anymore, like everything else is caving in around it.

Air. I need some air.

I throw my mouth wide open, pitch my head back and gulp a breath. I draw it down as if draining the last drops from a bottle of water. I swallow again, and again, trying to buoy my way back to the surface of my body.

Then my body lets go completely, like a puppet when the strings are cut.

Olofsbo, Falkenberg, home of the Bergströms
Saturday, 3 December 2016, 7.00 pm

IT WAS A THICK, heavy night that dimmed the light of the moon.

Alexis rang the doorbell and rubbed her thighs vigorously to stem the biting cold rising from her boots and through her whole body. When Lena Bergström opened the door, she had the phone wedged between her shoulder and ear, and was clutching the necks of two bottles of wine between the fingers of one hand. Stellan's sister motioned with her free hand for Alexis to come in, without interrupting her conversation.

Now accustomed to Swedish habits, Alexis took off her hat, gloves, scarf, coat and boots in the entryway, a fleeting pang of nostalgia for the gentle Provençal winters warming her heart. She walked through to the living room in her socks, trying to shake the unpleasant feeling of being not barefoot, but naked. Try as she might, she just couldn't get used to this custom. Walking around without slippers at home was one thing, but she still struggled with the idea of spending an evening in her socks at someone else's house.

'Sorry, Alexis,' Kommissionär Bergström's wife said as she hung up. 'Problems with planning permission for a villa in Stockholm.' She plonked both bottles on the coffee table beside four stemmed glasses on a round tray. 'Pinot gris or chardonnay?'

'Pinot, please.'

'Stellan's in the office. He's still on a videoconference with one of our clients, who's just decided to change the plans for his Majorcan villa, two weeks before we break ground. I'd be telling him where to stick his plans if I were the one in charge,' she scoffed, popping the cork and filling two glasses. She flopped herself down on the sofa and ran her elegant fingers through her silver hair.

'The colour really suits you,' Alexis said.

'Do you think so? I'm not sure Lennart's convinced. My hair-dresser twisted my arm to go grey, you now. The boys told me I look like a more "senior" version of Gunhild Stordalen ... Petter Stord-alen's wife. Oh, silly me, you might not know who they are.'

'The Stordalens ... aren't they the Bill and Melinda Gates of Norway?'

'That's right. A frumpier version ... ouch. But still – Gunhild Stordalen!' Lena winked.

'When are the boys getting back to Falkenberg?'

'Thursday the fifteenth, just to be sure they don't miss the rehearsal dinner with the family on the Friday,' Lena replied, reaching for her glass on the coffee table.

'How are things going for them in Madrid?' Alexis asked, between sips.

'Didn't Stellan tell you? They're in Barcelona now! They're opening a new restaurant down there. Seriously, I can't quite believe it. Though I am a bit worried about all this overnight success. They're still so young, and I'm not sure they're responsible enough to make the right decisions.'

'Well, they really seem to have their heads screwed on, Lena. It's quite remarkable what they've accomplished in the last two years.'

'It certainly is. Oh, before I forget, are you published in Spanish? The boys asked me to find out.'

'Spanish and Catalan, yes. My book about the Ebner Affair was a big hit down there, apparently. My Spanish publisher is having my books about Rosemary West and the profiler Micki Pistorius trans-lated right now, actually.'

'Oh, fantastic! The boys are thinking about doing some cultural and culinary soirées at the restaurant and they thought you might like to kick things off. Talking about criminals while you sip Rioja and nibble tapas – that's not such a bad idea, is it?'

'It's a fabulous idea!'

'Perfect. I'll tell them to get in touch.' Lena absent-mindedly brushed some dust from the armrest of the sofa with the back of her hand.

'Maman sends her love, by the way,' Alexis said, changing the subject.

'How is she?'

'Oh, she's fine. She was just feeling a bit tired by the whole day and decided she'd rather get an early night. The wedding preparations are stressing her out a lot more than me!'

'And how are things shaping up on that front?'

'Honestly, there really isn't a lot for me to do. The wedding planner's taking care of everything. The Strandbaden Hotel offered to handle it all for us, and with all my to-ing and fro-ing between here and London I couldn't say no to that. Other than the initial meet-and-greet to see the venue, choose the decor, the menu and the entertainment, we've only had a few emails back and forth. I'm supposed to be meeting her this week to iron out the finer details.'

'What about your dress?'

'Jeez, what an absolute shit show!' Stellan blustered into the living room. He kissed Alexis, losing himself for a moment in their embrace, before he carried on. 'There's no getting him to see sense at all. He says he'll pay for all the extra time he has to. Damn right he will. But he's adamant about expanding the spa area in the basement, whatever it takes.'

Lena sighed and drained her glass. 'Seriously? What a clown. He's going to be a royal pain every step of the way until the job's done, isn't he?'

'What were you talking about?' Stellan asked, pouring himself a drink.

'Your bride-to-be's wedding dress. Time to change the subject, I think!' Lena quipped.

'Well, I *can* tell you that it's my sister's wedding dress,' Alexis gushed.

Lena gave Alexis a soppy look and squeezed her future sister-in-law's hand between hers.

'I love the idea of there being a chain of love from one union to another in our family,' Alexis explained. 'I can't wait to show you the photos. It's a simple dress, but it's absolutely gorgeous, you'll see.'

The front door opened abruptly, and slammed shut. Seconds later, Lennart Bergström appeared in the living room and nodded a weary '*hej*' all around. His shoulders were hunched from fatigue, and his downcast eyes and mouth looked like they'd snagged on a fisherman's hook. The weary, sullen look on his face lent his imposing stature an almost menacing air.

Lena sprang out of her seat to greet her husband. 'You poor thing, you look like you've really been through the wringer.' She rubbed his thick beard before planting a kiss on his cheek. 'What was the big emergency last night, then?'

The commissioner furrowed his brow. He turned to Alexis. 'Haven't you seen Emily?'

Alexis sat bolt upright and shook her head in puzzlement. 'No … why?'

Bergström closed his eyes and rubbed the bridge of his nose. 'Aliénor's parents have been murdered.'

Alicante, Spain
Sunday, 26 December 1937, 11.30 pm

TERESA TILTED HER HEAD back to feel the sweet caress of the fresh air on her face, drawing it all in with a breath deep enough to make her nostrils clench. She held it at the very bottom of her lungs before releasing it slowly, eyes wide open to the clearest of skies filled with stars.

It had not been easy, but she had done what Tomeo said. By making herself answer a simple question: *Would I rather live or die?* It would have been easier to die. Provoke a guard and take a bullet to the head, like Sole. And Paco. But still, confined to her seat for five whole days in an Alicante cinema, as the excrement of the hundreds of women and children she was holed up with multiplied and festered on the floor, she had chosen to live.

When they first arrived, the cinema had been buzzing with the cries of lost women and hungry, thirsty children sucking in vain at their mothers' dry breasts. One by one, the sounds had faded to silence, snuffed out by fear and exhaustion. Only the occasional whisper or the creaking of a body changing position remained; even the moans and groans had subsided.

Teresa felt a hand shove her forwards. She tripped and grabbed at the jacket of the woman beside her as she fell. The woman smiled and helped her back to her feet. Her eyes were filled with the same anguish Teresa harboured within – the giant void that grew deeper and deeper by the hour.

Stretching her frozen limbs, Teresa stuffed her hands to the bottoms of her cardigan pockets and made her way through the sea of women's and children's sweaty, stinking bodies on the station platform and towards the carriage she had been assigned. At the cinema, she had given her coat away to help a mother cover up her shivering baby. Every other scrap of material they could find had been folded into nappies and soiled by dysentery.

She was the third to board. It must have been a goods train, or perhaps for cattle. There were no seats, and no benches either. Only a big tin can, abandoned in a corner. Her travel companions sat down on the floor with their young offspring. One was rocking the baby at her breast as the other stroked the forehead of her daughter, whose thirst had cracked her lips until they bled. These mothers were far from singing with joy; instead they huddled in silence. They had already resigned themselves to the worst and could only dab at the pain and suffering as they struggled to hold on to their children. Their lifelines, however threadbare they may be. The extensions of themselves. Themselves and their loved ones, for those lucky enough to have loved. Teresa creased up her eyes and shook her head to rid herself of the image of her baby nephew's body, left in the brush by the side of the road.

Suddenly, a raging torrent of women and children flooded into the wagon, herded by the Falangists, who then slammed the metal grille shut behind them.

The train coughed and spluttered, then creaked its way forwards.

○

The tin can was overflowing with urine and faeces. It was a sardine tin. Probably the same sardines they were feeding them. They had stopped the train three times so far to give them each a sardine and a sip of water. The fish only made them thirstier, stinging their throats all the way up to their ears, but none of the women had been able to resist.

They had counted three nights on board the train. Three nights and three days on top of one another, wallowing in the stench of bodies that were being treated like those of animals. In silence. Because they had nothing left to say. That's what a lack of hope will do to people. Her Tomeo had told her that. The sense of resignation people felt when they were staring death in the face.

Suddenly, two soldiers flung the metal grille open. A wave of relief swept through the wagon. Finally, some fresh air; perhaps some water, and a sardine. Perhaps even the chance to empty the contents of the tin can onto the train tracks.

The Falangists reeled back a step or two, covering their noses and mouths.

'*Los muertos fuera!*' they barked, moving their hands no further from their faces than they had to: *Bring out the dead.*

Two screams rang out and clashed. Two mothers, cradling their children's dead bodies in their arms. But in the silence that stood like a wall in front of these men, not one of the dozens of women and children dared move.

'*LOS MUERTOS FUERA!*' they screamed again, reaching for their belts, ready to draw their weapons.

Tears streaming down her face, one of the women stepped down onto the platform, clutching her daughter in her arms, nuzzling her face to hers, the girl's braids hanging limply in mid-air.

The second mother joined her, cradling her baby to her bare breast.

'*Al suelo!*' – *On your knees, now.*

The two women obeyed the order and kneeled, each hanging on to their child for dear life.

'*Los muertos al suelo! Vosotras dentro, joder!*' – *Leave the dead here, on the ground! No fucking stragglers!*

The first woman laid her dead daughter to rest on the station platform. She smoothed her dark braids over her shoulders, made the sign of the cross on her forehead and then kissed her on the lips.

'*Vamos, vamos!*' the militiaman shouted impatiently. *Get a move on.*

The woman stroked the sole of an icy little foot that no longer had sock nor shoe. Then she stood up and climbed back onto the train.

The other woman shook her head, nestling her lifeless baby to her bosom. The infant had succumbed to the journey, but she couldn't bring herself to let her baby go. Not here. Not now. One of the soldiers strode over and cracked the butt of his pistol down on the top of her head. Still, the woman refused to let go. She just kept rounding her back, whimpering with every blow, until she fell silent and collapsed to one side, still clutching her babe in arms to her heart.

The soldier stepped over her and slammed the metal grille shut.

Then the train rolled on.

A CLOUD OF SNOWFLAKES was dancing in front of the car head-lights like a corps de ballet on the stage. Bergström was right: the icy cold afternoon had set the scene for a blanket of white that night.

The driver slowed down as she turned into the driveway, trigger-ing automatic security lights that illuminated their way along the grand paved approach to the front porch.

Through the inky darkness, Emily noticed the floor-level lighting along the paving stones on either side of the house. She also observed that the lights over the spiral staircase on the east wall were on, and so were the lights inside the house – on the landing that led to the second-floor attic.

The moment the profiler stepped out of the car, she was struck by the cold. She swiftly zipped her parka up to the neck, slung her backpack over her shoulder and hurried around to the rear of the Lindberghs' house. The patio and garden were brightly illuminated too. Emily turned on her heels and walked into the house through the front door.

The uniformed officer was waiting for her in the foyer. 'If you need me at all, Ms Roy, I'll be—'

But *Ms Roy* was already halfway up the stairs.

Emily strode across the landing into the Lindberghs' master bedroom. She put her backpack down and pulled out a kraft paper envelope, from which she extracted a series of A4-size photographs. Those depicting the murder of Aliénor's mother she spread out on the mattress. Kerstin's naked body had been found at the end of the bed, stabbed in the chest multiple times. And her tongue had been cut out. One photo showed how the blood had oozed from Kerstin's lips, down her chin and pooled in the gooey mess that remained of her chest. Another showed a wound on the back of her head, which Emily suspected was connected to the blood stain she could see on the bed frame. Emily turned her focus to the three photographs of the mattress. The first showed a fitted sheet that had been pulled down towards the end of the bed. The corners had slipped off the mattress and folded in on themselves. The second was a close-up of a crumpled pillow in the middle of the mattress, and the third showed another pillow, teetering on the edge of the bed as if Kerstin had grabbed it during her fall.

Emily stood at the foot of the bed with her back to the window facing out to sea and her boots almost touching the large aureole of dried blood on the floorboards. She figured the killer must have dragged Kerstin onto the floor by her feet or ankles, over the end of the bed; the injury to the back of her head perhaps a result of it hitting the bed frame. That would explain the bloodstain. Once she was on the floor, unconscious, Kerstin had been stabbed about a dozen times, judging by the wounds visible on the photos. Her tongue must have been removed afterwards. Kerstin's petite frame, which was at most one metre and sixty centimetres and weighed only fifty kilos, lent credibility to that scenario.

Emily slung her backpack over her shoulder again, poked her head into the en suite bathroom and took a quick look behind the door, before leaving the master suite, envelope and photographs in hand.

Scanning the floor as she moved down the hallway, she observed a few droplets of blood along the skirting boards, which she presumed had dripped from the knife or the killer's clothes. Then she went into Aliénor's bedroom. The proportions of the room were gener-ous, to say the least, and it opened onto a balcony deep enough to hold a small table and two chairs. Emily opened the sliding door and stepped outside to find herself caught in a flurry of billowy snowflakes, which brushed her cheeks and caught in her hair and eyelashes. She leaned over the railing, observed the surroundings for a moment, then went back into the bedroom and perched on the edge of the bed. From where she was sitting, the balcony and wooden railing were barely visible against the dark sky.

Emily picked up a few photographs and scrutinised them. Unlike her mother, Louise had not been naked. She had been wearing pyjamas and socks. Her body had been found on the bed, arms outstretched, with the duvet pulled over her bloody torso. The killer had subjected Louise to an even greater degree of violence, dealing her a vicious blow to her left temple, then stabbing her about twenty times in the chest before cutting off her tongue too. One of the photographs showed a close-up of the right side of her scalp, where a clump of hair was missing, and another showed some strands mixed with blood residue on the headboard. This probably meant that Louise had been sitting on the edge of the bed, looking out to the balcony, leaning against the pillow with her back to the door, like Emily was now. The killer must have grabbed her by the hair and slammed her head against the bed frame before attacking her with the knife.

Emily left the bedroom and went downstairs, observing that there were no traces of blood visible to the naked eye along the way. She breezed past the officer still standing in the foyer, who gave her a nod that she didn't see. Emily hurried on to the living room, flipping through the envelope to find the photographs of Göran Lindbergh. When she got there, she stood behind the U-shaped sectional to cast her eyes over the images.

The crime-scene shots showed Aliénor's father lying on the sofa with his head resting on two cushions, wireless headphones still perfectly in place over his ears. The iron candlestick used to knock him out had been placed on a small table beside the sofa, and his four stab wounds had been inflicted through the blanket that was pulled up to his shoulders.

Emily walked around to the side and stood by the armrest. As with Kerstin and Louise, the position of Göran's body suggested that the blow to the head had come first, and was followed by a knife attack that was less frenzied than the ones to which they'd been subjected. Finally, there'd been the excision of his tongue. Clearly, the killer's method had been to render each victim unconscious before stabbing them to death and removing their tongues.

Emily was building a profile of the killer based on three key elements: the blow to the back of the skull to immobilise each victim; the frenzied stabbing of the two women; and finally, the aspect that said the most, so to speak: the removal of the victims' tongues.

The profiler turned to look out of the bow window. The moon was tracing a luminous path across the sea. The Swedish had a special word for that, Emily reflected: *mångata*.

The killer could have climbed in through that window. Other possible points of entry were through the front door, the door from the veranda or the outside door to the second-floor attic, if Gerda hadn't locked it. The balcony door in Aliénor's bedroom had no handle on the outside, and there were no signs of forced entry. The killer could just as easily have approached the house from the main road or the beach. Canvassing the neighbours might shed some light on that.

Emily braced her backpack against her knee and put the envelope back inside, then went back out to the hall.

'Would you like me to drive you back, Ms Roy?' the young police officer asked, as Emily zipped up her parka.

'Yes, thank you, Mona.'

The rookie officer's cheeks flushed. She would never have expected the profiler to know her name.

The profile of the killer was starting to take shape, Emily thought as she opened the door of the police car, but there were still so many questions. One of those questions was much more pressing than anything else: if Louise had been killed in Aliénor's bedroom, did that mean Aliénor was the intended target?

Could Aliénor be in danger?

Nino's hand trembles in mine.

The doctor flips through the document without lifting his eyes from the pages. As if he were taking pleasure in keeping me waiting, one foot in the grave.

'And you haven't had another episode since then?' he asks, still reading.

'No,' I reply, freeing myself from Nino's hold.

'Not even a suggestion?'

'No, nothing at all.'

He snaps the folder shut, shaking his head. He rubs at his thick beard with his fingers. The chafing sound it makes is unpleasant. Indecent, almost.

'Listen, there's nothing wrong with your heart. Your test results are normal. Just a bit of cholesterol to keep an eye on, but nothing to be worried about.'

'Oh, thank God,' I sigh, fidgeting in my chair.

'And you say you've never experienced anything like this before?'

'Never,' Nino answers for me.

The doctor smiles. 'Did this episode of, er, falling ill, occur at a time when you were particularly stressed or tired?'

'Not at all. Precisely the opposite, in fact. I was with my family.'

'Yes, well, family is no guarantee of a quiet life, you know.'

I feel like asking the doctor whether he's speaking from experience.

'It happened during my grandson's christening.'

'Were you involved in the planning?'

'Ha! You obviously don't know my daughter, doctor. She's quite the

matriarch. It was all she could do to let me give the christening robe a bicarbonate of soda and lemon treatment to whiten it. Then she relegated us all to the church pews, and even then, she told us all where to sit.'

Nino strokes my hand. To take my voice down a tone, coax me off my high horse. I do tend to go off at a gallop sometimes without realising. And I never know when to stop.

'Perhaps the christening did stress you out, after all,' the doctor says, tongue in cheek, as he leans into his chair's high back.

As if the discussion has somehow taken a more light-hearted, familiar turn.

'Oh, no. I wasn't stressed.'

'Irked, then?'

'Certainly not to the point of collapsing in the middle of the church.'

'What I mean to ask is, how did the episode unfold, precisely?'

I close my eyes and exhale deeply with a sigh that splutters and then stalls, like an engine dying at the end of a race.

'My God, when I think back to it … I spoiled the whole day. Oh heavens, doctor, I feel mortified…'

'Tell me about that.'

I shake my head as I recall the incident.

'It was … it was like my whole body was shutting down, bit by bit…'

I swallow, but the words won't come out.

Nino's hand, clammy this time, squeezes mine once more. He saw me slip away. And when I came around and opened my eyes, it was him I saw, the look on his face shifting from horror to relief.

'I felt myself dying, doctor.'

The doctor nodded blankly, as if I were telling him I had a cold. 'Which of your senses was altered the first?'

I squint, trying to remember.

'My hearing.'

'And then?'

'I couldn't breathe anymore … and I felt like…' I press my palms to my heart. Fold my arms. My breath quickens.

'Like there was a weight on your heart?'

'More than that. Like something was crushing me.'

'Like an elephant sitting on your chest?'

'No … it was more of a feeling of bursting from the inside. It's hard to explain. Then my body, my body just gave up…'

'Where were you when it happened?'

'I was sitting in the church. Fortunately, I might add. Otherwise I might have really hurt myself. It was Nino who caught me.'

Nino straightens his lips into a thin, awkward smile. A smile of pity.

'They laid me on the floor … My God, I feel so ashamed.'

The sound of my grandson crying as I came to. The touch of my daughter's hand on my face. As cold as the church flagstones.

And the pool of urine I was lying in. The recollection snags in my throat.

'I … lost control of myself, doctor…'

Again, the blank nod sucks the drama out of my story, my experience.

'Do you suffer from incontinence?'

I glance at Nino from the corner of my eye. Some things are better not shared. Even with my Nino. It's bad enough that he's seen me pass out in a puddle of my own piss.

'No. Not at all, no.'

'What was the last thing you saw before you passed out?'

I smile. That's the effect this child has on me. Like a flower blooming from my heart.

'My grandson…'

My sentence tails off into the void. So does the doctor's reply.

He springs up from his chair, hurries over to me.

My eyes close as his white coat descends over my face. Like a shroud.

KRISTIAN OLOFSSON SLATHERED VICKS ointment all over his upper lip and tossed two sticks of fruit-flavoured chewing gum into his mouth, knowing the artificial flavours would mask the putrid odours that always seeped their way into his mouth and turned his stomach.

Birgit Pedrén looked up as she heard the squeaking of Emily's and Olofsson's soles on the vinyl floor of the morgue. The medical examiner had whipped her blonde hair into a tightly braided ponytail that kissed her shoulder.

'*Hej* beauty!' Olofsson purred, forgetting all about his mentholated moustache. 'The big boss is on his way. He's just on the phone with the prosecutor. He won't be a minute.'

'No problem,' Birgit chirped, following Emily with her gaze as the profiler walked straight past her, without a word, and headed for the autopsy tables.

'What's *Negan* supposed to mean?' the detective asked, pointing to the medical examiner's black T-shirt. The slogan on the garment proclaimed 'I'm Vegan', but the V had been crossed out and replaced with a blood-spattered N.

'No, way, Olofsson! Don't tell me you've never seen *The Walking Dead*?'

'I haven't, but everyone keeps telling me I have to get into it.' Olofsson couldn't help but notice the skin-tight vinyl leggings Birgit was wearing. 'Well, well, well, it didn't take you long to get your figure back, did it?'

'Don't be fooled, Olofsson, I'm wearing a girdle. As soon as I strip off, my skin looks like melted ice cream dripping off a cone. My belly's an apron catching it, and my tits are a scarf. I'm not kidding!'

'TMI, Pedrén, TMI! You'd better start working out again, and quick.'

'Right now, the only workout I get is in the bedroom. And believe me, it's always quite a feat.'

'You've popped out too many sprogs already, Pedrén.'

'Tell me about it,' she quipped. 'You can have one of them if you want. Or two.'

'You're making my heart bleed; I'm almost tempted to take you up on the offer!'

The medical examiner smiled and pinched his cheek, the way she would a cheeky child's.

'*Hej* Birgit, how are you?' Kommissionär Bergström called, striding towards them across the autopsy room.

Olofsson stood to attention, puffed out his bodybuilt chest and straightened his lips to wipe the smile off his face.

'Ah, thank you, Lennart. Finally someone who thinks to ask after the mother. People are always asking how the little ones are doing, but they conveniently forget I'm the one who squeezed them out of a hole no bigger than a thimble. Seriously, sometimes I wonder why we do it!'

Birgit pulled on a pair of latex gloves. 'Right, let's start with the mother, shall we? God knows, she deserves that at least.'

She smoothed the braid down her back and approached one of the steel tables. 'The blow to the back of her head was hard enough to disorient her or knock her out for a while. I found splinters from the bed frame in her hair. Given the angle of the wound, it seems she was pulled down the bed and cracked her head when she went over the edge and onto the floor. Then she was stabbed eleven times in the chest – three of those in the heart.'

Birgit pointed a gloved finger at the criss-cross of stab wounds in Kerstin Lindbergh's chest.

'Any signs of sexual activity or assault?' Emily cut in.

'None,' she replied just as curtly, scratching at the chain of Latin words tattooed around her neck. 'Right, on to the father,' she continued, moving to the next table. 'Unlike his wife, he was completely unconscious when he was stabbed four times in the chest; twice in the heart, I should add. The head wound was inflicted with the iron candlestick, as you suspected. No other signs of violence or sexual activity either.'

Olofsson spread some of the mentholated ointment inside his nostrils and tossed two more pieces of chewing gum in his mouth.

'As for their daughter, she had a rough time of it,' Birgit continued, moving to stand on Louise Lindbergh's left side. 'The blow to her left temple knocked her out like a light.'

Birgit turned Louise's head to the side. Bergström and Emily stepped forwards for a closer look.

'The fistful of hair that was ripped out of the right side of her scalp suggests that was where the killer grabbed her and shoved her up against the headboard, where you found the traces of blood. She was completely out of it when she was attacked, dead to the world, but not because of the blow to her head. I found traces of a pretty heavy sleeping pill in her blood, a drug she had been prescribed for the last four years. Now, hold on to your hats for this one: she was stabbed nineteen times. There's nothing to suggest sexual assault, but there is evidence of sexual activity – sperm in the vagina – from several hours earlier. Perhaps early evening.'

The medical examiner pulled off her gloves, threw them into the waste bin beside the autopsy table, and rolled up the sleeves of her lab coat to reveal a kaleidoscopic mosaic of tattoos.

'That's it for the blow-by-blow details. Now, for the common factors. All three of them had blood alcohol levels consistent with having had a glass or two of wine with their dinner, but nothing more. They were all in good health and they were all killed around eleven pm, give or take an hour or two. Based on the blood transfer between the victims, it appears Kerstin was killed first, followed by

Louise, and finally Göran. The blade used was nothing special, just a bog-standard kitchen knife, but a long and very sharp one. The killer was right-handed. As for the strength it would take to kill this little cast of characters: with a knife like that it would have been as easy as slicing into a steak. The tongues were cut out post mortem.'

'No difference in depth or angle between the wounds or the three victims?' Emily asked, her eyes still glued to the tattered breasts of Aliénor's sister.

'Not enough to suggest there were two or more assailants, no. The slight differences in depth are likely due to the fatigue caused by the effort involved. Even with a very sharp knife, it would be pretty exhausting for anyone to inflict thirty-four stab wounds.'

Las Ventas Women's Prison, Madrid, Spain
Thursday, 30 December 1937, 11.30 pm

TERESA'S CELLMATES HAD PUSHED their straw bedrolls together to make room for hers, leaving just a foot's width down the middle to form a narrow pathway to the door. The cell had been designed for two prisoners but was now housing twelve of them, all piled on top of one another.

One of the women, María, had shown Teresa the way to the sanitary block. They'd had to step over no end of women and children, whose prone bodies covered the floor like a swarm of insects. Eleven thousand souls in a prison built for five hundred: it was a monstrous human sea for them to wade through.

They went to the latrines first. The bowls were overflowing and they had to trudge through pools of excrement just to relieve themselves. Only then could Teresa start to scrub away the filth that covered her body like a second skin. The water was icy cold and the bar of soap tiny, but Teresa scrubbed so vigorously to get rid of the smell, afterwards her body was streaked all over with scratches. The next day, she could wash her clothes, María had promised. They would find something for Teresa to wear in the meantime, she said. Because whenever one of their cellmates was hauled before the firing squad, the women usually managed to keep a few of her meagre belongings.

Teresa stretched out on her bedroll, numb with cold. It was a cold that chilled her to the beds of her nails and the tips of her ears, as if she were freezing from the inside out, her bones before her skin. She listened to the relentless clamour of sick, starving bodies in suffering. Then she closed her eyes and thought about her beloved Tomeo, out there in hiding. Those rough hands of his. Oh, how she would always sigh with the slightest touch of his fingers. Now she felt like she couldn't breathe without him. She wondered where he was sleeping tonight. Whether he had found something to eat. God forbid, whether he was hurt. She wondered, too, how long they were going to keep her here at Las Ventas. And whether this was where she would draw her last breath.

UNDER A DUSTING OF FRESH SNOW, the contours of the Skrea Strand beach took on a watercolour quality, the sand and pebbles streaked with white and the jetty lying still beneath its icy blanket. Snowflakes shimmered like sequins, rounding every angle, smoothing each imperfection and spreading a sweet, calming beauty that lent the wintry scene a fairy-tale quality.

After dropping Bergström at the police station, Olofsson and Emily were on their way to pay a visit to Carina Isaksson, the Lindberghs' neighbour and friend. To quell his nausea, the detective had pulled into a service station on the drive back from the morgue to buy himself a coffee and some freshly baked *kanelbullar*.

Seeing Louise's body, her torso torn to shreds, had done him in. In his mind, he couldn't help but transpose the image of Aliénor's sister's brutal stab wounds onto Mona's firm, milky-white breasts. The urge to throw up had grown so strong, he'd had to rush out of the autopsy room, clenching his fist in his mouth. Like a slap in the face, the icy air had helped him regain some of his composure, but none of his colour. He was as white as a sheet until the coffee and cinnamon buns brought the blood back to his cheeks. Now he was chomping at the bit for another dose of caffeine, and he hoped some would be on offer at the elderly neighbour's place.

Gerda Vankard, the Lindberghs' resident housekeeper, opened the door to them before they had time to knock.

'Detective. Sergeant,' she nodded, ushering them inside.

Olofsson had to stifle a chuckle. He found it oddly amusing how often people mistook the renowned profiler for his subordinate. Emily simply flashed the warm smile she reserved for witnesses. *Unbelievable*, Olofsson said to himself. *How can someone so socially handicapped turn on the charm whenever she pleases? Emily Roy's taking the piss out of all of us, but no one dares bat an eye.*

Ahead of their interview with the Lindberghs' widowed neighbour, Emily had said not to worry about her at all. She didn't speak Swedish, but she could sit there and observe. The witness's body language and hesitations were all Emily needed to do her job as a profiler.

Carina Isaksson was waiting for them in the living room. To Olofsson's surprise, she was dolled up hotter than a Finnish sauna, as he so delicately phrased it in his mind. Judging by her face, which was as smooth as a baby's bum, there must be a lot of plastic under the surface and skin behind her ears, but he had to hand it to her, this cougar knew how to sharpen her claws.

'Detective Olofsson and Ms Roy, if I'm not mistaken?' she said, greeting them in flawless BBC English.

'You're absolutely right,' Emily replied, with a smile so radiant it almost seemed genuine.

'Please, do sit down,' their hostess insisted. 'Gerda will bring us some coffee. Or perhaps you'd rather have something else to drink?'

'Coffee would be lovely. Thank you, Ms Isaksson,' Emily replied, the smile still glued to her lips.

'Oh, do call me Carina, please! You know how it is in Sweden – everyone goes by their first name. I used to try and swim against the tide, but I came around to the idea in the end, and now I quite like being unencumbered by all that stuffy old "Ms" nonsense. Kommissionär Bergström said you'd be dropping by today. I'm delighted to meet you both. Göran and Kerstin were extremely proud of the opportunity you've given their daughter. I should thank you on their behalf.'

She lowered her eyes for a moment and wiped away a tear. 'If you don't mind, detective,' she continued, with a discreet sniffle, 'I'd prefer to carry on our conversation in English, out of respect for our guest. And also, I have to admit, because I don't often get the chance to speak English, now that my husband has passed away.'

'Where was he from?' Emily asked politely.

'Buckinghamshire. But I only ever set foot there myself on our wedding day. We lived in Edinburgh. I was born just down the road from here, in Varberg, but I went over to the UK to finish my studies and never really left … until Rupert died, eleven years ago. I felt like I needed a change of scenery, so I came back here and took my maiden name again. It felt easier to move on that way.'

Gerda placed a tray on the ottoman in front of them with a pot of coffee, three china cups, some milk and sugar, and a plate of *kanelbullar*, then left the living room, closing the door behind her. Olofsson poured the coffee straight away to get the caffeine into his bloodstream without further delay. He couldn't wait to wrap his chops around one of those delicious, puffy golden cinnamon buns. Now that they had switched to English, he figured Emily was going to lead the interview anyway, so he might as well sit back and relax in the passenger seat for a while.

'How long have you known the Lindberghs, Carina?' Emily asked.

'Since they bought their house in the late eighties. I inherited this place from my aunt, and Rupert and I used to spend three or four weeks here every summer, from about 1985, if my memory serves me well.'

'Were they from the area originally?'

'No, they were from Stockholm, but they'd been living in Falkenberg for years.'

'How often did you see them?'

Carina creased her lips, trying to keep the tears at bay. She took a few sips of coffee before she carried on. 'We would see each other at least once a week. We used to play golf together. Sometimes it was just Göran and me. Kerstin made a hobby of it to please her husband, but she really didn't find it very enjoyable.'

'Any dinners, lunches?'

'Yes, but it was always very informal. I would often drop by for a drink and end up staying for a bite to eat, and vice versa.'

'Did you know their children well?'

'Aliénor more than the other two, because she lived at home for a long time. I only ran into Louise and Léopold occasionally, when they came home to visit.'

'How did they get on with their parents?'

'Perfectly normally, I'd say, from what I saw.'

'Did Kerstin or Göran ever hint at any family conflicts?'

'No, never. But I do know what a burden Aliénor's autism was for the whole family.'

'Were you aware of any run-ins with anyone else who might have been involved in their deaths?'

'Good heavens, no. I know their work at the clinic was stressful, but I never got wind of anything that dramatic.' Carina sighed, massaging the fingers of her right hand.

'And you didn't see or hear anything suspicious on Friday night?'

'Nothing at all, no. I was in bed at eight, with my e-reader. I must have been asleep about half an hour later.'

'What about earlier that day? You didn't see anyone near the Lindberghs' house? On the driveway or the approach, perhaps?'

'Sorry, no. I went out in the morning to run some errands in town. I was home before eleven and I pottered around the house all day after that.'

'When did you see the Lindberghs for the last time?'

Carina shook her head, then answered the question through trembling lips. 'On Thursday. Göran ... came to see me in the middle of the afternoon, while Kerstin was at the clinic, in Gothenburg.'

Emily marked a pause, then continued. 'How would you say he was?'

'He was fine; as fit as a fiddle,' Carina replied, wiping a fresh stream of tears from her cheeks.

'Do you know if they were expecting any visitors yesterday, or anytime this weekend?'

'Sorry, I have no idea.'

'And how did they get on as a couple?'

'Very well. Tremendously well, in fact. In every way, except in bed. That's why our arrangement worked so well – it balanced everything else out.'

Emily tilted her head to one side. 'Forgive me, Carina, but what kind of arrangement are you talking about?'

Carina clapped her hands on her thighs. 'Goodness me, I thought Gerda would have been falling over herself to tell you! Göran and I were lovers.'

Olofsson almost choked on his mouthful of *kanelbullar*. He had to take another swig of coffee to help it go down. Reeling from the shock, he watched as Emily poured them all a second cup of coffee, as if Carina the Cougar's bombshell had been the most natural thing in the world to discover.

'How did Kerstin take to your arrangement?' the profiler asked, reaching for her cup.

'She felt like she'd been set free. Sex was torture for her, even with the man she loved. She was relieved she didn't have to force herself to satisfy his needs anymore, with me seeing to them, so to speak. And as far as I was concerned, it did me the world of good – it made me feel far less lonely.'

'How did the arrangement work from a practical perspective, Carina?'

'Well, Göran came over here whenever he felt the need. And because it was just sex, nothing else, everyone was happy.'

'And the three of you were able to enjoy each other's company, regardless?' Olofsson chimed in, clearly baffled.

'Yes, absolutely. Let me be clear, detective, I wasn't taking anything away from Kerstin. In fact it was quite the opposite; I was giving her peace of mind.'

WHEN OLOFSSON AND EMILY entered the incident room, Mona was sticking photographs of the crime scene onto the whiteboard.

'Ms Roy … Detective Olofsson,' she blushed, seeing who had swished their way through the swing doors. 'The … the commissioner asked me to bring over the photos and I thought that if I…' For a moment, she was lost for words. 'I thought that if I stuck them up on the board, it might save you some time,' she eventually managed to say, her cheeks as rosy as if she had just come in from the cold.

Emily turned to Olofsson, leaving it up to him to take the situation, or rather Mona, in hand.

'Uh, yes … thanks. We'll take it from here,' he stammered, leaning on the back of a chair.

Mona nodded, fixed her gaze on her feet, and then scurried out of the room, running into Bergström who was on his way in.

'Good grief, Olofsson, whatever did you say to the poor young woman to make her run out like that?' the commissioner asked, placing a pot of coffee and three mugs on the table.

'I didn't say a thing, boss! I was actually thanking her, wasn't I, Emily?' the detective protested.

Emily didn't grace him with a reply. She was busy sticking up the photographs Mona had left behind.

'All right, Olofsson, don't get a bee in your bonnet,' the commissioner said as he poured the coffee. 'Tell me how things went at Carina Isaksson's.'

'Bloody hell, boss. Talk about a soap opera. Turns out the widow next door was having it off with Aliénor's old man. Can you believe it? I mean, I get it – she's as hot as a rocket. But that's not the half of it. Get a load of this: Aliénor's mum knew all about it! I know, right?' He winked in response to the shock on Bergström's face. 'And according to Isaksson, she was doing Kerstin a favour, because apparently she really wasn't into getting her rocks off…'

'Good grief,' was all Bergström managed to say, rubbing the bridge of his nose.

'Other than dropping that bombshell, she didn't see anything, didn't hear anything, blah, blah, blah. And she had nothing interesting to say about the family, or the clinic either. So that's that.' Olofsson stood up, pulled his phone out of his pocket and scrolled through his notes. 'So, where the hell do we start, then? Because right now, it's just one big shit show. We've got three victims, all from the same family, the same signature, same M.O., so…'

Bergström looked at him, unsure whether he should be worried or pleasantly surprised.

'Maybe it was an act of retaliation against the clinic?' Olofsson continued. 'Or maybe the old man was slipping it to a whole coop of other chicks, and one of them, or one of their husbands, got fed up and decided to take it out on the whole family. What do you think?' he asked, looking up from his phone.

'It looks to me like young Mona's turning you into quite the studious type, Kristian,' Bergström teased.

Olofsson opened his mouth in astonishment, as if he'd been caught red-handed. He couldn't help but notice a flicker of amusement in the corner of the Emily's eye too. It made him want to crawl under the table.

'We need to start with the crime scene,' Emily interjected, twirling her hair into a ponytail.

Relieved by the change of subject, Olofsson slumped down into the nearest chair.

'Kerstin is our first victim,' Emily continued. 'The killer was lying in wait under the Lindberghs' bed, then came out and dragged her onto the floor, most certainly by her heels. The blow to the back of the head might appear to be accidental, but seeing as Göran and Louise Lindbergh were killed the same way – knocked out then stabbed – that's our killer's modus operandi. Then the killer sliced off her tongue, and must have brought some kind of container or zip-lock bag to take it away in, before moving on to do the same to Louise, down the hallway, and then to Göran downstairs.'

'Hang on a sec,' Olofsson cut in, rocking forwards in his chair. 'We haven't got any results back from the lab yet, so what makes you think the perp was hiding under the bed? And are you seriously suggesting this psycho brought a Tupperware to carry the tongues home?'

Emily flipped the board over, popped the top off a marker and drew three rectangles to represent the various levels of the Lindbergh home. She marked the living room, veranda, bedrooms and attic on her diagram, then added the balcony, beds, doors and sofas.

'Let's assume the assailant enters the house around the time the crime is committed: approximately eleven pm. Both possible points of entry are on the ground floor. The two other access points – Aliénor's balcony door and the separate entrance to the attic apartment – are locked.'

Emily kept scribbling on the board as she voiced her theories. 'If the killer came in via the ground floor, Göran – who, according to Aliénor, was a night owl – would have seen a figure pass by on the veranda, which skirts around the living room, or come in through the front door, which is visible from the sofa.'

Emily pointed with the marker to the rectangle representing the sofa where Aliénor's father had been found dead. 'By the same token, this theory only works if Kerstin was asleep, otherwise she would have heard her attacker approach and would have got up to defend herself. But the crime scene suggests otherwise. When she was dragged onto the floor, Kerstin grabbed at the pillows and sheets, which means that she was awake – she was taken by surprise and didn't have time to get up. I think, therefore, that her attacker came out from under the bed, then dragged her off the end onto the floor in one quick movement, knowing she was no heavier than fifty or so kilos.'

'What a nightmare ... Imagine a guy with a knife lurking under your bed.' Olofsson shivered.

'Do you think we might be dealing with a woman, Emily?' Bergström asked, pouring himself another coffee. 'If we analyse the modus operandi and the need to immobilise each victim before killing them, that could tell us something about the killer's build or strength, could it not?'

'It certainly could be an indicator of strength, yes, but also the killer's own perceived strength, or self-confidence. That's a function of the killer's prior experience and mental state. Or it might be quite simple: the killer wanted to make sure the victims didn't fight back. And to answer your "tongues in Tupperware" question, Kristian: my deduction is linked to the killer's modus operandi. Someone who kills with such organisation and precision would treasure trophies like that, not just shove them into a pocket and let them drip all over the place.'

'Right, then, so we have no idea whether the killer's a guy or a gal,' Olofsson quipped, still balancing on two legs of his chair. 'But first, shouldn't we be asking ourselves why this whole massacre happened? What the hell is this all about? Revenge? Or a serial killer going after randoms because his mum once told him off for touching his itty-bitty private parts? I mean, the guy cut out their tongues, for chrissakes. There must be some secret message there, Em, don't you think?'

'Certainly. Either they talked too much, or not enough. But that's all in the killer's fantasies, so it's not necessarily linked to the Lindberghs.'

'So what the hell do we do now? Practically, I mean.'

'We work with what we have: the victims,' Kommissionär Bergström snapped, unimpressed by the detective's hypothetical musings. 'We're going to start by doing some DNA tests to make sure there are no family secrets and to confirm that Louise, Léopold and Aliénor are all biological siblings.'

Emily nodded.

'Kristian, I want you to look into the family's past and the clinic's history.'

'All by myself, boss?' Olofsson complained, a bit more abruptly than he intended.

'Ask Mona to help you.'

'Seriously, boss? You're pairing me up with Mona? You're kidding, right? Why can't we ask Mademoiselle Ooh-la-la instead? – Alexis, I mean. I'm sure she must be getting fed up with choosing centrepieces and canapés by now.'

'Kristian!'

'What? I bet she is. And you have to admit, this kind of stuff is right up her street.'

Emily closed her eyes. In her mind, the image of Alexis in her wedding dress merged with the vision of the Lindberghs' massacred bodies. A sea of blood washed over the white dress and Aliénor's face emerged from the glossy red surface.

Emily grabbed her backpack and parka and left the room without a word. Without batting an eye, Bergström and Olofsson carried on divvying up the tasks at hand.

The cold struck her full in the face as Emily stepped outside the station. Greedily sucking in a few breaths of icy air, she crossed the street and went to sit on a low stone wall beside the pavement. Then she took a little black box out of her inside coat pocket. She opened it and gazed inside for a few seconds.

That was always the hardest part. Being in tune with her senses, without letting her emotions overwhelm her.

Emily tucked away the image of Aliénor in the empty box. She contemplated her friend's face for a moment, then closed the lid.

'HELLO AND WELCOME, *Madame* Castells. I'm Serena; so pleased to meet you. *Mad-oh,* is that right?'

Mado shook the hand proffered by the wedding planner, who was not only a picture of Swedish beauty, but also spoke French. Visibly impressed by the sublime Serena's linguistic talents, she turned and went to sit beside her future son-in-law, miming a wide-eyed '*Mad-oh*' to Alexis, who had to bite her lip and squeeze Stellan's hand so she wouldn't burst out laughing.

Her mother had been in fine form all day and seemed to have forgotten about all of yesterday's moaning and groaning. Over breakfast, Alexis had told her that Lennart was busy investigating a triple murder and would be mostly unavailable in the lead-up to the wedding. Mado hadn't asked for any details; but shaking her head, she had mustered up the appropriate pain and spread it all over her face, living the drama as if it were her own, with the eternal empathy she liked to say was a Mediterranean thing.

The rest of the day had been a race against the clock: collecting the bottles of Bandol rosé from the Systembolaget shop that were to be given out as wedding favours, trying on her dress for the seamstress to make her finishing touches, and finally, shopping for the shoes that would take her down the aisle. She was yet to find the right pair. But in spite of Mado's breezy good humour and all the wedding preparations, Alexis couldn't stop thinking about Aliénor and her family. After several attempts to reach her, she had ended up leaving a message. Then she had called Emily and arranged to meet her for dinner that evening.

On the phone, Emily had been just as curt as usual, but Alexis knew not to take offence. The two previous cases they had worked on together had taught her not to search the surface for Emily's emotions. Alexis simply accepted the profiler's misanthropic façade and even found herself appreciating it sometimes. She had only seen Emily twice since the Tower Hamlets case was closed, but that was twice more than the year before. Alexis was still the one to initiate their get-togethers, but at least now Emily responded and occasionally accepted her invitation. That was a huge step in the right direction.

'Well, perhaps I should continue in French then?' Serena asked, pouring her clients a coffee.

'*Absolument*,' Stellan replied, with his customary hint of a Belgian accent.

'The big day is fast approaching, so I'd like us to go over the timeline and clear up a couple of questions. But before we get into any of that, can I just clarify something? Alexis, you'll get dressed in this suite here, with your mother, your maid of honour and your bridesmaids. Stellan, we'll put you and your best man in a junior suite. Is that all right with you?'

Alexis and Stellan nodded.

'No changes to the witnesses or bridesmaids, I presume?'

Alexis and Stellan exchanged a look of surprise before confirming there weren't any changes, no.

'Believe me, it does happen,' Serena explained. 'And who's going to have the rings at the ceremony?'

'My niece and nephew, my sister's children,' Alexis replied.

'Perfect. I have your sister's email, so I'll get in touch with her. Did you manage to order the wine for the wedding favours?'

'Yes, it's in the car.'

'Perfect, I'll get someone to unload it before you go. And have you chosen a toastmaster for the evening?'

'Yes, my sister Lena,' Stellan replied.

'Very well. Would you like to be kept abreast of the number of speeches, so you can get one or two out of the way during the cocktail hour?'

'I don't think there'll be that many,' Alexis laughed.

'Twenty-two, last I heard from Lena,' Stellan chimed in.

Alexis's eyes flew open in surprise. 'Twenty-two ... speeches?'

'Er ... yes.' Serena crossed and uncrossed her legs, smoothing out the creases at the knees of her trousers.

'But that's going to be at least two hours of blah, blah, blah!' Alexis sputtered. 'That's not a wedding, it's a United Nations convention.'

'That's the tradition, *älskling*,' Stellan purred. People look forward to the speeches – it's when they express their love and friendship for the newlyweds, and—'

'*People?* The Swedes, you mean! Because everyone else, the other half of the guests, is going to die of boredom. Can you imagine anyone listening to all that "tudubrrrutudubrrrutudubrrru" droning on for two hours? I get that our parents and my maid of honour and your best man should give a speech, of course, but twenty-two people, Stellan, seriously?'

'Thirty-one, actually, but a lot of them are pairing up for their speeches—'

'Oh, what a relief. And here I was thinking it'd go on forever and a day!' Alexis rolled her eyes.

Mado reached out and gently rubbed her daughter's hand.

'Why didn't you say anything to me?' Alexis went on.

'You asked me to take care of the dinner, so I took care of the dinner,' Stellan argued.

'And you didn't think to tell me our wedding dinner would go on for five hours?'

'Listen: I don't see why it's such a big deal. It's a fantastic tradition. It's not all speeches, you know. It's like having lots of little cabaret numbers. Some people sing songs or recite poems—'

'Oh, wonderful, like an end-of-term show, you mean?' Alexis

raised an eyebrow. 'I've never heard of anything more ridiculous in my whole life!'

'Really, Alexis?' Stellan protested.

'Now just a minute, Alexis Castells, can you hear yourself?' Mado's voice boomed over her daughter's and future husband's. 'Don't you be getting on your high horse now, young lady! For the love of God, you've been in a foul mood since this morning. Let's just get through this meeting in one piece, shall we, then we'll drop you at the station with your crime-fighting friends so you can sniff a few dead bodies and leave the rest of us in peace.'

'Maman?!'

'Yes, I'm sorry, may their souls rest in peace, those poor people … But at this rate you're going to beat around the bush until you trip and fall into it, so we might as well throw you right in!'

Silence.

'Right, then,' Mado barrelled on. 'And what if, as Serena suggests, we were to move five or six speeches to the cocktail hour to lighten the load during dinner, and ask everyone to keep it short, eh? Like three minutes max for the parents, best man and maid of honour, and two minutes tops for everyone else? Then, I suppose the toaster—'

'The toastmaster,' Serena corrected.

'Yes, sorry Serena, I suppose the *toastmasteure* will be given all the speeches ahead of time so she can introduce the speakers, *non*?'

'The toastmaster can ask for the speeches ahead of time, yes.'

'Right. So, here's how we'll do things – because I agree with my son-in-law-to-be on this; it's a fabulous tradition. And you are marrying a Swede in Sweden, aren't you, *ma chérie*? So anyone who speaks English will give their speech in English, whether they're French, Swedish or from Whocareswhere-on-Sea. Then, someone will translate the Swedish speeches into English and French, and someone else will translate the French speeches into English, because we all know the Swedes understand English perfectly, unlike us linguistically handicapped Frenchies. Then we'll put all these little texts in a booklet that we'll give to all the guests with some embarrassing photos of the two of you in nappies and dental braces, and it will make such a lovely souvenir for everyone. That way, the guests will be able to follow all the speeches, poems, songs and whatnot with a kind of simultaneous translation in front of them, and if they still get bored out of their tree, then they'll keep on munching their meal, chugging their wine or leering at the person next to them at the table. How does that sound to you two lovebirds? And what about you, Serena?'

'*Mad-oh*, you're a natural at this!' the wedding planner gushed, giving her a wink.

Stellan kissed his future mother-in-law on the cheek.

Alexis flushed with emotion – and a tinge of embarrassment – and acquiesced with a nod. Her mother was right: it was time she saw Emily.

TERESA TRUDGED ALONG BEHIND Sister Marcela, accompanied by the clicking of her rosary. Nearly seven years had passed since she had first set foot in these corridors strewn with bruised, battered bodies.

She hadn't wanted to stay in the infirmary. She had already spent two nights there. She needed the girls by her side; their presence was like a cocoon. Or rather, a wall to keep the outside at bay. She needed to hear them going about their day, arguing over scraps of orange rind and moaning and groaning when they were trying to go to sleep at night.

When they arrived back at Teresa's cell, Sister Marcela slipped a little chamomile and two aspirins into Teresa's hand, then promptly turned on her heels and went on her way.

The girls got up from their straw bedrolls. Slowly. Juana's little one hid behind her mother, and started crying and asking who Teresa was.

'Oh, Tere…' they all gasped, almost in unison. The sound echoed off the damp walls.

Not one of them dared wrap their arms around her, fearful of hurting her battered body even more. Teresa could see in their eyes the ravages she had suffered three days earlier. The slightest touch to the cuts and bruises on her face made her flinch.

Her cellmates made sure she took an aspirin. Then they helped her out of her dress, gently lifting it free from her scabs, and dabbed at her wounds with compresses dipped in the chamomile. Teresa could feel from their touch they were surprised she was still alive. She too had thought she would never be going back to them in that cell. There had been so much force and rage behind the blows, each one had felt like it might be the last.

For the first few hours, she had tried to keep the flavour of her beloved Tomeo fresh in her mouth and her mind. It was for him that she kept getting up – after every single blow. There were two of them fighting so they could be together again after the war. He was battling in the resistance, and she was struggling in here. Every time a blow came, she thought back to the taste of the scraps of paper her Tomeo would have someone slip to her on visitors' days. She would read the message twice, loving every curve and peak of the letters he had written on the little slip of paper, then crumple it up and place it under her tongue, like a holy communion wafer, before chewing and swallowing the pulp. She savoured every moment of this communion.

But when they placed his wedding ring on the table in front of her, she understood. Suddenly, she felt empty. Hollow and empty. The spirit of Tomeo had kept her stronger than she could ever have imagined. If she were a tree, he had been the roots and the branches. And so she had asked one of the guards to open the window. She was suffocating, she had said, spitting the words through her swollen lips. If he had believed her, and if he had opened that window, she would have hurled herself out of it. Because she understood there would be no more scraps of paper showered with kisses and folded with hope. There would be no joyful reunion. No more future for them. This was where their story ended.

The girls clothed her in a loose tunic, and piled a few straw mattresses on top of one another and helped her to lie down. Teresa closed her eyes to connect with her Tomeo. She was going to tell him she had changed her mind.

Now, she would far rather die than live.

LÉOPOLD LINDBERGH. His parents could not have chosen a more fitting name. He wore it like the family coat of armour. All he was missing was the haughty chin tilt and arrogant power pose. He reminded Bergström of the old-moneyed sons of aristocrats certain British TV detectives always encountered brushing horses in their stables.

'Mr Lindbergh, thank you for coming to see us under such tragic circumstances.'

'No, not at all … It's my pleas— Er, not at all.' Léopold's gaze flitted from the commissioner to Emily before falling to the floor, as if suddenly burdened by a weight too heavy to bear.

'Please accept our deepest condolences.'

Léopold nodded, his eyes still rooted to the floor.

Bergström mentally corrected himself. There was something about the image the Lindberghs' son projected that didn't fit with his personality. His gentle voice, imbued with hesitation, contrasted with everything else about him, from his meticulously groomed hair to his sleek, velvet corduroy trousers.

'Perhaps we could start by talking about the last time you saw your parents and sister, Mr Lindbergh?'

Léopold coughed into his fist then spread his palms as wide as suns on his thighs. 'It was Friday night. We … we all had dinner together at home.'

'Just the four of you?'

'No … there was Albin too – Louise's partner; and Esther, Albin's mother.'

'Do they live in Falkenberg?'

'No. Albin just moved to Gothenburg and his mother was visiting him.'

'What time did you finish eating dinner?'

'Quite early. Albin wanted to get back to Gothenburg that night. He was flying to Russia the next morning.'

'To Russia?' Bergström reflected in surprise.

'Yes, for a business trip.' Léopold suddenly looked up and cast a gaze of bewilderment around the room, as if he had only just noticed the bare walls, two-way mirror and plastic cup of water on the table.

'Didn't your sister want to go back to Gothenburg with him that night?'

'No … Louise … she was spending the weekend at home.'

'What about you? Weren't you planning to stay as well?'

'I … I had to work … the next day … Saturday … yesterday.' His brow knitted and his face seemed to go limp, as if it were caving in from the grief.

'What time did Albin and his mother leave?'

Léopold paused and swallowed, then reached for his water and took a few careful sips. 'Nine pm,' he murmured.

'And what time did you leave?'

'About a quarter of an hour later.'

The thin plastic cup crunched between his fingers as he put it back down on the table.

Bergström observed Emily. In spite of her relaxed posture, she was watching the Lindberghs' son like a hawk, analysing every micro-expression, every pause and every movement he made. He knew that when Léopold had left the interview room, they would go over the recording and the profiler would stop the video from time to time and ask the commissioner to translate a word or sentence from Swedish. And she would not take a single note, content to simply observe with the keen eye of a predator stalking its prey.

'Why didn't you travel with them? You were all heading back to Gothenburg, weren't you?' Bergström pressed.

'That's what we said at dinner … that we should have arranged to all drive out here together.'

'How did the dinner go? No tension or arguments? Nothing that might have struck you as strange or surprising? How did you find your mother? Your father? And your sister?'

Léopold shook his head after every one of the commissioner's questions. 'It … it was all … it was…' He closed his eyes for a moment and exhaled deeply through his nose before continuing. 'It was just a family dinner. That's all it was.'

'You're not aware of any conflict there might have been between your father, mother or sister and anyone else?'

'No … no,' he replied, shaking his head adamantly. 'I don't understand … I can't wrap my head around…'

Léopold suddenly looked up at Bergström in horror. 'Do you know who … who attacked them?'

'No, Mr Lindbergh, not yet.'

'But do you have any leads? Any idea who might have done it, I mean?'

'I'm sorry, not yet. You work at your parents' clinic, don't you?' Bergström continued.

'Yes, I'm an embryologist.'

'And how are things at the clinic?'

A crease appeared between Léopold's eyebrows. 'Good … very good. But do you think their … Do you think this is connected to the clinic somehow?'

'Have you had any threats from patients? Or former employees? Any legal disputes?'

'No. Not at all, no.'

'That will be all, then,' the commissioner said, getting up.

Léopold hesitated for a second, then pulled himself together and stood up, almost as tall and firm as Bergström. 'Can I…?' he asked, gesturing to the door with his eyes.

'Yes, you're free to go. I will just ask you to prepare your employee and patient files for us to inspect,' the commissioner said as Léopold shook his outstretched hand. 'All the way back to when the clinic opened. We have a warrant to access these documents.'

Léopold Lindbergh hardened his stare and looked from Bergström to Emily, who was still seated. He nodded a curt acknowledgement and left the interview room.

'Good grief, Emily, if you hadn't asked me to listen out for it, I don't think I would have noticed it at all,' Bergström sighed, tossing the used plastic cup into the bin. 'He didn't say Aliénor's name, or refer to his parents directly, a single time. Not even once.'

Emily turned towards the door with a scathing look in her eyes. It was a primal kind of stare. She looked like a lioness on the prowl, every muscle in her body poised to attack.

Thursday, 22 November 1990

I take a pew at the back so I can make a quick exit. As soon as I feel the urge. I'm not planning to sit through the whole mass. Even though I probably should, so I can gather my scattered thoughts. Pull myself together and try to make sense of what's happening to me.

The next step is a brain scan, the doctor explained after the episode in his office. Because even though it feels like it's my heart that's caving in on itself, maybe it's what's happening up there that's the problem.

I unbutton my coat and rest my handbag on my lap.

I've never taken the time to think about the end. About the end of me. I have never contemplated the punctuation at the end of my life sentence. Being confronted with it all of a sudden feels like having to slam on the brakes at the edge of a cliff, stretching my arms out wide to try and keep my fragile but vital balance.

I've never liked ending my sentences with full stops, anyway. I've always preferred exclamation marks. 'Excitement and enthusiasm, and at the very least a pause, but never a full stop,' my editor-in-chief liked to tease, back in the old days.

A young woman sits down next to me. The church pews are chock-full of believers, or desperate souls, like me. On a Thursday evening, believe it or not. I smile.

'Believe it or not' indeed – how so many people have faith, or want to believe, in God.

I suppose there is a certain beauty to this gathering in the name of love, because after all, it is the love of God that's drawing these men and women here. Perhaps some of them, like me, are searching their souls.

They could be reclining in a shrink's office, or nursing a bottle of whisky, but instead, they're here, in the House of the Almighty.

Still, it would never have occurred to me to go soul-searching in a church, if my daughter hadn't suggested it. When she was a child and had misplaced a toy, I used to tell her that retracing her steps would help her find it. Now she was giving me my own advice. 'Why don't you go back to church, Mum?' she suggested. Because that's where it all started.

So Mum has decided to return and retrace her steps. During Mass, no less. Might as well go the whole hog, mightn't I?

Speaking of Mass, the priests (plural) are making their entrance. They're crossing the nave and heading towards the altar. There are three of them. Perhaps it's a special occasion. Theirs is a careful, paced and solemn procession. In communion with their god already. The one in the middle is wearing a sort of chasuble over his cassock. He must be the one officiating. No choirboys this time, only three cassocks – or perhaps the proper word is albs – that's it, three albs. Since I was only a child I have only ever set foot in church for weddings and christenings, and I can count on the fingers of one hand how many of those I've been to, so forgive me if my vocabulary's a bit rusty.

The church murmurs with the rustling of liturgical vestments gliding over flagstones, brushing against one another, the age-old silence of God reducing us to a whisper before we kneel before Him.

In their wake, the priests trail a smell of incense, candles and damp stone. As if these men of the cloth were reviving the perfume of prayer.

The priest on the right cranes his neck and holds on to the pulpit as he adjusts his stole.

I shiver. Turn up the collar of my coat.

Another wave of chills washes over me. It swells in my chest and rolls out through my whole body, making me hot and cold all at once. My tongue feels thick, heavy, and my heart heaves with nausea. A taste sticks in the roof of my mouth and makes me want to throw up. All of a sudden, there's an image in my mind, together with that awful sensation; then another, and yet another. Memories that have no roots in my past, like orphaned recollections.

Yet these are memories so intense, they root me to the spot.

The awful taste in my mouth and shivers on my skin have gone. Now all I can feel is the pool of urine wetting my clothes on the church pew.

Gustaf Bratt Restaurant, Falkenberg
Sunday, 4 December 2016, 7.00 pm

'*HEJ*, NICE TO SEE YOU!' called Jonas, the owner of Alexis's favourite restaurant in town, enveloping her in a Scandinavian embrace. 'So, how are the final preparations coming along? You must be run off your feet!'

'Not really. Actually, it feels like I'm just getting started,' Alexis replied, taking a seat at a table in a quiet corner of the room.

'Oh, that's good, because I've got a job for you. Beata's tearing her hair out because you haven't confirmed the menu option for your dinner yet.'

'Oh my God, Jonas, I'm so sorry!'

The night before the wedding, Alexis and Stellan were hosting their families at the restaurant for a rehearsal dinner, and they had completely forgotten it was up to them, not their wedding planner, to organise that evening. The chef's email must have been gathering dust in her inbox for weeks.

'You know what, I'm going to get on that right away, before Beata decides there's no cheese and pizzettes for me tonight!'

'Wise idea,' Jonas replied with a wink. 'What do you feel like now: red or white? We've just brought a 2014 Barbaresco into the cellar. It's exquisite. How does that sound?'

'Perfect.'

'With an order of pizzettes?'

'You must be a mind-reader.'

He vanished, and Alexis scrolled through her phone to find the menu options the chef had sent. She decided to go with Beata's second option, which featured a typical Swedish dish for every course, from finger food through to dessert. It was a perfect tasting menu for the occasion.

Jonas returned with a glass of Barbaresco for Alexis and a plate of miniature pizzas topped with cherry tomatoes and smoked mozzarella.

'*Voilà, Madame!*' he announced in a rough, guttural rendering of French.

'*Tack så mycket,*' Alexis replied, thanking him in her Gallic-tinged Swedish. And please tell Beata I'd like to go with option two; I'm sure she'll be thrilled.'

'*Parfait.* Shall I bring you a carafe of water and a bread basket now, or would you rather wait for your plus-one?'

'I'll wait, thanks.'

He smiled and breezed away to another table to take a couple's order.

Alexis tasted the Barbaresco – robust and full-bodied, just the way she liked it – and let her eyes wander around the room. Bratt's had become her evening bolthole whenever Stellan was away. She loved the familiar, cocoon-like feeling of the place as well as the exquisite cuisine, not to mention the all-French cheese board, which they had renamed 'Alexis's Choice' in her honour. Sometimes she would bring her laptop and spend the evening working – and nibbling, of course – at a table to help combat the solitude of her Swedish days. Her mother was right about that, at least. She was going to miss the frenetic pace of London and Londoners, although she was keeping her Hampstead flat and planning to spend ten days or so each month there. She had no children, so it was a little luxury she could afford to treat herself to. No children, indeed. It was a conscious decision, as she had no desire whatsoever to start a family. Her biological clock must be broken. Her sister swore the urge had come to her 'like she had to pee', but Alexis had never felt the slightest hint of that kind of pressing need. She loved her niece and nephew to bits, but she never had to bombard their ears with a constant stream of no's, as her niece put it. She could treasure them without the responsibility of educating them, and she loved to spoil them rotten like every good auntie should.

When she had announced to Stellan how determined she was to reject motherhood, she had been expecting the discussion to last more than a few seconds. He had simply replied that he didn't want kids either, and before they knew it, they were in bed together. But could a couple live happily ever after without any offspring? Was it unnatural – against human nature – to reject the idea of parenthood and not pay it forwards? Besides, how much of a role did conformity and social pressure play in all of this? Perhaps it was all one huge conspiracy – by parents who hated the thought of others perpetually living the free and easy life they had sacrificed when they decided to start a family and were now driving this widespread desire to reproduce? In spite of them all professing to *adore* being bound by family ties. Bloody masochists, she thought, relishing a mouthful of pizzette.

Suddenly Emily appeared in Alexis's field of vision, making her jump. The profiler put her backpack down by her feet and, as she always did in a public place, buckled the straps around the leg of her chair.

'Would you like a glass of wine?' Alexis asked without further ado, knowing that Emily wouldn't grace any pleasantries or rhetorical questions with a reply.

'Just water.'

Alexis gestured to the waitress, who glanced at their table and brought over a carafe and a bread basket.

Emily poured them each a glass, then pulled a large envelope from her bag and passed it to Alexis.

'Crime scenes and autopsies?' Alexis asked.

'Crime scenes.'

Emily scanned the menu as Alexis examined the photos in her lap, wanting to be somewhat discreet about it.

As soon as she put her true-crime writer hat on and dove into a case, Alexis disconnected from all empathy. She had the ability to detach herself from the underlying human drama and create a separate compartment in her mind for the other victims: the family, who had to suffer not only the loss of their loved ones, but also come to terms with the brutal violence that had snatched them away. They had to grieve twice; Alexis knew that from personal experience. A decade earlier, the man she loved, Samuel Garel, had fallen victim to a notorious serial killer, Richard Hemfield. As if the loss of her partner at the time hadn't been bad enough, Alexis had had to confront her grief again years later when a case she and Emily were investigating pointed to Hemfield's involvement.

The waitress came back to take Emily's order and breezed away again.

Alexis suddenly looked up, smoothing her creased eyebrows with the tips of her fingers.

'The killer cut their tongues out?'

Emily's gaze shifted to meet hers.

'Were they sexually assaul—'

'No,' Emily cut her off. 'The mother was sleeping naked. The sister had had consensual sexual relations, but earlier in the day.'

'What order were they killed in?'

'Kerstin, the mother, in the master bedroom on the first floor at one end of the hallway; then Louise, the sister, in Aliénor's room, again on the first floor at the opposite end of the hallway, near the top of the stairs; and finally Göran, the father, in the living room on the ground floor. That's based on the blood transfer between the victims.'

Alexis froze in astonishment. 'Louise was killed in Aliénor's bedroom? Did the killer force her in there?'

'No, there's nothing to suggest that she was dragged or carried there. That wouldn't be consistent with the head injury she sustained. Still, I don't know why she was in there.'

Emily's never more expressive than when she's talking about death, Alexis mused as she flipped through the photographs again.

'So … the killer started upstairs … then went down again? Do you think they were hiding in the Lindberghs' bedroom?'

'That's what I'm thinking, yes.'

Alexis paused for a moment. 'Wait a second: you said the killer started with the mother, but from the crime-scene shots, it looks like the sister, Louise, was subjected to the most violence, unless I'm mistaken?'

'That's right. Nineteen stab wounds for Louise, eleven for Kerstin and four for Göran.'

'So the sister was the primary target,' Alexis said, shuffling the photographs of Louise's lifeless body to the top of the pile. 'Or perhaps it was Aliénor – since Louise's body was found in her bedroom…'

Alexis reached for her Barbaresco. She swirled the wine around her glass, stretching its legs and letting it breathe before she took a sip.

'Are you thinking revenge?'

'Some kind of retaliation for sure, but not necessarily directed at the Lindberghs personally. It could be a fantasy thing, something that's all in the killer's mind.'

Alexis shook her head with a sigh. 'Bloody hell, Emily…'

'I know,' the profiler whispered, as the waitress placed a plate of gravlax in front of her.

'No drama in Aliénor's past or rivalry we should be aware of?'

'She walked out before we could finish her interview.'

Alexis placed her hand on Emily's, just for a second or two. 'How's Aliénor coping?' she asked.

'I don't know.' Emily glued her eyes to her plate and made a start on her gravlax.

Alexis didn't push it. 'For now, what do you know about the Lindberghs? Where did Aliénor's sister work? And the parents?'

'Louise worked for SKF, the big Swedish engineering firm; Kerstin and Göran owned a medically assisted reproduction clinic in Gothenburg.'

'An IVF clinic? Is there anything fishy about that? Well, I suppose you haven't had much time to look into the clinic yet. You should get in touch with any patients' associations for people who've resorted to IVF. Anyone with a vested interest in sperm or egg donation will know a lot about the market, because that's essentially what it is. You'll probably learn a lot more about the Lindbergh Clinic from them than you will from the employees.'

Olofsson was right, Emily thought. Once again, Alexis would come in handy down at the station.

TERESA OPENED UP HER BEDROLL, kneeled beside it on the ground and started to squash the lice and bedbugs that emerged from the seams.

María looked at her out of the corner of her eye.

'Everything all right?' Teresa asked, still squashing away.

María shrugged. 'How are you feeling?'

'What do you mean, how am I feeling?'

'Just that: how are you doing?' María shook her head.

Teresa looked up at her without saying a word.

'You don't have to hide your feelings from me, you know.'

'I really don't think you want to hear it.'

María tilted her head to one side and gave her a sad smile.

Teresa lowered her gaze and got back to work eradicating the vermin swarming over her mattress.

'You know what the silver lining is here, Teresa?'

Teresa stopped what she was doing, but didn't look up.

'There's a meaning to all of it.'

'Don't talk to me about your wretched God, María.'

'I'll talk to you about yours, if you'll let me.'

'No.'

María pursed her lips. She paused for a moment, then carried on. 'You know it's quite extraordinary, what connects you to your Tomeo, Teresa.'

'He's dead.'

'Perhaps.'

Teresa responded with an exaggerated sigh, her eyes still focused on her fingers and their tireless work, catching and killing.

'When you came back to us after those three days, and we saw the state you were in … we understood, you know…'

Teresa smoothed her palms flat on the mattress. She was shaking.

'We understood what those monsters had done to you.'

Teresa bowed her chin to her chest. She clenched her teeth to hold back the tears.

María took a step closer and kneeled beside her friend, then rubbed her shoulders as the tremors rippled through her. 'Oh, my Tere … this child will be your greatest strength, you'll see.' María ran her fingers down Teresa's dark braid. 'You'll make this child yours, and Tomeo's, believe me.'

Teresa's sobs were no louder than a murmur, but they rocked her whole body with spasms.

'You have created light from all the darkness in here, my Tere. You must stop seeing the faces of those men who raped you. See your Tomeo instead. Make it his face you see every time you rub your belly. Your child will be who you raise it to be.'

Suddenly, they heard a loud cry from the direction of the latrines. A cry that stretched into a wail.

Teresa and María took to their heels and hurried over towards the sound.

There they found an old woman surrounded by half a dozen tiny dead bodies, doubled over on the floor.

'It's the milk,' the old woman sobbed. 'I told the nuns not to give that milk to the little ones … I told them it had turned … I told those witches the babies would be sick if they drank it. I did … Oh, the poor souls … Those poor little angels…'

Old Town, Falkenberg
Sunday, 4 December 2016, 9.00 pm

ALIÉNOR TOOK A SIP of her pear cider.

Léopold was going to be late. He always was, a good ten to twelve minutes. And he would breeze in as if it was only natural. Just like when they were growing up. Gerda would have dinner on the table at six sharp, every day without fail, but Léopold would never show up before ten or fifteen minutes past, and she and Louise were always kept waiting. Gerda would lecture him, and he would turn bright red and apologise, only to slip back into the habit a few days later. Aliénor had never understood her brother's lack of punctuality.

Right then, she saw him, weaving his way through the tables in the bar. He was seven minutes late.

Léopold gave his sister a furtive kiss on the cheek and slid onto the velvet bench seat beside her.

'You've lost weight. You're not as handsome.'

'Hello, Aliénor.'

She pushed the second bottle of cider towards him. 'We have to sort out the estate and plan the funeral, Léopold. Gerda will take care of the finances. But we have to arrange for the ceremony. Carina texted me to ask how she could help, and whether we wanted to hold the wake at her place. I think that's a very good idea. Have you been home yet?'

Léopold shook his head. He was tracing circles on the table with his bottle of Kopparberg as he listened to her.

'We'll have to sell the house,' he said.

'Why do you want to sell it?'

Léopold twisted his mouth in disgust. 'Seriously, Ally?'

'I don't like that nickname.'

'Honestly, do you really have to ask why?'

'Yes.'

'For fuck's sake, our family was butchered to death there!' he hissed, through clenched teeth.

'It's also where we grew up and spent most of our lives.'

'I don't get it. I just can't understand what you're saying,' he muttered, shaking his head.

'I think you know exactly what I'm saying. The problem lies in the fact that we're reacting differently to the same thing. You want to get away from those memories, and I want to feel closer to them.'

'Just for a change, eh?'

'A change of what?'

'It's nothing new for you, is it – reacting differently from everyone else?'

Aliénor leaned back on the bench and looked her brother in the eye. 'Do you want me to apologise for being different?'

'Oh, come on! You're not going to play the victim again, are you? We all suffered just as much as you, you know.'

'Not Louise. You and Mum and Dad, yes, but not Louise.'

'OK then, the three of us. You fucked up our lives, Aliénor.'

'I know, Léopold; you all made that very clear to me. You, more than Mum and Dad, as it happens.'

They each gripped their cider bottles as if the floor had started shaking beneath their feet. The silence mounted to a deafening level before Léopold pulled the plug.

'Even so, can you please explain to me how you can even entertain the thought of spending time in that house again? That's where they were…' He clapped his hands over his eyes and gasped to stem a flood of tears.

Aliénor took a long swig of her cider. 'I should feel the desire to wrap my arms around you, Léopold, but I don't,' she said, putting the bottle back down on the table.

He gulped and sniffed back a tear.

'I'm scared that I'll start crying, Léopold. And that I won't be able to stop.'

'Louise,' he stammered, as if to himself, his eyes glued to the table.

'Yes. It's Louise. I can't think straight without her. It's like … she would often show up in my mind, and help me figure out the proper way to behave, or tell me the appropriate way to react. Louise helped me make sense of the world.'

'She helped you *make sense* of the world…'

'Yes. That's what I just said.'

Léopold pushed his cider bottle to the side of the table.

'I want to spend time in the house because it's the only place where I'll still find her appearing to me,' Aliénor continued. 'That house is all I have left of her, Léopold.'

Monday, 7 September 1992

I've never accepted the invitation to lie down. The psychoanalyst's couch – it's such a cliché, and that's what bothers me. Most of the time I stay standing. I pace up and down the therapist's office. My arms and hands say almost as much as I do. I find the movement helps me express things.

It's not proper psychoanalysis, anyway.

I couldn't handle the shrink's silence, so Nino encouraged me to bring it up with her. I did, and we changed our sessions so she would intervene, focus on certain words, ask questions. The back and forth works better for me. I think it's more productive.

'Is that a metaphor?' she interrupts, shifting forwards in her armchair.

It takes me a moment to realise what she's referring to.

'No,' I say, without a second thought.

'How does it manifest itself?'

'The images from that time come to me in black and white. The people, the places, all of it.'

'Even yourself?'

'I don't see myself. It's as if I'm the one holding the camera.'

She holds the silence for a moment, looks at me with those intimidating blue eyes.

She's sizing me up, seeing whether I can take the next blow.

She smiles when she sees I'm on to her.

'Do you think we could try to name these images?'

I swallow my fear.

'Can you?' she presses.

I shake my head.

She sits back in her chair. 'Is there anything about that time that really marked you?'

'The word "no" wasn't part of my vocabulary. I was taught to say yes to everything. "Yes, of course." "Yes, thank you." I always had to say yes to adults.'

'Do you think that's why this is happening? Because you didn't know how to say no?'

'I'm sure it didn't help.'

'Will you let me say the word?'

Fear grips me in a stranglehold.

I acquiesce in the end.

Because even now, I'm afraid to say no.

She shifts forwards again to the edge of her armchair. Her eyes are filled with empathy, but there's determination in there too.

'The memories of your rape are in black and white.'

I close my eyes. The word makes the images more vivid, as if I've suddenly turned up the sound. The sounds of my distress and his gratification.

'Do you think I'm fabricating these memories too?' I ask the question without opening my eyes.

The last shrink I saw thought I had never been raped. He was convinced my subconscious self had made up these pseudo-memories to protect me from some trauma or situation he said he could get to the bottom of, with my help. I couldn't bring myself to hear a word of it. I ran out of his office.

'I'm leaning more towards post-traumatic amnesia,' she says.

I open my eyes and release a long sigh that seems to form a bridge between us.

Suddenly, I feel a colossal wave of appreciation and gratitude for this woman, who has just replaced the 'crazy' label with one that says 'victim' instead.

'Why?' My question takes me by surprise. Am I really asking her why she isn't filing me away in the insane folder?

'I'm going to have to give you the short and simple answer,' she smiles again. She crosses her legs under her pencil skirt before she continues.

'First of all, because of what you've told me and the way you said it; second, because you're depressed; and third, because of your age. It's generally in middle age that memories start to return following post-traumatic amnesia. Especially in cases of sexual assault. A similar phenomenon has been observed in members of the armed forces suffering from PTSD. But if you want to make progress, you're going to have to put specific words to these events. You have to retrieve them to make them yours, and accept them so you can digest them all.'

I sit down on the couch, which I usually only use as a place to toss my handbag. Every time until now.

'If you want to climb out of your depression, you'll have to dive into your past first. It's likely to stir some things up.'

TOBIAS BLOM shook Bergström's hand. It was a firm, brief hand-shake, just the way the commissioner liked.

'Gym gear?' he asked, nodding to the two sports bags dumped on the floor by the front door.

'My twin boys,' Tobias grinned. 'I coach their hockey team. Want a coffee?'

'Yes, thanks.'

Bergström took off his shoes and followed his host into the kitchen. Emily had told him about Alexis's suggestion: that information about the Lindbergh Clinic might be gleaned from associations for medically assisted reproduction patients. 'Consumer organisations', as Olofsson had put it, with all his usual delicacy, before reaching out to Parents Another Way, an influential country-wide association with a regional branch in Gothenburg, run by Tobias Blom.

'Rugby was always more my thing,' Tobias replied, setting two mugs down on the kitchen table. 'But my boys are mad about the ice, so I had to adapt. Milk, sugar?'

'No, thanks.'

Tobias was built like a rugby player, or at least he fit the tall, strapping stereotype.

'I read on Twitter this morning about what happened to the owners of the Lindbergh Clinic. What a nightmare.' He poured the coffee and slid a basket of saffron pastries across the table. 'How can I help you, commissioner?' he asked, taking a seat.

'I was hoping you might be able to enlighten me a bit about the medically assisted reproduction process.'

'Don't you think an embryologist or scientific journalist would be a better person to ask?'

Bergström felt a flicker of doubt about Alexis's suggestion.

'I think your experience must have made you a bit of both,' he said.

Tobias took a sip of his steaming coffee. 'Look, why don't you simply say that you want to hear whatever rumours might be going around about the Lindbergh Clinic?'

'That's not what I'm here for at all,' Bergström smiled, raising his own mug to his lips.

Tobias Blom's lips also curled – but with the hint of a mocking smile.

'OK, then, let's start at the beginning. There are two types of couples who turn to medically assisted reproduction: they're either able to conceive using their own DNA, or they aren't. If they aren't – in other words, if the sperm or eggs are unusable – they have the option of bringing in a donor. And that's where the business gets really lucrative. Because some organisations, like the Lindbergh Clinic, operate sperm and egg banks, and store embryos. Try to imagine for a second that you're in the same situation as me and my wife. We're what you might call an extreme case. There are no swimmers in my pool, as the lab so delicately put it. And here's the icing on the cake – they even opened up my testicles, searching for what they call "sperm pockets", in other words, trying to find a few stray swimmers that might be lurking in some dark corner of my masculinity. And there were none at all. So our only option was to turn to a sperm donor.'

A knot of sadness caught in Bergström's throat. He thought about his own sons. About Lena getting pregnant the first month they started trying. About how her pregnancies had been free of complications. About seeing it all as a perfectly natural process – and taking it for granted.

'I'm sorry, Tobias.'

'Don't be. Twelve years ago, when we found out I was sterile, I would have said my life came crashing down. I felt like a lesser man, incapable of procreating, having children of my own. It was like the very essence of the survival of our species had been snatched out of my hands. After the operation, I couldn't bring myself to look my wife in the eye. Somehow I felt like I was on the outside of the world, looking in. I grew up in a foster family, and I always dreamed of being a father. For me, starting a family was all about passing on my blood line and my genetic makeup – having descendants who looked like me, who I could see myself in. Planting my seed, you know. But finding out I was sterile turned out to be the best thing that ever happened to me. It helped me to understand the challenges of fatherhood and educating a child. I came to see how being a father wasn't something I was born with; it was a role I could build into my life.'

Bergström took another sip of coffee to hide his discomfort. He could never paint a complete picture for himself of all the pain this man had been through. He could only imagine the broader strokes, and those were more than enough.

'Kommissionär, I know what you're thinking. That I'm a raging optimist who's out of his mind. Obviously I would rather have jumped into bed with my wife than see her give herself injections thirty or more times a week for months on end, and watch the treatment make her as sick as a dog. I didn't want to see her have to take time off work to go to the clinic every second day for a whole bunch of tests, blood samples, ultrasounds, the whole shebang, all because I'm sterile. I'm not exactly thrilled, either, at the thought my sons might have dozens of half-brothers and sisters all around the world. I wouldn't have chosen any of that, but I'm a much better father and husband today than I ever would have been if my body hadn't let me down.'

Tobias paused for breath and topped up their coffee mugs. His face showed no signs of sadness whatsoever. In fact, he seemed even more radiant and at ease than at the start of their conversation.

'So, where was I? … Oh, yes. So we started to look for a sperm donor. To give you an idea of the different stages of MAR, the patient is pumped full of hormones for several weeks to stimulate egg production, then her eggs are harvested and inseminated in a test tube, hence the name "test tube babies" for babies conceived by in vitro fertilisation, or IVF. Two to five days after fertilisation, one, sometimes two embryos – that was the case for us – are transferred to the patient's uterus, and then you cross your fingers that one of them will implant. The other viable embryos are generally frozen and stored in case of miscarriage, or for use if the couple wants to have another baby without having to go back through all the other stages of IVF treatment. None of this comes cheap, though. First, there's the cost of the IVF treatment, which in a private clinic like the Lindbergh can be as much as the price of a second home; then there's the cost of the sperm or eggs, not to mention the fees for storing your embryos.'

'Did you and your wife go through the Lindbergh Clinic for your treatments?'

'Yes, we did, and not just once.'

'I'm sorry, it was insensitive for me to—'

'Oh, not at all. I just meant to say that it took two tries before my wife got pregnant with the twins.'

'Did you ever see the Lindberghs themselves?'

'Never. We had two consultations with the clinical manager, Signe Skår: one before we started the treatment the first time, and another before we started the second round. Then my wife only ever saw the nurses and ultrasound technicians.'

'Is there a lot of competition or rivalry between MAR clinics?'

'I was coming to that. The war these clinics wage between themselves is all about results. On the one hand, the percentage of women who get pregnant, and then how many of them manage to carry a baby to term. Clinical protocol is what makes the difference – in other words, the kinds of treatment they prescribe and then the quality of the patient follow-up. The Lindbergh Clinic's treatments have generated some phenomenal pregnancy rates – even in challenging age brackets, like the thirty-eight-to-forties. They get fantastic results, but it shouldn't come at the price of neglecting the mother's health, or pumping her full of so many hormones she'll end up with generalised cancer ten years later. You can see where I'm going with this, can't you?'

'Do you mean to say there's something iffy … er, unconventional, about the Lindberghs' clinical protocols?'

'That's the rumour, anyway,' Tobias said.

'What are you insinuating, exactly? That the clinic has been experimenting with illegal drugs and using its patients as guinea pigs?'

'That's exactly what I'm saying,' Tobias said, finishing his coffee. 'And I'm not the only one who thinks it.'

THEIR LATEST CELLMATE had gone into labour the day before, in the early hours of the morning. She had been in Las Ventas for seven months but had only been transferred to their cell three weeks ago. She was as thin as a toothpick, yet her belly was enormous. The girls had pushed two bedrolls together for her to lie on and rolled up a third for her to lean against.

Teresa was waiting outside, with her back against the cell wall. She could see the courtyard from there. She had been doing the same for the last two months, every time there was an execution. María had pleaded with her to come back inside; to stop watching the killings. But Teresa wanted to prepare herself. She knew that as soon as she gave birth, they would drag her out into that courtyard and shoot her. They were no longer allowed to kill Republican women who were pregnant; so instead they waited, and as soon as the baby saw the light of day, they hauled its Republican mother before the firing squad.

Teresa had started by listening. The executions generally started with the soldiers giving orders. Then came the chanting. Republican chanting. Or rallying cries, punctuated by machine-gun fire. Then came the *coups de grâce* – the shots, that always made Teresa sick to her stomach. They made her skin crawl. She wouldn't have that kind of courage. The courage to keep proclaiming her ideals when death was staring her in the face. Acts of heroism like those were only for the great. No, she would just close her eyes and wait for the end to come, thinking of Tomeo and her child, and holding their memory in her eyes so she would see only them as she departed.

The new girl groaned like a heifer. The others told her to push. When her contractions had started, she had pulled out a robe she wanted them to give to her sister when she came to get the baby. A grey woollen robe with blue piping, which her own mother had sewn.

She was from Valladolid, the new girl. She had told them how the local bourgeoisie would dip churros into their hot chocolate as they watched the executions. What was more, she had said, the same well-heeled townsfolk would turn out to see their own sons shoot in the firing squads – on Sundays, after Mass.

Two guards arrived while the new girl was breastfeeding her new son. She looked like the Virgin Mary, with her tall forehead, creamy skin, fine, straight nose and plump baby in her arms. It was a wonder how the infant could have been born so big, with the diet of rotten potatoes and turnips they were served day in, day out. He was latched on to her nipple like a leech, his tiny mouth sucking the milk with the strength of a three-month-old.

The new girl looked up and noticed the guards. Creasing her eyes, she leaned forwards and kissed her baby on the forehead, as if she wanted to engrave her love there with her lips. Then she unlatched his tiny mouth from her breast and placed him in María's waiting arms. The little one wailed and screamed, and María had to start jiggling and bouncing to calm him down.

The new girl leaned on one of the others to get up and staggered her way between the guards, not bothering to cover up her breast. Her legs were shaking so much, she could barely stand, and had to stop several times on her way down the corridor.

Teresa went to stand at the window. But as soon as she saw the new girl in the courtyard – her bare chest bursting with life – Teresa's legs gave way. She slumped to the floor, her round belly nestled between her thighs, eyes staring down at her own bosom.

The new girl didn't chant or sing. She didn't scream either. There was a silence that seemed like a moment of hesitation. Perhaps that's what it was. Then the shots rang out. Teresa closed her eyes and counted.

Bang, bang, bang, bang, bang, bang, bang … Bang. Bang.

When she opened her eyes, she saw one of her cellmates nursing the newborn baby. The little one was sucking away greedily without complaint, as if he had already forgotten his mother. His heroic, stoic mother, only just turned nineteen. María was busy writing the new girl's name on the tiles, below the names of all the others who had gone before the firing squad.

As Teresa watched the baby's cheeks pulse, she wondered when her name would be added to the list.

THE DOOR OPENED to reveal a slender young man with long chestnut hair coiled on the top of his head.

Seriously, a man bun? Olofsson thought, looking Louise's boyfriend, Albin Månsson, up and down. *Soon these arseholes are going to be slapping on lipstick.*

He pulled himself together. 'Good morning, I'm Detective Olofsson. And this is my colleague, Emily Roy.'

Albin shook their hands without a word, the briefest smile of courtesy on his lips. He turned on his heels, and Olofsson and Emily followed him to the living room and made themselves comfortable on an L-shaped sofa. Albin Månsson barely seemed to notice.

'Please accept our deepest condolences,' Olofsson began. 'We're terribly sorry for your loss.'

Albin nodded, his lips curling again, this time in appreciation.

'We have some questions to ask you about Louise and her family.'

'All right, yes, of course,' he agreed, every letter of his words seeming to fray at the seams.

A woman hurried into the room and cantered over to the investigators with an outstretched hand. 'I was just calling my neighbour to ask her to feed the cat … Sorry…' she said, all of a fluster. 'I'm Esther, Albin's mother. I should have been home yesterday, and…' She closed her eyes and breathed a long sigh. 'I was the one who took your call, Detective Olofsson,' she explained, taking a seat on the sofa next to her son.

Olofsson tipped his chin in acknowledgement. 'I was just about to ask Albin to tell us about the evening you had dinner at the Lindberghs' house.'

Her son's pale-blue eyes wandered to the dozen or so boxes piled up in one corner of the room.

'Had Louise just moved in with you?' Emily asked, in English, discreetly tapping Olofsson's thigh with the back of her hand. He was happy to let her lead the way.

'I'm sorry, I don't speak Swedish yet,' Emily explained, her expression now the picture of empathy.

'No problem,' Albin replied. 'I work in English. And Mum always used to speak to me in English when I was growing up.'

'I was raised by a British nanny,' Esther explained. 'And it seemed so important that he learned a foreign language from an early age. I won't bore you with how much that used to get on my husband's and in-laws' nerves!'

Albin's gaze had strayed back to the pile of moving boxes.

'We were supposed to be unpacking her things when I got back,' he suddenly blurted, as if to himself.

Emily wanted to give him time to savour the moment – to breathe in the essence of Louise while her scent and touch were still fresh in his heart, while her memory still filled him as much as her presence had. While he felt as if he could still embrace the one he'd lost.

'Had you known each other for long?' she asked.

'Three years. We met in Copenhagen, through SKF. She's in communications, and I'm an engineer. I got a transfer to Gothenburg a few months ago, and Louise is … was … joining me here…' Creases spread across his forehead. He swallowed and rubbed his throat.

'Was the dinner at the Lindberghs for a special occasion?' Emily continued.

'My mother hadn't met Louise's family yet. And since she was coming to spend a few days with us, it seemed like the ideal opportunity.'

Esther took his hand and squeezed it in hers.

'Where do you live, Esther?'

'In Malmö. To tell you the truth, Albin really had to twist Louise's arm to get her to introduce him to her parents. And I was starting to think I'd never get to meet them at all.'

'How did the dinner go?'

Albin shook his head. 'Fine. Nothing special, really. We had to leave early, though, because I had a flight to Tver to catch at the crack of dawn the next morning. Louise decided to stay a bit longer to go through some of her things. Obviously, I cancelled my flight as soon as I heard what had happened.'

'How did Göran, Kerstin, Léopold and Louise seem to you?'

'Fine.'

'You didn't get a sense of any tension? Nothing strange, nothing out of the ordinary?'

Albin gestured a no. His mother crossed and uncrossed her legs.

'What would you say, Esther?'

'Oh, they seemed very nice. It was a very pleasant, enjoyable dinner.'

'There was nothing that … jumped out at you?'

Esther stole a fleeting glance at her son. 'Well, I did find the atmosphere a bit … tense, I suppose – between Göran and Kerstin.'

Albin pulled his hand away from hers and slapped his thighs. 'Seriously, Mum? You're not going to start again, are you?'

'I'm sorry, but yes, I have to,' she insisted, shaking her head stubbornly.

'You don't even know them! Who are you to judge?'

'You don't have to know people to feel something's not right, Albin.'

'What makes you say things were tense, Esther?' Emily cut in.

'They didn't say a word to one another.'

'What are you going on about?' Albin scoffed.

'I'm telling you, they didn't talk to each other all night. We were all laughing and joking, and chatting about this and that, but the two of them did not say a word to each other, I guarantee you.'

'And how did you find Louise, Esther?'

'Louise and Léopold were both fine … yes, fine. Well, Léopold isn't the chatty type. He's a bit of a … what do people say these days?'

'Geek? Hipster?' Olofsson suggested.

'Yes, that's it; a bit of both. And Louise seemed happy. Still, I wouldn't say she had the best relationship with her mother…'

'Bloody hell, Mum…'

'Well, it is what it is, Albin, no matter how much of a bee you get in your bonnet. There was no affection between them.'

'Not everyone has to hug or kiss their child all the time to show their affection.'

'Actions aren't the only measure of affection, Albin. There are words and looks too.'

'What about with her father?' Emily asked.

'It was strange – as if they had never connected, if you know what I mean. But she did have a lot to say about her sister, Aliénor. She was brimming with love and pride for her.'

'The tension you mentioned, did you notice it more around any specific topics of conversation?'

'Not really. It was more the general atmosphere. But, wait a second: Göran did have a dig at his son at one point. When Albin and Louise went down to the cellar to fetch some wine, before we sat down to dinner.'

Albin ran a hand over his face and sniffed.

'What was it, again? Oh, yes! We were talking about Aliénor, and how she was living in London now. Göran said something begrudging to Léopold – very subtly, I might add – about him not wanting to step up and take over the clinic. He gave him a compliment first, then he said something like "if only you would agree to take the helm at the clinic". And then he mentioned how Louise had left the family business a few years earlier.'

Olofsson stiffened. Louise had worked for her parents' clinic?

'Did he mention the reasons why she left?' Emily continued, not revealing that this was news to her too.

'No, not at all,' Esther replied.

'When was the last time you talked to Louise or exchanged messages?' Emily continued, turning to Albin.

'I sent her a text to say good night when I got home, around ten. I didn't wait for her to write back; I went straight to bed,' Albin replied, smoothing the creases on his forehead with his fingertips. He released a deep sigh, the dark circles of his saddened eyes flitting back and forth between the profiler and the detective. 'Do you have any idea what … what happened?'

'Not at the moment, Albin. Not yet.'

Emily paused for a moment, then stood. 'Could we have a look at Louise's things?'

'Yes, of course…'

'Are there any more boxes, besides these?' she asked, pointing to the far wall.

'Yes, in our bedroom.'

'Could you show me the way?'

Olofsson stood, ready to follow them.

'Detective, would you kindly take care of the boxes here in the living room, please?'

Kristian had to stifle a laugh. Any more of this politeness, and the profiler would end up choking on it. As far as he was concerned, a guy needed an instruction manual to understand any woman, but with Emily it would take nothing less than translation software.

Emily followed Albin down the hallway. He led the way into a palatial bedroom with high, moulded ceilings.

'Did Louise talk to you about her reasons for leaving the clinic?' Emily asked, kneeling beside a box on the floor.

'SKF basically headhunted her. Louise had always wanted to work for an engineering firm. Her work at the clinic wasn't very fulfilling. She only did it to make her father happy.'

'Is that what she said?'

He gave a silent nod.

Emily pulled her keys out of her pocket and used one to cut open the tape on the first box.

'You don't have to stay, Albin.'

'Thanks … I'll wait in the kitchen, then.'

'Albin?'

He turned around.

Emily flashed him a big smile. 'The two of you … snuck off for a moment alone, when you went down to the cellar to fetch the wine, didn't you?'

The young man's eyes were veiled with tears, making the blue even more intense.

'Yes, we … snuck off for a moment.'

5 Calle San Isidro, Madrid, prison for nursing mothers
Wednesday, 21 January 1948

EVERY MORNING FOR EIGHT YEARS – the whole time she had spent at Las Ventas prison – Teresa had got up not knowing whether she would lay her head on her bedroll again that night or face the firing squad before the day was out. Whenever one of her cellmates was taken away, they were never sure to return. And so, ever since her little Gordi was born, one stifling hot July afternoon, Teresa had spent every moment she could clutching her daughter to her breast, telling her all about Tomeo and the endless olive groves of El Palomar. She wanted to tell her little Gordi everything about her roots and her ancestors' struggles, before she was snatched away from her. She whispered the sounds of her village and the words of her beloved Tomeo into her daughter's ear. To imprint their love in her memory like a song she would come to know by heart.

One January morning, two years earlier, the guards had come for them, to take them away from Las Ventas to this prison for nursing mothers on Calle San Isidro. Gordi had barely been six months old. It had been such a cold night that Teresa and her cellmates had all huddled around their precious little girl, to protect her scrawny little body as best they could with their own skin and bones. The guards had woken them before dawn in a shroud of chilling silence. Teresa was sure they had come to take her to her death, so she was surprised when they ordered her to follow them without tearing her daughter from her arms. She'd had no idea why she'd been spared. María had sighed with relief. Her sweet María. Teresa had not even had the chance to say goodbye. But even in her absence, she could feel her near. They were united by blood, as María said. Spilled blood.

There had been a lot of talk inside Las Ventas about Calle San Isidro, where mothers were allowed to stay with their children until they turned three. And then the children – Republican offspring – were sent off to boarding schools or orphanages to be brainwashed into Franco's disciples. On Calle San Isidro, there were said to be blue cribs for baby boys, pink for baby girls, and separate beds for older children. Proper beds with clean sheets and blankets.

Now a shiver ran through Teresa. She was sharing the window with two other women, fists clenched and eyes riveted to the court-yard below. It was a miserable day. Cold and damp. It had even rained that morning. But the children still spent the whole day outside in the courtyard, frozen from head to toe. They were unsupervised, so their mothers tried to watch over them from the surrounding build-ings. The guards only stepped in to beat the children, retrieve babies for their feed or walk the older children to the refectory. Dinner time was another 'fun' experience. Day after day the children were forced to swallow the same old lentil and carob bean stew. It was full of insects, which they would often vomit right back up again. It was no wonder some kids would instinctively lick the plaster on the walls to make up for the lack of calcium.

Teresa caught sight of her daughter. Gordi emerged from behind one of the cribs scattered around the courtyard. She was helping a little girl back to her feet. The poor mite was just learning to walk and had tripped and fallen face first in the mud. Her teeth were black with dirt, and she was screaming.

Gordi took it upon herself to clean her up with the water from a puddle. Then she hugged the child with her scrawny arms before returning to sit in the centre of the courtyard, where the sun offered a little warmth, pulling her skirt over her bare legs.

Gordi. That was the nickname María had given her. Teresa's daugh-ter had been born so skinny, her friend had given her a pet name that would put some meat on her bones. *Gordi*: 'the chubby one'.

Teresa smiled. Her daughter was a good soul. Gordi knew that if the little girl cried for too long, one of the guards would come outside and beat her. Because on Calle San Isidro, there were no blue cribs, no pink cribs, and even fewer beds. The infamous cribs had been abandoned in the courtyard, and so had the children. Separated from their mothers all day long, except for one precious hour they were allowed to spend together.

Gordi hugged her arms to her chest to warm herself up, and looked up at the windows surrounding the courtyard, trying to spot her mother. She knew better than to wave at her, though. She mustn't draw the guards' attention. Looking at each other had to be their little secret. Teresa had explained to her daughter how they could communicate with the language of the heart. She could use her eyes to tell her about her nightmares and fears, and whisper messages only her mother would hear, while she, Teresa, could hug her tight in return and kiss her forehead and snub little nose, the way she always did in Las Ventas. Gordi had caught on straight away. Because she had seen that the children who cried until their voices cracked were beaten.

Suddenly one of the guards appeared with a screaming baby in her arms. She left the infant in the nearest crib without a blanket, and promptly went back inside the prison. The cries of the starving newborn echoed around the walls of the courtyard. Babies were only allowed to suckle their mother's breast twice a day – so for an hour at most. The bare minimum, to make sure they weren't poisoned by their mothers' Communist milk, the guards kept saying.

The baby's mother was echoing the cries from inside her cell. She was banging at the window, screaming her son's name, her blouse soaked with her milk, which kept on flowing.

Gordi searched for Teresa with her eyes, and nodded when she saw her. It was the very tiniest of nods, just as they had agreed. Teresa felt a weight like a sledgehammer slam into her chest. As if her heart was beating so hard, it would burst out of her body. She placed one hand against the window in reply to her daughter, as she said she would. Just for a few seconds.

The newborn was still screaming when they took Teresa away. His tired little voice would fade away for a few notes, before coming back loud and strong.

Teresa felt the gaze of her daughter's brown eyes on her shoulder when she left the prison. She could hear last night's nightmare and sweet whispered nothings, cupped in those dirty little hands and blown like kisses. She hoped that one day, her Gordi would start dreaming instead. That she would have children of her own. Children who would dip churros in hot chocolate and get sugar all over their fingers, not dirt. She held her so tight in her heart it ached and, with a sigh, she called out to her Tomeo. Reached out for him to join them in their little bubble of love. To say goodbye, or perhaps hello again, because surely this couldn't be the end, could it? There must be something on the other side, after all this. Surely, after all these battles. Not God, but something else.

When she looked down the barrel of the gun, Teresa was surprised to find herself raising her fist and chanting '*No pasarán!*' over and over, a little louder each time, thinking about her fallen comrades and those still fighting, and holding her Gordi and her Tomeo tight to her chest, until a bullet silenced her cry.

BERGSTRÖM MET EMILY AND OLOFSSON at the entrance to the clinic. The compact reception area was all white, with a few photos of round bellies and tiny newborn feet adorning the walls.

On the narrow sofas in the waiting area four couples sat in uncomfortable proximity to one another. Bergström noticed the resignation on their faces, the torture of not having a child. These couples seemed to be grieving, suffering under the weight of their quest. They were preparing to challenge God, perhaps with the help of a stranger who would become the progenitor of their child. Some stared at their phones or their own clasped hands, while others gazed at the snapshots on the walls flaunting what they couldn't have – or couldn't have yet. But they all shared the despondent look of those on whom Mother Nature frowns. Bergström paused for a moment to compare his good fortune to their struggle.

The receptionist gestured to the commissioner and directed him, Emily and Olofsson up to the fourth floor. Léopold Lindbergh was waiting for them behind a glass-paned security door. With the swipe of a card, he opened the door and nodded a greeting, before leading them into a vast office where two desks faced each other. Along the wall on the right was a three-seater sofa, flanked by two armchairs. The wall on the left was chock-full of books from floor to ceiling.

'You wanted to see my parents' office, well here we are, Kommissionär, and here are all the clinic's files,' Léopold said, holding out a USB stick. 'The prosecutor has assured us that none of this will be disclosed, and that you will notify us before contacting our patients, so we can make the necessary arrangements.'

Bergström nodded.

'If you need anything, I'll be in my office. Third door on the left on your way out,' he said, walking to the door.

'Before you go, Mr Lindbergh, could you tell me whether the clinic was involved in any ongoing legal action, or whether it was dealing with any dissatisfied clients?' the commissioner asked.

Léopold Lindbergh turned around reluctantly. 'We have never been involved in legal action, Kommissionär. As for unhappy patients – yes, of course there were some. Those who weren't able to conceive; but there aren't many of them. You can see all that in the files.'

'No issues or disagreements with any ex-employees?'

'*Hej hej.*' A voluptuous woman entered the Lindberghs' office and stood beside Léopold, as generous in her presence and gestures as he was sparing. She flashed them a radiant smile that creased her face from ear to ear.

'Signe Skår, I'm the clinical manager.' She pressed her palms together, as if she had just been applauding.

'Signe is running the clinic now as well, until—'

'Until we find someone more capable,' she interjected, her smile never faltering. 'I'm not doing too badly, but I'm not really cut out for running a business.'

Léopold swept his eyes across the floor and out the door.

'Feel free to leave us,' she said in a gentle voice.

He nodded in silence and disappeared down the corridor.

Signe shook her visitors by the hand, touching a warm, protective palm to each of their arms. When Emily introduced herself, Signe paused for a moment before switching to English.

'Emily Roy, you're the police officer who took Aliénor under her wing, aren't you?'

'That's right, Aliénor works alongside me now,' Emily answered, returning the smile.

'Kerstin told me about you. What a pleasure it is to meet you!'

'Signe, do you mind if we continue in English?' Emily asked.

'Not at all. It's easier for me, in fact, because English is the language we use here at the clinic, even among ourselves. I have to admit, sometimes I feel like I'm forgetting my Swedish!'

She sat in one of the armchairs and invited them to take a seat on the sofa. 'I interrupted you when I came in. What were you saying?'

'I was asking whether the clinic currently has any issues with patients or former employees,' Bergström explained.

'We have a very high success rate, so disappointed clients are a rarity. Nevertheless, sometimes we're simply not able to give Mother Nature a helping hand, so we do come up against a few desperate patients who are unfortunately let down by medically assisted reproduction.'

'Has the clinic ever been taken to court?'

Signe shook her head vehemently. 'No, never. Patients who don't manage to conceive walk away dejected and exhausted from their months of treatments. The last thing they feel like doing is fighting the clinic that moved mountains to try and find a solution to their problem. These couples need peace and quiet, not confrontation or a legal battle, believe me.'

'What about by other MAR clinics? Any disputes with them?'

'No, not at all.'

'How about employees who left to work for the competition?'

'No problems there, that I'm aware of.'

'What are some of your most challenging cases?' Emily suddenly asked.

Signe uncrossed her legs. Her chest swelled, stretching her beige velvet blazer.

'It might come as a surprise, but it's not the cases that are related to the sterility of one or both members of the couple that are the trickiest. It's the cases of unexplained infertility that cause the greatest difficulties. In other words, perfectly healthy couples who are unable to conceive for reasons we can't discover.'

'Were you aware of any problems at the clinic that might explain what happened to the Lindbergh family?' Emily continued.

Signe's fingers strayed to her short hair, shifting a few brown strands. 'Nothing that could explain anything like that.'

'Did you know the Lindberghs well, Ms Skår?'

'Yes. Göran and I have known each other for more than forty years. He and my husband met at business school in Stockholm. Not just any business school, I might add. The *Handelshögskolan* is the most renowned business school in the country.'

Signe paused and held the silence for a moment, staring into space as her mind wandered.

'Göran was a brilliant man,' she suddenly continued. 'Truly brilliant. In everything he set his mind to.'

'And Kerstin?'

'Kerstin was more than just a pretty face. She was the secret of Göran's success. She set his boundaries. And frequently adjusted them.'

'In what sense?'

'Göran always aimed too high, too quickly. He was impatient. He never left time for time, as the French like to say.' She flashed Emily a smile, one of those mechanical ones that don't spread to the eyes. 'So Kerstin used to put up roadblocks – to slow him down a bit. He would protest, of course, but he always ended up listening to his wife. They had a ... symbiotic relationship.'

'There was a strong bond between them, according to their children.'

'Oh yes, there was.' Signe looked down at her hands. She turned a ring around her middle finger, then placed her palms on her thighs and sat up straight, all prim and proper.

'Were you aware of any conflicts in the family? Any tension or quarrels? Or issues with people outside the family?'

She shrugged her shoulders slightly. 'Only that raising and educating Aliénor was a challenge. That child threw the family off balance when she came along. The pregnancy was unplanned, and by the time Kerstin realised she was expecting, it was far too late to abort. Their family was growing again, whether they liked it or not.'

'How did Léopold and Louise take to the new family dynamic?'

'Léopold has always been very reserved. Exceptionally intelligent, but a bit inept, socially speaking. Not on the autism spectrum, in case you're wondering; let's just say he's happier working with lab rats than people. He earned his doctorate with flying colours, but he's always had trouble finding and keeping a girlfriend. He doesn't … know how to take care of the people he loves. Louise was the complete opposite of Léo. She wore her heart on her sleeve. Always brimming with kindness and empathy. The kind of smile that lights you up from head to toe. She was a beautiful person inside and out; she would give you a little part of herself with that smile of hers. And Louise adored her sister. Kerstin, by contrast, used to joke that Aliénor was her own personal charity case.'

'Charming!' Olofsson scoffed.

'Yes, I know,' Signe agreed. 'It's a pretty harsh thing to say. For a mother, I mean.'

'It's a harsh thing for anyone to say,' Bergström added.

'Yes, I suppose you're right,' Signe replied, blinking a few times.

'Do you know why Louise left her position here at the clinic?' Emily pressed.

Bergström raised an eyebrow. Emily and Kristian must have gleaned that piece of information from Albin Månsson.

Signe sighed deeply. 'She didn't like working with her father. And to be honest, having the two of them here together was a pain for the rest of us, because all they did was shout at each other. It was exhausting.'

'Was it a big conflict that pushed Louise out in the end?'

Signe shook her head. 'No, I wouldn't say that. They just weren't made to work together and were incapable of communicating. It was unbearable.'

'Have you been working at the clinic for long, Signe?'

'Ever since it opened, in 1990.'

'Do you know Carina Isaksson?'

'Their neighbour in Falkenberg, yes.'

'And Göran's mistress, too.'

Signe blinked and her mouth dropped open a little.

Olofsson felt a sudden craving for popcorn. This was like a scene from a movie. Emily was going for the jugular now. Talk about a sly character. She had buttered the witness up, flashed a couple of warm, friendly smiles, and then BAM! In came the uppercut, followed by a little jab in the back to throw her opponent off and draw a natural reaction, not a calculated response. He bet she really knew how to dig her claws into a man.

Signe shook her head in disbelief. 'I … Are you sure?'

Emily let it sink in. It was enough to keep looking the witness in the eye.

'How come your success rate is so high?' she asked finally.

Signe stared at her, lost for words. She swallowed before delivering her reply. 'Because we have excellent treatment protocols.'

'That's what we've heard. We've also heard you use experimental treatments.'

'Excuse me?' Her brown eyes drilled into Emily. 'I would never allow such a thing, Ms Roy. Never.'

Signe Skår paused, still glaring at Emily as a mask of determination hardened her face.

'If this is the way our conversation is going, Ms Roy, commissioner, detective, I must refer you to our solicitor. My secretary will see you out.'

She stood up and left the room.

ALEXIS PUSHED A MUG in front of Emily. She cupped her own between her palms, held her nose to the edge to breathe in the aroma of the steaming black tea. Her eyes flicked from one crime-scene photograph to another.

Alexis had called Emily earlier that evening to find out whether the medically assisted reproduction association had shed any light on the Lindbergh Clinic. By way of reply, Emily asked her to come to the station. And so, like an eager child, Alexis had left Stellan to his own devices and hurried off to see what the profiler had to say. Stellan had only held her back for a moment, pulling her body to his, stroking her neck with his fingertips and pressing his lips to her hair. She had surrendered to his embrace, basking briefly in what had felt like the afterglow of passion.

When Alexis arrived at the police station, Emily had just started combing through the hundreds of patient files they had been given at the clinic. They were all in English, reflecting the international profile of its clients and staff. Alexis had rolled up her sleeves straight away and started examining the interviews, autopsy results and police and forensic reports with the giddy excitement she always felt at the beginning of a new investigation.

'There's no DNA evidence to prove it, but the forensics experts seem to share your opinion that the assailant must have been lying in wait under Kerstin Lindbergh's bed,' Alexis announced.

Unsurprisingly, Emily didn't say anything in response, so Alexis kept on reading.

Alexis was scrutinising a photograph of Louise's bloodied chest when it dawned on her how quickly she always glossed over a victim's identity. It was a salutary reflex, one she had honed through years of researching the most gruesome of news stories. She swallowed a mouthful of tea and pushed away the image of Aliénor that had floated into her mind.

'Don't you think it's strange that Louise was the second victim but appears to have been the main target?' she asked, keeping her eyes on the photograph.

'Or perhaps she wasn't,' Emily replied.

'If she wasn't, how do you explain her nineteen stab wounds versus eleven for Kerstin and only four for Göran? Well, not "only", that's a poor choice of words, but you know what I mean. Starting with the mother and then going crazy on the daughter sends two contradictory messages.'

Emily stood and moved over to the whiteboard. Her finger landed on a photograph of Göran's body lying on the sofa.

'The killer smashed Göran's skull, then put the headphones back on his ears and replaced the candlestick where it was. Louise was also covered up with the duvet. But Kerstin was left on the floor with the bed sheets scrunched up at her feet.'

'Do you think Kerstin Lindbergh was the killer's main target?'

'Yes, if we trust what the crime scene is telling us.'

'What about Louise being stabbed nearly twice as many times, though? How do you explain that?'

'The killer might not have intended to kill Louise. She didn't live at home, and her being there might have been a surprise. It's quite possible Louise messed up the killer's plan, so he or she took their frustration out on her.'

'He or she? Do you think the killer could be a woman?'

'There's nothing to prove we're dealing with a man, and nothing to contradict the theory of a female perpetrator. And let's not forget, Louise was killed in Aliénor's bedroom—'

They were interrupted by the swing doors creaking open.

Mona poked her head into the room. 'I'm sorry to interrupt, Ms Roy, but Aliénor Lindbergh wants to speak with you. She's waiting in the corridor.'

Emily nodded.

'I'll send her in,' Mona said, as Alexis flipped the whiteboard over so Aliénor wouldn't see the crime-scene photographs of her family.

Aliénor stepped into the conference room a few seconds later, still bundled up in her parka.

'What are you doing here, Alexis?' Her abrupt tone was like claws scraping a blackboard.

'I'm here to help Emily.'

Aliénor looked from Alexis to the blank whiteboard, then focused on Emily.

'I forgot to tell you: Louise used to work for the clinic. Up until three years ago. She left because things weren't going well with Dad. I should have told you on Saturday, but … I couldn't get my thoughts in order.'

'It's all right, Aliénor.'

Aliénor shifted her gaze to the whiteboard again. 'I want to know how they were killed.'

Emily shook her head. 'No, Aliénor.'

'I know why you don't want me to know. Because those images will stay with me. But I have other images in my head anyway and my mind keeps conjuring up more. They're horrible. They leave a taste of blood in my mouth, and they smell of death, or rather the way I imagine death smells. The images in my mind are terrifying me. They're making me ill. And they're always there, even when I close my eyes.'

'You'll need help and support if you want to know the details.'

'I do have support. But I need to know what happened to them before I can start to grieve. And I want to help too, like Alexis.'

Emily sat back down at her computer and looked up at her protégée. Alexis saw resignation in Emily's face, but no compassion.

'Nothing significant in your past?' Emily barked. 'Any tension or conflict? Any relationships that ended badly?'

'Absolutely nothing,' Aliénor replied, taking no offence at Emily's onslaught of questions. 'Any interactions with my classmates were almost nonexistent. It exhausts me – applying and adhering to all the social codes that seem necessary for maintaining friendships. My relationships with my teachers were always cordial. And I've never had a boyfriend. Or a girlfriend. Only sexual partners – of both genders. And I've had no conflicts with them either.'

'Was your sister in the habit of sleeping in your bedroom?'

The question hit Alexis like a slap in the face. She would never be able to explain the profiler's emotional viciousness to the people she cared about.

A stunned Aliénor managed to blink. 'No. Louise wasn't in the habit of sleeping in my room.'

Her gaze sank to the floor. She unbuttoned her parka, giving her childlike body room to breathe.

Alexis felt her throat knotting with anger.

'Did Louise die in my bedroom, Emily?'

'Yes.'

'She was in my room. Surrounded by my books. And my things. In my bed.'

'Yes.'

'So I was with her when she died.'

'Yes, you were there, Aliénor, as if you were holding her in your arms.'

Alexis froze in amazement. She had been too quick to judge her friend.

'Do you think I was the target?'

'I have considered the possibility, but now I doubt that was the case.'

'All right.'

Emily stared at her screen and let the silence sink in, giving Aliénor time. Time to slow her breathing. Relax her face. Unclench her hands. Time for her to register the brutal shock of this information in her body and mind before analysing and digesting it.

'Can you have a look at Louise's computer?' Emily eventually asked, looking at Aliénor to gauge her reaction.

'Yes. Is it here?'

'No. Forensics are still examining it. You should be able to pick it up in a day or two.'

'What am I looking for information about? Albin Månsson? The clinic?'

Emily nodded. 'If it's not all right, just stop, OK?'

'I'm with Louise, Emily. It's going to be all right. You'll see.'

La Virgen de los Desamparados Orphanage, Madrid
Monday, 8 January 1951

GORDI WAS ALREADY AWAKE when the morning whistle blew.

In the other orphanage, she had developed the habit of getting up long before anyone else, so she could go and drink without alerting the nuns and risking a thrashing. They had only been allowed one glass of water a day, at noon, and it was often salty. In the morning and evening, they were given milk. One glass each time. So Gordi was thirsty. All the time. It was the kind of thirst that burned her throat, and the pit of her stomach when she urinated.

And so, before anyone else was awake, she and two of the others would always sneak into the courtyard to siphon any stagnant water from the plant pots after they were watered. And if there was nothing left, they would drink from the toilets.

Last night, when she got up to drink, she had lost her way in the maze of corridors. She must have thought she was still back in the other orphanage. She had been trying to get to the yard, but had gone the wrong way. Fortunately, she had run into another girl, who had helped her find her way back to her bed.

'You'd better figure things out for yourself, new girl, and quick, or Sister Fernanda will be on you like a ton of bricks.'

Gordi turned. It was the girl who had helped her back to the dormitory in the early hours of the morning.

She has a smile like the sea, Gordi thought. *A smile that makes you want to look and sigh.*

'I'm 101 and my sister there, she's 102; but we call each other Launa and Lados,' she went on.

'And I'm 134. Reme,' a little blonde-haired girl with a short fringe said, from the bed opposite.

'I'm 145. Dulce,' another girl followed suit; her face was peppered with freckles. 'What about you?' she asked, pulling on her dress, socks and shoes.

'Gordi. 162.'

'Gordi. That's funny. How old are you, Gordi?'

'Five … nearly six.'

The girls began their morning ritual and Gordi followed their lead: get dressed; make the bed.

'Where were you before?', Dulce asked.

'In another orphanage, in Barcelona.'

'Whatever you do, don't speak Catalan,' said Lados, 'or Sister Fernanda will wash your mouth out with soap.'

'I can't speak Catalan.'

'Just as well. That'll save you some hassle. They didn't chop off your curls, then?' Lados carried on, smoothing her bed sheet and folding back the thin blanket. 'They cut mine off because they were things of the devil, they said. And my hair was so short I could almost have gone to hear Mass with the boys!'

They all burst into a chorus of laughter. But it quickly fell flat. They sprang to attention beside their beds, standing as still as statues, hands clasped behind their backs, as Sister Fernanda breezed into the dormitory in a shroud of silence. Her rosary brushed against her habit, which swished as she walked. Holding a whip in her hand – fashioned from leather belts Father Murillo had taught her to braid together – she inspected every bed, one by one, stripping some of the sheets back to make sure the mattresses were dry.

'Attention! Forward, march!' she shouted, once the last bed had passed inspection.

The entire dormitory scrambled to form one long, meticulous line, and all the girls began to march forwards in unison, like an army of ants. Only one dark-haired girl, who was as white as a sheet, tripped out of line every few steps.

'Forward, march!' Sister Fernanda commanded, giving her a shove in the back.

Gordi wondered whether this scrawny girl was the one who had sobbed all night long, or the one who had moaned in her dreams and called out for her mother.

Gordi would not have been able to call to her mother, because she could not remember her. Try as she might, she could conjure up no image of her mother. Nor could she recall the sound of her voice, or the way she smelled. All that came was a curious sensation that swelled in her chest and filled her with both joy and sadness.

The little dark-haired girl fell out of line completely now. Sister Fernanda grabbed her by the hair and flung her against the wall. The other girls stopped marching and waited with bated breath. The only sounds to break the silence were a thud and a crack as the child's face hit the wall, and the damage was done.

Shaking, the girl rose to her feet. She quickly wiped away the blood that was gushing from her lips, and ran her tongue over her broken tooth before shuffling back to her place in line with the others.

'That'll teach you not to step out of line!' Sister Fernanda chided. 'Attention! Forward, march!'

Gordi did like the others and marched forwards. The clicking of the nun's rosary was like a metronome setting the pace of their steps. She wondered where they were going. To the refectory, for breakfast? To the showers, perhaps? She hoped they weren't. That had not been a pleasant experience when she arrived the previous day. The stream of water was so cold, it had felt like it was drilling into her head. The numbing pain had seized her skull in a vicelike grip and not let go until it was time for bed.

The nun suddenly hastened her pace and stepped ahead of them to push open the door to the big courtyard. A glacial wind swirled its way beneath their dresses, whipping their faces and legs.

The march slowed to a crawl, and the line splintered into five rows before breaking out into a rendition of 'Cara al Sol'. Gordi knew that song. She had learned it in the other orphanage. She didn't understand what the lyrics meant, but she knew the most important thing. That she had no choice but to sing the praises of *El Caudillo*. Señor Franco.

If she wanted to live, she had to sing.

May these flags return victorious,
at the joyful pace of peace.
May there be five roses tied
to the arrows of my quiver,
May the springtime smile once more
on the sky, the land and the sea.
May a new day dawn on Spain,
Now onwards, legions, to victory!
Spain united! Spain the great! Spain the free! Now onwards, Spain!

EMILY ENTERED THE CONFERENCE ROOM, followed by Alexis and Bergström, who was carrying a tray of croissants, mugs and a Thermos flask. Olofsson was leaning against the table, waiting for them, his muscular torso stretching the seams of a sweater that left little to the imagination.

'What, no *kanelbullar* this morning?' the detective protested, grabbing one of the flaky pastries.

'We can ask Mona to bring you one, if you like,' Alexis teased as she poured everyone a coffee.

'Oh, come on. Not you too? I wish you'd all give it a rest about Mona. Anyway, aren't you supposed to be off somewhere, choosing your centrepieces or something?'

'Ooh, look at you, Kristian the wedding planner!'

Olofsson rolled his eyes and conceded a smile to Alexis, just as Mona glided through the swing doors. She nodded good morning to everyone and took a seat at the far end of the conference-room table, avoiding eye contact with Olofsson. The detective mumbled a quick hello, trying to shake from his mind the image of Mona in the skimpiest of attire, moaning with pleasure earlier that morning. He flicked a few flakes of croissant from the corners of his mouth and went to sit beside Alexis.

'Why don't we start with you, Mona? Then we can let you go,' said Bergström.

'Yes, of course, Kommissionär.'

The young rookie smoothed a lock of dark hair behind her ear before continuing.

'There was a regular audit of the Lindbergh Clinic eighteen months ago, and that didn't detect any irregularities. No legal action has ever been taken against the clinic either. Léopold Lindbergh, Signe Skår and Albin Månsson had nothing in their pasts that we could find. Stockholm also got back to me: all other cases of victims being stabbed and having their tongues cut out were very different kinds of murders from the Lindberghs'. I've emailed you the details of them all, and here's a printout.'

Mona passed the papers to the commissioner. Bergström gave the document straight to Emily, who started leafing through it.

'To give you an idea, the Lindbergh case is unprecedented in Sweden; there's been no other family massacre with this kind of modus operandi. Any other cases involving tongues being cut out were gang related, and any other knife murders were committed in completely different circumstances, and most of those cases are closed. As for Interpol, Kommissionär, they'll be sending you their report today; this evening at the latest.'

'Perfect. Thank you.'

Mona nodded and left the room as discreetly as she had entered, again averting her gaze from her lover across the table.

'Kristian, you spoke to Gerda Vankard, didn't you?'

'Yes,' the detective smiled, thrilled to avoid another swipe at his private life. 'She confirmed that Göran Lindbergh and Carina Isaksson were having an affair, and that Kerstin Lindbergh knew all about it. Gerda was tight-lipped about the whole thing, but I certainly got the sense she would have had plenty to say, given the chance. I also spoke with Gerda's, er, companion, who confirmed her alibi. It's true that Nicole's daughter popped a sprog that night, but she really can't stand Gerda, so Gerda decided to go back to the Lindberghs' – or *home to her place*, as she puts it.'

'Where are we at with the Lindberghs' phones, computers and tablets?'

'The techies didn't find anything to write home about, besides the fact the old man – Aliénor's father – was watching Redtube videos back to back.'

'Redtube?' Bergström asked.

'Online porn,' Emily interjected, without looking up from the file Mona had put together.

Olofsson wolfed down the last mouthful of his croissant with a swig of coffee. This profiler was always full of surprises, he thought.

Bergström raised his eyebrows briefly before continuing. 'And what about Louise's computer?'

'Nothing there either, at least for now,' Olofsson replied.

'I've asked Aliénor to take a look at it,' Emily said.

Bergström whirled around and glared at her as his surprise turned to anger.

'Seriously, Emily?'

'She knew her sister very well, Lennart,' Emily coolly replied.

'How am I supposed to explain that to Møller?' the commissioner thundered.

'Maybe the prosecutor doesn't need to know about it, boss,' Olofsson volunteered.'

'Oh, come on! Don't give me the Olofsson method!'

'And somehow, I'm always the one who takes the flak,' the detective muttered to himself, slumping back in his chair.

'Good grief, Emily! You're going to get me up to my eyes in trouble,' Bergström hissed.

'We've done a first round of sorting through the patient files from the Lindbergh Clinic,' Alexis cut in.

Still seething, Bergström turned to look at his future sister-in-law.

Without losing her cool, Alexis carried on explaining her findings.

'We started by isolating those cases where MAR treatment failed, which were about a quarter of all patients. That might seem like a colossal percentage, but the Lindbergh Clinic's success rate is actually as phenomenal as they claim. It's far higher than their competitors'.

Two-thirds of those patients are either from abroad or have since moved overseas. The other third live in Sweden.'

'OK, good,' Bergström ceded in a calmer tone of voice. 'Let's start with them, then we'll cast the net further geographically. Emily?'

The profiler was staring into the empty space behind Bergström, as if thoughts and images were commanding her mind, and her body was somewhere far from the room. At the sound of her name, she gave a start and pulled herself together.

She rose and went over to the whiteboard.

'We're dealing with an organised killer who prepared meticulously for these crimes and acted with great precision. The perpetrator knew when and how to get into the house without breaking in, and they knew about the Lindberghs' habits and flaws, so it was easy to enter the premises in their absence. This was a familiar hunting ground for a trained and seasoned killer who tracked the victims' movements, as we can see from the precise sequencing of the MO. This probably isn't the first time they've killed, and the sequence has likely been honed for maximum efficiency: take the victim by surprise, knock them out to render them immobile, stab them, cut their tongue out, then take the time – somewhat arrogantly, I might add – to stage their bodies for the benefit of the police, like we saw with Louise and Göran. I'll come back to Kerstin in a moment. The killer also came prepared with protective overalls, which would explain the absence of fibres under the Lindberghs' bed and the droplets of blood right by the door in the hall, where the killer must have taken their suit off before leaving the house. The killer brought their own weapon, and the way the tongues were cut out – in one slice, without any hesitation – suggests this is a familiar act. And the tongues were almost certainly taken away from the scene in a sealed container, which would explain why there were no trails of dripping blood.'

Olofsson stifled a gag.

'These few elements, combined with the best profiling data, tell me a lot of things,' the profiler continued. 'They suggest that our killer is someone who is well integrated in society, is of above-average intelligence, is in a relationship and perhaps even has a family, and is employed. They choose strangers as their victims, people living nowhere near the killer's home. This profiling work suggests we're dealing with a serial killer who has struck before and should have a history in the judicial system.'

Emily returned to the table, sat back in her chair and crossed her legs before turning to address her audience.

'However, there are two elements inconsistent with this profile. First, the killer attacked Kerstin and Louise in a frenzied manner, stabbing them far more times than was necessary to kill them. Second, the bodies were left at the crime scene. These elements would tend to suggest an unplanned or unexpected aspect to these murders, which contradicts the profile I just explained.'

'Oh, that really helps, doesn't it?' Olofsson scoffed. 'And where does Aliénor fit into all of this?' he asked, as he poured himself another coffee. 'Do you think she might still be in danger?'

Emily shook her head. 'I said earlier I would get back to Kerstin. Unlike her husband and her daughter, Kerstin Lindbergh's body wasn't covered up, and her bed wasn't remade, so the crime scene wasn't altered. That wasn't something the killer forgot or didn't have time to do; rather, it was intended to punish. Kerstin was the main target of this massacre. The killer clearly expressed a desire and a need to chastise the mother and wife in the family.'

'Or rather, as you say, to chastise the bad mother and the bad wife,' Olofsson deduced.

'Right,' Bergström breathed, at the end of a weary sigh. 'Let's keep looking into the clinic and digging away at the Lindberghs' pasts. We'll wait and see if Interpol turns up anything interesting.'

RS SINCE the blanket of night had settled over Stock-
darkness was tinged with colour. What was black took
ue in the snow, and the lights from the buildings shim-
in the sea.

sitting in the bar of the Diplomat Hotel in Östermalm,
part of the city. The hotel stood in pride of place on
, a grand waterfront boulevard that stretched from west
ecting the hub of Nybroplan square to the Nobel Park
of land that reached out to embrace the Baltic Sea. She
but gaze out at the strip of frozen water surrounded by
es. No matter where you went in Stockholm, the water
whispering sweet nothings to the land and the stones of

ed the wine around her glass before she took a sip. White
preferred colour. Still, she had succumbed to the wait-
ence that she should try a glass of something that would
red pale in comparison. This Burgundy certainly was
Alexis had to admit, but nowhere near as satisfying as a
red.

ame in and took a seat across from her.
red one for you too,' Alexis said, sliding a second glass to

swished the wine around a couple of times and took a sip.
eir meeting that morning, Emily and Kristian had started

Nino gives me a hug with my herbal tea. Our eyes meet, then avoid each other.

Nothing has really helped since I finished my last round of therapy, five years ago. I still feel like I'm going round in circles. I still dwell on the same memories, the same anxiety, the same anger, and I can't bring myself to move on. I stay fixated on the facts that I carry with me wherever I go, like travel companions. I don't know how to talk about anything else.

Nino sits me on the bidet and pulls down my incontinence pants.

I don't know how he can stand being by my side, day in, day out. Listening to me ramble on about the same old things. I know it's an obsession, this kind of bulimia I have about that chapter in my life. But I can't stop myself from talking about it, regurgitating, chewing, swallowing it again, but never, ever digesting it.

'Come,' Nino says.

I can hear the bath water running.

'I don't really feel like it.'

'You have to wash. Please. I don't want to have to manhandle you.'

'Do I smell?'

With downcast eyes, he nods.

It's true. I do smell. But I've lost so much over all these years. Much more than myself.

'Hey,' he says, as he helps me into the bath. 'You didn't say a word over dinner.'

He could have replicated my monologue without me opening my mouth. Starting with my funny turn in the church on the day of the baptism, twenty-two years ago. Then followed by that drastic change, when what was such a simple, serene pleasure turned into the nightmare that has tormented me and torn me away from the people I love. That's what I would have talked about at dinner. For the umpteenth time.

It's been eighteen years since I've seen my grandson. Or my daughter, for that matter.

I forgot to give my little man his bottles. Not during the daytime, but at night. I still managed to get him back to sleep, though. Then I forgot to give him his morning feed, and our little man became dehydrated. I don't know how I could have not thought about it. Not remembered.

After that incident, my daughter never left me alone with him again. She started to pull away from me. Daily visits became weekly, then even our Sunday dinners grew further apart. Until it was just Nino and me on Sundays.

I yelp. The water is too hot.

I think addiction is a better word, really. Because I just can't stay away from the subject. From the rape. The rapist. And the rest of it. I always find a way to bring him back to the conversation. Invite him to join us.

I know I'm wallowing in the past, but I simply cannot detach myself from it or change my approach to it, which is even more upsetting. I've become as dependent on revisiting my memories as an alcoholic nursing on a bottle.

I realise I haven't replied to my Nino, but he's already turning up the volume on the plasma TV he installed in the bathroom to keep me in the bath.

The news is on. He sits beside me, on the edge of the bath, takes my hand and kisses it, still avoiding eye contact. Perhaps he doesn't want to lay eyes on the woman I've become. Perhaps he's trying to remember the woman who filled his life before all of this.

Or maybe he just wants to watch the news in peace.

Nino inches the volume higher, as if he can hear me thinking, dwelling.

I hear the voice before I see the images.

I release a whimper.

Nino doesn't even turn ar...
listening to the journalist com...
on the screen, and the video...
with Franco.

The voice that sends shivers...

IT WAS HOU...
holm, yet the...
on a bluish h...
mered yellow...

Alexis was...
the swanky...
Strandväge...
to east, con...
along an arr...
couldn't hel...
the quaysi...
was always...
the wharve...

She swi...
was not h...
ress's insis...
make any...
exquisite,...
full-bodie...

Emily...
'I orde...
Emily.

Emily...
After...

to contact patients of the Lindbergh Clinic whose treatments had failed. Most had not been keen to talk about their experiences and were even less inclined to explain their whereabouts at the time of the murders. Only one woman had agreed to see them: Lydia Olsen, a Dane who lived in Stockholm. She had told Emily she would be happy to meet with her that very evening. Emily and Alexis had jumped on a train to the capital city later that morning, leaving Bergström and Olofsson to keep combing through the patient files, much to Kristian's horror, who was worried they'd be at it all night.

Just an hour ago Emily and Alexis had checked in to the hotel where Lydia Olsen had arranged to meet them.

'Emily Roy?'

Emily looked up to see a smiling young woman extending a friendly hand over the tops of their wine glasses.

'Good evening, I'm Lydia Olsen.'

'Hello, Lydia. Thank you for agreeing to meet with us,' Emily replied, clasping the woman's hand in hers.

'Thank *you* for coming all this way! My office is just over the road, so this place couldn't be handier. You've travelled from Falkenberg, haven't you?' She looked from Emily to Alexis, her warm, generous smile creasing the corners of her eyes.

Emily nodded and returned a gentle, maternal smile. 'This is Alexis Castells, the colleague I mentioned on the phone.'

'Can we offer you a drink?' Alexis asked, after a brief handshake.

Lydia's straight, dark bob brushed softly against her jawbone. A few stray locks briefly veiled her light eyes; she flicked them away.

'I'd love a glass of what you're having, thanks,' she replied, taking off her coat.

Alexis ordered a third glass of Burgundy. The waitress beamed a triumphant smile, sure she had succeeded in converting Alexis from red to white.

'What terrible news! I can't believe such a horrific thing could have happened to the Lindberghs,' Lydia said as she sat down. 'I dread to think what it must be like for their children to come to terms with something like that. My God, it's horrible. They have another daughter and a son, don't they?'

Emily nodded.

Lydia briefly scrunched up her eyebrows then smoothed them with the tips of her fingers. 'What do you want me to talk about, exactly? Our journey through the desert lasted for years,' she joked, 'so we might be here all night.' She took a glass from the waitress's outstretched hand.

'About your experience at the clinic, and about the Lindberghs, if you ever met them.'

Lydia's gaze wandered through the window to the quayside and its dusting of snow, before falling on the table in front of them. She slid the three glasses away from each other, as if to make room for her memories.

'I met Göran, Kerstin and their daughter Louise at a talk about infertility. That man was like a magnet; he had such a presence. He certainly had that effect on his wife, in any case. She was like his shadow, following him everywhere with this strange sort of devotion.'

'How do you mean, strange?'

Lydia shook her head, and her hair rippled in time. A wrinkle formed at the bridge of her nose.

'It's hard to explain. It was as if he was the only reason she existed. I don't know, it's just a feeling. They were both charming, and that's the reason we chose their clinic.'

'And you met Louise Lindbergh too?'

'Yes. As a matter of fact, she was the one who came over to talk to me. She had a … a talent, or rather, a gift for putting people at ease. She made people feel not just heard, but special, as if her whole world revolved around them. She was an exceptionally good listener.'

Lydia savoured the wine on her lips, never taking her eyes off the glass as she set it down again.

'My husband Terrence and I, we're one of those infertile couples whose infertility is – how shall I put it? – unexplained. Well, that's not entirely true, because my husband's sperm aren't the strongest swimmers, but in vitro fertilisation should have worked. That wasn't the case, though. Over the course of three years, I had nine treatments that all ended in failure. Month after month, you live in hope, but the longer you try, the harder that hope is to find. You spend all your time listening to your body; it's like you're constantly eavesdropping on a stranger. You end up feeling reduced to a cluster of cells, not a woman. You lose every bit of sex drive and you're guided only by the desire to reproduce. It's like you're just a womb on legs, you know?'

Lydia shifted in her chair. She wasn't smiling anymore.

'Our relationship started to fall apart. I found myself resenting my husband for standing in the way of me becoming a mother. And it pained him to see me going through all that torture because of his physical shortcomings. It made him feel so inadequate. We both ended up cheating on each other.'

She downed a long swig of wine and stared at the table.

'And then I got pregnant. By the other man I was seeing.'

Lydia hunched her shoulders, gazing at her fingers as she ran them along the grain in the wood.

'Right then, that moment when I told him another man had given me what he couldn't – and his reaction…' Lydia pursed her lips and tightened her grip on the wine glass. 'He put his hand on my belly. "There's life inside you." That's what he said. He rubbed my belly, and he told me he wanted to be a father to that child.'

Her chest swelled with a sigh of relief.

'I know, I know how strange that sounds. You can think what you like, but it seemed to us that it would be even more bizarre and unnatural to go through a sperm donor. One of my friends, Melinda Gorp, and her wife Vera, had some unbelievable and frankly inhumane experiences with sperm banks. Most of them are based in Denmark, where I come from, actually. Melinda was already pregnant when they got an email to notify them that I don't know how many babies fathered by the donor they had chosen were born with serious heart problems. I mean, hearing about something like that by email: can you imagine? Basically, a message telling you the child you're carrying is doomed. And then they had a ridiculous email from another sperm bank announcing a Boxing Day sale – two vials for the price of one!'

'My God,' Alexis muttered.

'I'm not joking. Most of these places treat their clients as if they're umming and ahhing over two jars of jam on the supermarket shelf, whereas they're actually choosing the progenitor of their child – making decisions about their genetic heritage. It's tragic. Tragic and completely insane. Anyway...' Lydia smiled a dejected, weary smile. 'I lost the baby. But strangely, it gave us, I don't know, the strength to carry on, I suppose. And so, we decided to try IVF again. For the tenth time. And I got pregnant on the first cycle. Now our little girl Ella is four.'

'Oh, that's wonderful, congratulations, Lydia.'

'I suppose you could say we needed to take a break for a while. The same thing happened with Vera and Melinda. After they took a break, Melinda got pregnant on the first try. With twins.'

'Which clinic did you go through?'

'What do you mean?'

'When you had your daughter.'

Lydia gave them a look of surprise. 'The Lindbergh Clinic, of course. The last thing I wanted to do was start again with all the tests we did when we first tried the treatment. As far as we were concerned, the clinic didn't do anything wrong, so there was no need to go elsewhere. Vera and Melinda stayed with the Lindbergh Clinic too. It really is an excellent facility.'

'But we found your name on the list of patients who hadn't managed to conceive.'

'That's probably because I was registered under my husband's name, Roberts, when I got pregnant, whereas I went by my maiden name, Lydia Olsen, the first nine times. I still can't get used to it; I keep introducing myself as Lydia Olsen. I never really made a conscious decision to change my name, but I took the leap when we started trying again so we'd all have the same last name when our child was born. I thought it would be a symbolic way to lay the foundations for our family. The clinic must have forgotten to merge the two files.'

Forgotten? Certainly not, Alexis thought.

ALEXIS SLIPPED ON THE HOTEL BATHROBE and opened the door. A young woman wearing a crown of blonde braids stood in the corridor, holding a room-service tray.

'*Bonsoir, Madame Castells.* Here's the dinner you ordered,' she announced in French, and two dimples dented her milky white cheeks. 'Would you like me to put the tray on the desk or the coffee table?'

'On the bed, please.'

The young woman blushed. She looked like one of the porcelain dolls Alexis used to collect as a child. The only thing missing was a frilly satin dress and shiny shoes.

'Your French is excellent, Estelle,' Alexis said, having glanced at the name on the badge pinned to the woman's breast.

The young woman smiled, and her blue eyes sparkled with a glint of childlike joy. 'Thank you, I'm flattered,' she replied, smoothing the bedspread flat around the tray. 'Have a lovely evening, *Madame Castells.*'

She made her way towards the door, but turned around at the last second. 'I don't mean to bother you, but I just wanted to let you know I loved your books. I devoured them, in fact. *The Ebner Affair* really resonated with me, because I used to spend summers in Falkenberg when I was growing up,' she explained, dropping the 'g' the way a local would, and making the word dance. 'And I'm sorry for your friend, Linnéa Blix.'

A wave of goosebumps spread across Alexis's skin. She still found it touching to meet her readers, and even more so when they rekindled the memory of Linnéa.

'You're very sweet; thank you so much. It means a lot to hear that Linnéa lives on in the thoughts of people like you.'

Estelle smiled at her and walked out of the room, leaving Alexis in the glow of the happiness her few words had ignited.

Alexis sat down on the edge of the bed, her mind filled with thoughts of Linnéa and the imprint her friend had made on her life. On the morning of their wedding, she and Stellan were planning to lay a wreath at Torsviks Småbåtshamn in Olofsbo, the tiny marina where Linnéa's body had been found two years earlier.

Alexis pulled her laptop towards her. Propping the computer on her legs, she opened the document containing the list of patient files from the clinic with one hand, and dug into her cheese board with the other. There were thousands of names – and stories – on the list. They had already started singling out those patients whose treatments had failed. Alexis wondered whether she should take a different approach, though, and look at the treatments that did succeed. The unexpected success stories. The sudden ones. Like Lydia Roberts and Melinda Gorp.

There was a knock at the door. Alexis finished chewing her chunk of bread before getting up to open it. Stellan was standing in the corridor, suitcase in hand.

'Babe?' Alexis gasped, more concerned than surprised. 'But I thought … Weren't we going to see each other tomorrow morning? Are you—'

'I needed to see you.'

'What's wrong? Is everything OK? What's happened? Did something happen with your job? And you; are you all right?'

Stellan closed the door behind him.

'Mado, what are you doing inside Alexis's body!' he joked, wheeling his suitcase into the space beside the luggage rack. 'Everything's fine. I just wanted to see you. *Needed* to see you.'

He cupped her cheeks in his hands. 'Oh, Alexis, my *älskling…*'

He kissed her gently, tracing the edges of her mouth with his lips. 'My wife…'

He paused and gazed at her with tender, eager eyes.

'You're going to be *my* wife.'

He relished the possessive pronoun with passion and pride.

Alexis smiled between two kisses. Stellan teased her dressing gown open. Still pressing his mouth to hers, he let his fingers wander down her hips, between her thighs. Alexis moaned. She fumbled a few steps back against the door, yielding to the warmth of Stellan's tongue and fumbling to unbutton his jeans. He pressed himself tightly against her, and Alexis felt her legs quivering as he lifted her up.

'*My wife,*' he whispered in her ear.

La Virgen de los Desamparados Orphanage, Madrid
Tuesday, 10 April 1951

GORDI REACHED FOR LAUNA'S HAND on one side and Reme's on the other. Petrified, Lados was clinging to her sister.

Gordi knew the routine by heart now: all hold hands in a circle around whichever of the girls had wet the bed that night, and loudly chant 'Pissy pants!' and 'Filthy wench!' in unison.

It wasn't like that in the other orphanage. Gordi figured everywhere had its own methods. In the old place, the nuns had a different way of dealing with the children who had wet the bed. They used to lock them in a cage in a dark room, and leave them there until they stopped crying and screaming.

Sister Fernanda set the name-calling in motion, and the chorus of girls followed suit.

Dulce was the one in the middle of the circle again. Rooted to the spot, she was staring at the floor, trying to shut everything and everyone out, trying to hide from all these horrible words thrown around by her friends. They didn't mean any of the words, of course, but they still repeated them harshly enough to ward off the dreaded floggings.

A few weeks earlier, Gordi had come up with an idea. Since Dulce had such a hard time staying dry at night, she suggested she might offer to wash the blood from the nuns' soiled menstrual towels. Perhaps then they would go a bit easier on her and stop banishing her to the pissy-pants attic.

Dulce shivered when she talked about that place. First they would flog her with stinging nettles, or, if Sister Fernanda had anything to do with it, burn her with a candle right there, between her legs. Then they would shut her in in the dark.

Dulce had spent a whole afternoon cleaning their soiled towels, plunging her hands into ice-cold water to rub the blood away.

A few nights later, she had wet the bed again. In the morning, Sister Fernanda had flogged her with her braid of leather belts in front of all the other girls. She had made them all watch, as Dulce bent double on her bed, her eyes full of pain and her body writhing with every blow as blood streamed down her back and buttocks. Sister Fernanda's eyes had blazed with glee, as they did every time she beat the girls. She had forced them all to listen to Dulce's pleas and her screams of agony, before delivering the same litany and banishing her to the dark, her buttocks smarting from the blows and her privates swollen and puffy from the stinging nettles.

Gordi squeezed Reme's and Launa's hands hard. They had no choice but to do what they were told. And cling to each other as tightly as Sister Fernanda's leather-belt whip was braided.

Gordi's mind was made up. The next day she would go to the chapel. She would kneel down, say her prayers, and tell Jesus he was a murderer.

Grand Hotel, Falkenberg
Wednesday, 7 December 2016, 8.00 pm

ALIÉNOR TOOK A BITE of the last slice of her pineapple pizza and put the rest back in the box, wiping her hands on the paper napkin. As her fingers touched the computer keyboard, she thought of her father. He couldn't stand paper napkins. He always thought cloth ones were better. Just like handkerchiefs were better than tissues. *Whatever were they going to do with all Göran's cotton handkerchiefs?*

Olofsson had brought Louise's laptop to her at the hotel that morning. Aliénor hadn't left her room all day. She had only changed positions, moving to the bed at 7.30 to work with the computer on her knees and her dinner on the duvet beside her.

Aliénor had never been asked to sort through the contents of a computer before. It was a colossal undertaking. She had soon developed a way to stay focused: she was alternately going through emails, files and photos, dividing everything by year and going back a decade, to 2006. Aliénor would never have expected that her sister – who was always so impeccably methodical, she used to organise her underwear by colour and books by their author – would have such an unstructured email inbox. It looked like it had never been organised. Louise's two email accounts – one Yahoo address and another connected to their parents' clinic from when she worked there – were both set up in Outlook. She only had three folders, entitled 'Travel', 'Bills' and 'Clinic'. All the remaining messages were jumbled together in her inbox, right down to the very last, which was one of those insufferable chain emails from one of Louise's friends, promising great fortune in exchange for forwarding the chain, which she had duly done several hours before she died. Judging by her deleted items folder, she only ever got rid of spam and newsletters, and kept everything else.

Aliénor took a long swig of Ramlösa mineral water. She had just finished going through everything from 2011. It had been both fruitful and exasperating to go through every document in every folder and look at every single photo. Seeing Louise time and time again made Aliénor want to dig into her chest with her bare hands and tear her heart out. But at the same time, she would have spent all day cycling through those photos, just to feel the bright spark of joy, even if it only lasted a split second, when Louise appeared on the screen, flooding her mind with happy thoughts and setting her heart aglow. But as the sentiment passed it felt like a bubble had burst, leaving the horror and emptiness behind. Aliénor had to keep bringing her mind back to the task at hand. This was her mechanism for coping with the panic and the pain: click on the next email, read the next line, draw the next conclusion.

That said, she was only doing a quick scan of each of Louise's emails at this point. She had created a folder in Outlook, where she dragged any messages that jumped out at her because of their subject, sender or recipient. She would read the messages properly the second time round.

Aliénor closed the lid of the pizza box and made a start on her tiramisu. It was time to tackle 2012 now.

With the spoon still in her mouth, she opened the folder containing Louise's photos. She only found three albums: One entitled 'Ko Phi Phi' from January, another named 'Anna W. Wedding' from October, and one more labelled 'New Year's'.

Aliénor frowned. There were four times fewer albums in 2012 than any of the previous years she had sorted through. She quickly checked to make sure Louise hadn't filed her photos under the wrong year, but everything seemed to be in order.

Aliénor spooned some more tiramisu into her mouth and opened the 'Ko Phi Phi' album. Her sister had gone on a girls' trip to Thailand with her friends and taken the usual snapshots: beaches, parties and local delicacies. Louise was radiant. In October that year, she had been to the wedding of a friend from university, Anna. That album only contained a few photos of the couple in church together with their children, the youngest of which must have been around five. There were no photos of Louise herself. The 'New Year's' album was similarly sparse, showing just a dozen or so photos of a group having dinner and then dancing. Louise was absent from these photos too.

Aliénor set her spoon down and moved on again, to Louise's emails. Around 21 March, her sister had started to send fewer and fewer messages. Then, from 17 June, most of the emails in her work inbox had gone unanswered. That had led to a message from their father telling her to come and see him in his office, followed by another two days later asking her why she wasn't at the Danish conference, where she was supposed to be representing the clinic.

Louise had not responded, which had provoked a flurry of furious emails from Göran.

Aliénor closed her eyes.

Something had shaken Louise enough to make her neglect her work and forget about a conference in Denmark – inconceivable behaviour for someone as diligent and conscientious as her.

2012...

Aliénor tapped at her eyebrows.

Had something happened in their family that year?

Nothing significant, otherwise she would remember. The last family drama she could recall was eighteen years ago, when her autism came to light.

Could Louise have fallen seriously ill?

Aliénor shook the thought out of her mind.

Back then, Louise was working with her parents and brother Léopold. They used to see each other six days a week, because they always had Sunday lunch together as a family. If Louise had lost weight or seemed frail, Göran, Kerstin, Léopold and Gerda would have noticed. *And so would I*, Aliénor thought. *I would have noticed the changes in her face.* Sickness had a tendency to yellow, hollow and shrivel a person. It went hand in hand with sadness, draining the face and withering the gaze.

Aliénor looked up at the window and cast her eyes towards the arches of the Tullbron bridge, straddling the Ätran river. 'A bridge older than the Royal Opera House at the Palace of Versailles,' Louise had told her, the first time they'd come here to fish for salmon. Aliénor remembered the two green benches down below, by the river, perched on a narrow strip of land splashed by the current. There they had leaned back and enjoyed a punnet of fat strawberries, the sweet red juice coating their lips, running down their chins as they squinted in the sun. Aliénor had kept the hook as a souvenir.

As the memory flooded back to her, Aliénor swiftly closed the screen of the laptop.

Yes, of course. The hook. She had kept the hook.

Aliénor jumped out of bed and donned her boots and her down jacket. She pulled a hat over her ears, grabbed her bag and left the hotel room with her phone glued to her ear.

Now she knew where to look.

La Virgen de los Desamparados Orphanage, Madrid
Friday, 15 August 1952

GORDI HAD SEEN FATHER MURILLO doing his rounds in the dormitory during the night. Without his leather-belt whip this time.

But she was far too thirsty to wait until the next morning. So she got up and went to drink from the toilets. After a year and a half of wandering these hallways, she knew her way around with her eyes closed.

It had been a good day for the five of them. Gordi had asked them to talk about their parents. She wanted to know what it was like to have a mother. A father. A grandmother. She wondered what it must feel like to exist in someone else's world. And see your life play out in their eyes.

Reme told the others how her father would rub her and her brother with tobacco when they went to see him in prison, before he died, so that his smell would linger with them when they went home. Launa and Lados showed them their shoes with the names of their parents written on the soles. Dulce talked about her mother and the braids she would wrap around her head like a crown. The salty smell of her hair. And the way she would always snort a little bit after she laughed. Gordi had listened and tried to conjure up memories of her own. But nothing came to her.

She'd had trouble falling asleep that night. When she finally did, she soon woke feeling as if she had thorns in her throat. So she slipped out of bed and went to the toilets.

From the corridor, she heard some strange noises. Whispering.

Hissing. Rustling. As she inched closer to where the sounds were coming from, she saw Father Murillo first, from behind. He was grunting and rocking back and forth on his knees, his cassock covering his legs, brushing against the floor. He kept going like that for a while, until he shuddered and gasped a funny, muffled sort of cry. As he stood up and shuffled away, Gordi saw the naked body huddled in silence on the floor, curled up tightly like a grub in the sudden silence. The body started to shake, and only when it unfurled from a foetal position did Gordi see who it belonged to.

Launa pulled her nightdress back on, slipped a towel into her underwear and tottered towards Gordi without noticing her in the doorway. As she drew closer, Gordi threw her arms around her.

'Good heavens, whatever did Father Murillo do to you? Are you hurt?'

'Shh,' Launa said. 'Don't worry about me, my sweet Gordi, it's all right. Come on, let's go back to bed,' she whispered, planting a kiss on the top of her head.

Gordi started to sob. She didn't understand why this wave of sadness had washed over her, but she cupped her hands over her mouth to stifle it.

Launa gazed softly at her face and brushed away the few locks of hair the tears had matted to her cheeks.

'Listen, my sweet Gordi, if Father Murillo comes to see you during the night, and if he brings you here, try to think about your mother, all right? Think about her. Somewhere in your mind, you must have some fragments of memories of your mother. Take those pieces, stick them back together, and think about her.'

Gordi tried, but no images came to her mind. Nothing but the immeasurable heartache that made her want to go to sleep and never wake up again.

'I can't…'

'What do you see in your mind when you feel the warmth right there in your chest?' she asked, placing her hand on Gordi's heart.'

Gordi thought for a moment, and she saw the sea.

'Your smile, Launa. The smile you gave me when I first came here. If I had a mother, she would smile at me the way you do. With the same kind of light in her eyes.'

'Well, think about me then, my sweet Gordi. And the smile I draw on my face for you.'

ALIÉNOR WENT UP the outdoor staircase to Gerda's attic. She walked straight through the apartment without turning on the light and then went down the stairs into the main house. She stopped on the upstairs landing and flicked the switch, filling the hallway with light. White walls, pale floorboards and black fingerprint powder. No streaks of red staining the floor, and no spatters arcing across the ceiling. Only black and white. Aliénor leaned against the door on her left – Louise's bedroom door – and gave a loud sigh. She closed her eyes and listened to the echoes of her short breaths and pounding pulse. Aliénor could feel her heart quaking in her chest. Or maybe it was her whole body that was shaking.

As she made her way to the family home, Aliénor had thought about nothing more than going into Louise's room, lying down on her bed and feeling her spirit. To breathe her scent and conjure up her presence. To be with her. And by touching her clothes, leafing through her books, looking at her photos and stirring her sister's world to life, Aliénor would be able to hear her voice. That wasn't how it worked, though. Because Léopold was right. Now the only thing left in that house was death.

She shouldn't have come here alone, she thought. Emily could have come with her. Or Gerda. Or Alexis.

On Monday, she had sensed a certain closeness with Alexis, as if they were grieving together and shedding the same tears. That was strange, because Alexis didn't know Louise or their parents. Aliénor had thought about seeking comfort in her arms. The idea had come to her spontaneously, so that meant it was an urge. She was sure that Alexis would have embraced her with open arms. She had pictured Alexis resting her cheek on the top of her head, sweeping a few stray locks of hair from her face and hugging her tight. All of that had run through her mind in a matter of seconds. Maybe it was because Alexis reminded her of Louise. They had the same gentle nature and air of determination.

Aliénor lifted her hand from the door and crossed the hallway to her own room. When she turned on the light, it struck her that it was no longer her room. It was the room where her sister had died. She found the sight of the blood-soaked mattress sickening. The grief felt like an arrow piercing her heart. Aliénor groaned and bent double. Gripping her thighs in her hands, her arms as stiff as sticks, she sobbed a fit of heavy tears that sent shudders through her chest. The tears stretched out into a cry. A cry of rage. A battle cry. Someone had killed Louise. Someone had taken Louise away from her.

Anger pulsed through her limbs and gave her the strength to stand up again.

Someone had killed Louise. Someone had taken Louise away from her.

Aliénor pulled the step stool out from between her desk and the wall. She slid it in front of her wardrobe, climbed to the top step and stood on tiptoe to open the narrow cupboard above. She pulled out two cardboard boxes and stepped down carefully. Placing the boxes on the floor, she removed the lid from one of them. The box contained around a dozen thick journals, all stacked up against each other. Each journal had a year written on the spine.

Louise had encouraged her to start writing these journals just before she hit puberty. To set goals for herself every year, figure out strategies for achieving them and keep track of her thoughts and triumphs. In the beginning, Aliénor had baulked at the idea of writing in her journal. So Louise had helped her make it part of her routine. After brushing her teeth at night and before reading in bed, Aliénor would take five minutes to reflect on her day and make a note of her feelings and accomplishments, with her sister sitting on the end of her bed to watch over her. Little by little, Aliénor had found that reading over what she had written gave her such great pleasure, she came to enjoy filling the pages and devoted more and more time to the endeavour.

Aliénor pulled out the journal dated 2012, sat down on the floor with her back against the wardrobe and started to read. If she had noticed something strange or unusual about her sister, or if she or her family had experienced anything disturbing, there would be a note of it in here.

2012 was the year she had read *Bonjour Tristesse* in French. It was also the year she had finally seen the film *Snabba Cash*, starring Joel Kinnaman. The English title was *Easy Money*, she recalled. Aliénor tried to turn to the next page, but the sheet only bent a little, as if it were suddenly too stiff and made from heavier-weight paper. She pinched the folded-down corner between her thumb and middle finger and turned the page.

Her eyebrows crinkled to a frown and she gasped, her mouth half open with surprise for a few short seconds. Then Aliénor closed her journal with shaking hands.

OLOFSSON STIFLED A YAWN with his fist.

Talk about harsh, having a team meeting at seven in the morning. It didn't help that he'd still been awake at four. He really had to get a good night's sleep by himself, otherwise he'd crash and burn. He just couldn't get enough of Mona, though. And that was really weird. He'd never felt anything like it before, such an insatiable need to be with a woman. He spent his days trying to take his mind off her, trying to stop the images of the nights they spent together from flashing before his eyes. He could spend his every waking minute thinking about her. Seeing her in the throes of passion, watching her smile, laugh, eat and even sleep. Yes, sleep. He loved the pouty crease of her lips and the little wrinkle that appeared between her eyes. *For fuck's sake, why was she making him go all soppy? Soft in the head. But still hard in the—*

'Kristian!'

Bergström's voice crashed like cymbals in his ear.

Olofsson blinked himself back to reality. 'Yes, er, what, boss?'

'For the third time: coffee?'

'Er … sure.'

'Nights are for sleeping, Olofsson!' the commissioner thundered as he filled his subordinate's mug.

Kristian sipped at the steaming coffee. Emily and Alexis were sitting at the conference room table, each turning their laptop on. He hadn't even heard them come in.

'Right, well, Interpol got back to us,' Bergström began, closing his eyes and pinching the bridge of his nose. 'They don't have anything that fits with our case.'

Emily frowned.

'Well, not technically nothing. They did send us a few leads,' the commissioner clarified, seeing Emily's reaction. 'But nothing that I feel speaks to our perp's profile. Emily, I uploaded their report to our internal server so you can read it. Kristian, where are you with the list of patients whose treatments didn't pan out?'

'I've been having a hell of a time checking their alibis. It's taking forever to get anywhere.'

Bergström turned to Emily and Alexis. 'Ladies, what's new with your theory about the sudden and miraculous MAR success stories?'

'That's Alexis's theory,' Emily corrected.

In spite of the headache making his forehead throb, Bergström had to fight a smile. Those words could just as easily have come from Aliénor's lips.

For a brief moment, Alexis placed her hand on Emily's and flashed her an even briefer smile. She knew her appreciation would only glance off the profiler's skin. Subtle and stealthy was the only way to avoid ruffling her feathers. The commissioner was treated to a longer smile.

'We focused on what I would say were the most desperate cases,' Alexis explained. 'In other words, patients who got pregnant after five or more tries. We compared the treatments that failed with those that succeeded by examining four aspects of data: the drugs used and the quality of the eggs, the sperm and the embryo.'

'Well, that must have been a hoot,' Olofsson scoffed.

'Tell me about it … Anyway, we waded our way through no fewer than a hundred and twenty-two files yesterday, starting with Lydia Olsen/Roberts and her friend Melinda Gorp, and we think we're on to something. Even though there was no change in the quality of the eggs and sperm, the quality of the embryos improved dramatically to reach an optimal level.'

'And the treatment itself wasn't modified in any way?' Bergström asked.

'Oh, it was.'

'Wait a second … What are you suggesting?'

Alexis paused and swallowed. Her theory made her feel sick to her stomach. 'That it wasn't their own embryos that were implanted. What I mean is that these women didn't realise it, but they were carrying someone else's child.'

A dense, heavy silence descended on the room, muffling the sounds of the hustle and bustle elsewhere in the station that crept its way through the thin walls.

'*Hej.*'

Aliénor was standing in the doorway to the conference room, looking pale and dishevelled. No one had heard the double doors creak open.

'I haven't slept,' she announced, her voice raw with fatigue.

'We'd never have guessed, Google,' Olofsson quipped, taking a sip of cold coffee.

'I've found something else.'

'On Louise's computer?' Emily asked.

'No. In my room.'

With a subtle nod, the profiler urged Aliénor to continue.

Aliénor moistened her chapped lips. 'I found a SIM card in a small envelope taped into my journal for 2012, on the page for the first of June.'

Bergström turned to Emily, wondering whether she was as lost as he was.

Aliénor unbuckled her messenger bag and pulled out a spiral-bound notebook protected by a freezer bag.

Emily reached into her own backpack for a pair of latex gloves. She tore open the protective plastic packaging and pulled the gloves on.

'And you didn't open the envelope?' she asked, taking the journal from Aliénor.

Aliénor shook her head.

Emily unzipped the plastic freezer bag and took the journal out. She flipped through until she got to the page for 1 June 2012. A tiny envelope made of tracing paper, the same kind that individual safety razor blades came wrapped in, was taped to the middle of the page.

'Kristian, go and find me a phone and a Stanley knife in—'

'Yep, I'm on it, boss!' the detective replied, and hurried out of the room.

'Only Louise could have put that there,' Aliénor murmured, as if the thought were meant for her sister's ears alone.

'What makes you say that?' Bergström asked, staring at the journal.

'Louise was the one who got me into writing these journals every day. Neither of my parents, nor Gerda, knew about them. Maybe Gerda did, actually, since she was the one who cleaned my room, but I never saw her clean inside my cupboards. I suppose she could have peeked inside, but I doubt it. Only Louise and I knew that these journals existed and what was in them. That's why I think she put the SIM card in there.'

'What made you think to look in your diary?'

'It's not a diary, it's a journal.'

'All right, Aliénor, I understand.'

'It was the Tullbron bridge – the one beside the hotel.'

Bergström shook his head. 'What do you mean?'

'You asked what made me look in my journal, Kommissionär. The idea came to me when I saw the bridge from my hotel room. It made me think about the first time Louise took me fishing, and the hook I kept as a souvenir, and what I had written about that day in my journal. I was in the middle of going through Louise's inbox, and I realised that her behaviour really started to change in the second quarter of 2012. She let her work and personal emails go unanswered or replied very late; she failed to report for work without telling my father, which made him furious; and she forgot her friends' birthdays, that sort of thing. And so, I wondered what might have happened in her life or ours – our family's, I mean – for her to behave like that. Otherwise, Louise was always such a responsible, upstanding and loyal person. Something serious, or at least very troubling, must have happened in her life for her to neglect her responsibilities as a daughter, friend and employee.'

Aliénor pressed her dry lips together, tilted her head back to stretch her neck and swallowed.

'But 2012 was four years ago, and I couldn't remember what had happened that year. So I thought about my journals. I figured I might have made a note of something that probably seemed insignificant at the time but would make perfect sense now. And I went home to look through them. When I opened my journal from 2012, that's what I found. Then I spent the night reading the rest of the emails from that time in their entirety, trying to uncover more specific details, but I couldn't find anything.'

'Were you in the habit of rereading your journals from time to time?' Emily asked.

'No, not before now.'

'What about your sister?'

'She never read them, so no, she never *re*read them either.'

'But she knew where you kept them.'

'Yes,' Aliénor admitted with a nod.

The double doors swung wide open, and Olofsson hurried back into the conference room.

Emily took the Stanley knife from the detective's outstretched hand. Delicately she sliced through the few millimetres of adhesive tape holding the flap of the envelope down, and extricated the SIM card. She inserted it into the slot of the phone that Olofsson had just plugged in to charge, and passed the phone to him.

The detective turned the phone on as Bergström, Emily and Alexis all huddled around him. Aliénor sat down on the chair closest to the double doors, crossing her fingers and placing her hands on her thighs.

The touch screen only contained a few app icons.

Olofsson opened the list of contacts first. It was empty, as was the messages folder. He moved on to the call log, which showed no incoming calls, but did list around a dozen outgoing calls over a four-month period from May to September of 2012. The calls were made to only three numbers.

'Norway, Spain, and Spain again,' Bergström observed, pointing at each of the numbers in turn.

'Aliénor, do you want to come and take a look at these—'

'I don't need to. My sister never talked to me about anyone who lived in Norway or Spain.'

'Would you like some water, Aliénor? Or maybe a bite to eat?' Alexis offered, reaching a hand across the table, as if to touch her.

Aliénor shook her head weakly.

'You're very pale, Aliénor,' Alexis persisted, pouring her a glass of water.

'Because I haven't slept.'

Alexis stood up and set the glass down in front of Aliénor.

'Drink it … please,' Emily insisted.

Aliénor acquiesced and gulped the water down greedily. She kept the glass cradled in her hand and stared at the commissioner.

Bergström pulled the conference room phone towards him, pressed the internal speakerphone button and dialled the Norwegian number.

The line disconnected straight away. He tried again, and the same thing happened.

'*Helvete,*' he hissed.

Staring at the phone, he took a deep breath and moved on to the next number. The phone rang five times before it was picked up by an answerphone. The robotic voice repeated the number he had just dialled, and ended with a beep.

'*Buenos días,*' Bergström began, in a very Germanic-sounding Spanish. '*Soy el Comisario Lennart Bergström de la policía de Falkenberg, en Suecia. Le contactamos en relación con una encuesta. Por favor, llámenos urgentemente al 00 46 77 11 41 400.*'

He hung up and dialled the third and final number. After three rings, the call went to voicemail.

'*Hola! Si, es Paola, pero no estoy. Déjame un mensaje si quieres, y te llamaré cuando pueda! Besos!*'

Taken by surprise, Bergström paused for a second or two before repeating the same message, this time mentioning the name he had just heard on the voicemail greeting. He hung up and immediately made an internal call to initiate a search on the Swedish number associated with the SIM card, as well as the three numbers he had just dialled.

'Well, apparently I'm the only uncultured person here, but it's not the end of the world,' Olofsson joked once Bergström had finished his conversation. 'Can someone translate for me what Penelope Cruz just said on the phone, please?'

'*Penelope Cruz's* name is Paola,' Alexis grinned. 'And that's the only information she gave in her voicemail greeting. Lennart just explained that he was calling about an ongoing investigation, and he said to please call the Falkenberg police urgently.'

'Well that's a real help, isn't it?' Olofsson snorted, rubbing his eyes. 'Sweden, Norway, Spain, Paola … For fuck's sake, Google, you've really opened Pandora's box for us, haven't you?'

Aliénor stood up, took off her parka and draped it over the back of her chair.

'For once, Kristian, I agree with you,' she said as she sat down again.

La Virgen de los Desamparados Orphanage, Madrid
Sunday, 17 August 1952

THE SUMMER SUN was choking everything. The parched earth smoked, cracked and crunched underfoot. The air was stifling everywhere, except for here, within the stone walls of the chapel, where it was as dark as night, but at least you could breathe. Life was always good when Christ was near, Sister Fernanda would have said.

Gordi inhaled the scent of the incense and candles. So many things were burned in the House of God. She sat in a pew, two rows behind two young girls. She knew who they were. They were in the pink dormitory, but Gordi often saw them in the refectory.

Every day for the last two weeks, Sister Fernanda had been bringing them to the chapel to pray for their father, who was due to be hauled before the firing squad. They were to plead for God's mercy and forgiveness. The nun would begin the prayers by counting down the remaining days until the execution, before asking the Lord to absolve their father of his crimes.

Today, however, Sister Fernanda had groomed them carefully and dressed them in the uniform reserved for official visits. The two young sisters were looking up at the effigy of Christ with gratitude and respect, because He had saved their father.

Gordi mused about the very different message she was going to deliver to Jesus when it was her turn to speak. She wouldn't be telling Him everything out loud; she wanted to be sure she wouldn't be punished, not like the time she had been locked up for four hours for crossing her legs. She would be content to use her inner voice to address the Lord (lord of what, precisely? she had to wonder).

Because apparently He could hear everything: the words that ran through her thoughts as well as those that slipped out of her mouth, in spite of herself. *Ah, Lord of the Kingdom of Heaven.* Now she remembered. She was going to tell this Lord of the Kingdom of Heaven that he was a murderer.

After all, someone had to tell Him, didn't they? Perhaps He would finally hear their prayers. All five of them – she, Reme, Dulce, Launa and Lados – had been pleading for the same thing for months. Five identical prayers. Yet still He turned a deaf ear.

Sister Fernanda made the two young sisters stand up and led them to the altar. Then she wrapped her arms around them. They both shuddered in unison, since Sister Fernanda only ever touched the orphans with her braid of leather belts. Her hand only ever whipped, and never stroked.

'It's time to ask Christ to take your father into His home now,' the nun said, in a calm, collected tone, smiling with the deference and gratitude she usually reserved for her God.

The young sisters turned to one another with a look of astonishment on their frozen faces, then both turned deathly pale. The older girl reached for her little sister's hand.

'Papa's dead?' the younger girl asked, glaring at the man on the cross. Her gaze drifted to her older sister's dress, then her carefully coiffed Sunday-best hair. 'But we prayed so hard…'

'Yes, and God heard your prayers, but He was not able to save your father.'

The older girl retreated a step, pulling her sister close. Her lips creased with suffering.

'He was executed today,' Sister Fernanda replied. 'Let us pray for him now. Sit there and start with an "Our Father".'

The two children staggered to the nearest pew and clasped their hands in prayer. Gordi was sure it wasn't a prayer they were going to say, though. They too were going to tell Jesus He was a murderer.

Sister Fernanda walked over to Gordi. Gordi instinctively bowed her head, tucking her chin to her chest as if to take refuge in her shell.

'162, it's good that you're here to pay your respects.'

Gordi lifted her gaze and looked the nun in the eye. She hesitated for a moment, weighing up the pros and the cons, then took the plunge.

'I came to have a word with Him. With Jesus.'

The nun steeled her gaze. And her fist. She had found her rage again. Or rather, her rage had caught up with her.

'What did you come here to say to Him?'

'That Father Murillo is hurting my friends.'

Sister Fernanda's opened her eyes so wide, wrinkles crazed across her forehead.

'And what exactly is Father Murillo doing to your friends?'

'He's hurting them ... between their legs.'

Sister Fernanda grabbed her by the ear so hard that Gordi had to stand on tiptoe to quell the fire that was burning all over her face.

'You should be ashamed to say such ungodly things, you dirty little rat!'

Sister Fernanda let her go as suddenly as she had grabbed hold of her. 'Look what you made me do in the House of God.'

She clenched her teeth and clasped her hands tightly together, probably to stop herself from lashing out at her again, Gordi thought.

'I'm not lying, Sister. He makes 101 and 102 bleed every night. Right here, between—'

'That's enough, you little rat!' Sister Fernanda spat. 'I'm going to have to teach you a lesson to rid you of the demons inside you! You horrible little pest. How dare you insult a man of God?'

Sister Fernanda grasped Gordi by the scruff of her neck and frog-marched her to the door. She was going to grab her leather belts and whip her back to shreds, Gordi was sure of it.

But she had still been right to come here and try to make herself heard. Even though she knew now why God had not heard their prayers: he only listened to Sister Fernanda and Father Murillo.

God only had ears for His soldiers, not His victims.

ALIÉNOR GREEDILY TUCKED INTO her meatball and beetroot salad sandwich. It wasn't lunch time yet, but they were all hungry by mid-morning, so Alexis had gone to fetch some goodies from the local bakery. Bergström was in his office, on a conference call with Møller. Emily had excused herself, but Aliénor wasn't sure where she was, and Alexis and Olofsson were still working their way through the list of patients. Whenever the phone rang, the detective picked it up straight away, hoping one of the Spanish numbers was calling back.

Aliénor opened the next email. She had spent all morning reading Louise's messages. So far, she hadn't found anything remotely of interest.

One of the swing doors creaked open. The sound alone told Aliénor it was Emily entering the room; the energy and emotion the profiler put into every gesture and every word were strictly measured. Aliénor had never heard Emily raise her voice – or laugh, for that matter. A fleeting smile, a mere hint of a chuckle were the closest she ever came to expressing joy. She seemed to have more in common with cats than people. Just like a feline, she was a hunter too. She shared their strategy of keeping a watchful eye on their prey until they were sure to overpower them, then emerging from the shadows to finish them off.

Emily took a seat across the table. 'Aliénor, we have the results of the DNA test. Louise and Léopold are your siblings and Göran and Kirsten, your parents.'

Aliénor found Emily's efficient way of communicating information immensely gratifying. She always delivered a message directly. None of those pointless preludes that always ended up drawing out the suffering.

'That only proves we have the same genes. It doesn't add anything to our family or our kinship, and it doesn't take anything away.'

Aliénor promptly returned to reading the emails. But then she paused and looked up at Emily, who was still sitting on the other side of the table as if she knew their conversation wasn't over and was patiently waiting for it to resume.

'Do you think that's why Louise was in my room when she died? She was leaving the SIM card in the journal?'

'We don't know yet if she was the one who put it there.'

'Perhaps, because she was moving out, she wanted to leave it in a safe place,' Aliénor continued, as if she hadn't heard Emily's words. 'Maybe she had read my journals even. I wonder if that's why she was in my room.'

'Have you been able to identify when her behaviour returned to normal?' Emily said, nodding at Louise's laptop to steer Aliénor back to the present moment.

'At the end of November 2012,' she replied, after a brief pause.

The phone rang, interrupting their conversation. Olofsson quickly swallowed the mouthful he was chewing and pressed a button to take the call on speakerphone.

'*Falkenbergs polisen.*'

'*Buenos días. Soy Paola Cuevas. Usted me llamó…*'

'I'm sorry, I don't speak Spanish,' Olofsson apologised, in English. He sat up straight and pulled his chair closer to the table, as if the caller were sitting across the table from him.

'No problem. My name is Paola Cuevas. You called me this morning about a current investigation.'

'Yes, of course. Thank you for calling us back.'

'Can you tell me which investigation this is concerning? Is it something to do with the deaths in the Lindbergh family? The story made the headline down here in Spain.'

'Yes, it is.'

Paola Cuevas kept them hanging for a moment. They could make out a few muffled words in the background.

'I have some things to share with you,' she said at last, 'but I don't want to say anything over the phone. I'm afraid I can't come to you either. You'll have to come and see me. Let me pass you over to my lawyer, who'll be happy to give you all the information you need to organise your visit.'

'Señora Cuevas, can you at least tell us who was calling you from the Swedish mobile number 00 46—'

'I was in touch with Louise Lindbergh.'

Calle de Alfonso XII, Madrid
Friday, 9 December 2016, 11.00 am

POWERFUL COLUMNS OF LIGHT were streaming in through the taxi windows. Alexis turned her face to the sun and breathed a contented sigh. In the south of Europe, the sun shone with pride, washing the sky such an intense azure shade of blue you couldn't help but smile. It oozed with the very essence of excess. If light could talk, this would be a heated debate full of gesticulation.

It had not taken long for them to get their act together the previous day. Bergström couldn't leave the station, so he had asked Emily to fly down to Madrid and back in a day, to take a statement from Paola Cuevas. Alexis had been keen to go too, and the commissioner had immediately agreed. He just had to persuade the prosecutor to give them the green light. If he sold the idea as Emily's, he figured, Møller's gratitude for the profiler's assistance in previous cases would hopefully spare them his usual wrath.

Emily paid the taxi fare and they stepped out onto the pavement. They were greeted by a porter at the door to the building, his radiant smile lifting the pointy ends of his dark moustache. He pushed open the ornate glass and wrought-iron door and directed them towards an equally good-humoured concierge. The way the Spaniards whistled their S sounds and rolled their Rs sounded like drum rolls, every sentence a celebration, Alexis thought.

The concierge asked them to wait while he dialled ahead to announce their arrival, before calling the lift and sending them up to the third floor.

When the lift doors opened, Emily and Alexis saw a petite woman wearing a figure-hugging suit waiting for them in a doorway down the corridor. They followed a red carpet that looked like a tongue snaking over the black and white tiles.

As they approached, the woman extended a slim hand with heavy rings weighing down every finger. 'Hello, I'm Montse Romero, Paola's lawyer.' She introduced herself in English, her carefully crafted curls bobbing between her ears and shoulders. 'I have to ask you to leave your bags and phones here,' she announced, closing the front door behind them.

Emily stiffened. Alexis almost fainted. She was so averse to being separated from her laptop, at airport security she always had to fight the urge to jump onto the conveyor belt and go through the X-ray machine with it.

'I'm afraid we can't take the risk that our conversation might be recorded and leaked to the press,' Montse said.

'We've already signed a confidentiality agreement,' Emily argued.

'I'm sorry,' the lawyer replied, pressing her ruby-red lips together.

Emily slipped her backpack off her shoulder and placed it on the floor, and Alexis followed suit with her laptop case. Montse led them further into the apartment, down a dark hallway dotted with half a dozen doors. When they reached the last door on the left, Montse knocked to announce their arrival.

The palatial bedroom was bathed in a warm light that seemed to lend an air of summer to the late-autumn day. A woman toying with her thirties was lying in a high, generously proportioned bed with a sheet draped over an impressive circumference of belly.

'Yes, I know,' she smiled in response to the look of astonishment on Alexis's face. 'It's huge, isn't it? I know it looks like I'm expecting triplets, but it's only twins. Two big, bouncing boys, as you can probably guess; but just the two of them. Well, perhaps "just" isn't quite the right word.'

Montse invited Emily and Alexis to take a seat on the velvet chaise longue facing the end of the bed.

'I'm sorry I couldn't get up to meet you, but I've been on forced bed rest for the last two months. Our two little cherubs gave us quite a scare,' Paola explained with a stroke of her belly.

'Coffee?' Montse interjected, with an enquiring look.

Emily and Alexis graciously accepted, and Montse disappeared down the hallway for a moment or two.

Paola waited until her lawyer returned before speaking again.

'I must apologise for all these precautions, but my husband is a professional footballer and there are some things we really mustn't divulge.' She lowered her eyes for a second and pulled the sheet up to the very top of her belly.

Emily's gaze wandered to the drapes framing the windows.

'I read in the papers about what happened to Louise and her family,' Paola continued. '*Dios mío* … what a terrible thing. … I was thinking I should contact you. I spoke to my husband and Montse about it…'

Emily blinked as if she were just waking up, and indulged Paola with a quick smile.

A housekeeper wearing a black dress and white lace-trimmed apron brought a tray into the room and set it down on the coffee table in front of the chaise longue.

'Anything for yourself, *Señora?*'

'*No, gracias,* Letizia.'

The housekeeper obediently nodded and left the room.

'I think it would best if you started at the beginning of your story,' Montse suggested to Paola, playing with one of her rings. 'To explain to these ladies how you came to be in touch with Louise Lindbergh.'

Paola sat up in bed, moved a cushion out of the way and pulled the sheet down. A white T-shirt hugged her belly like a second skin and tapered into a strange crinkly shape at her waist. She stretched her legs, then tucked them beneath her to sit cross-legged.

'My husband is sterile. We decided to have a baby with the help of a sperm donor,' she explained, running the tips of her fingers over her belly. Our doctor told us about the Lindbergh Clinic, which had an excellent reputation and could guarantee our anonymity. So I flew to Gothenburg to start my treatment. We rented an apartment across from the clinic, and I stayed there for four months.'

Paola paused to smile, gazing tenderly at the mound of her belly, which must now always be in her field of vision.

'I didn't offer any explanation to my friends here; they thought I was keeping my distance because of complications from a cosmetic-surgery procedure. Anyway, I got pregnant on the third try and came home to Madrid. But I lost the baby after ten weeks. The hormonal treatments caused all kinds of respiratory symptoms and ovarian cysts, and I put on a lot of weight. So we decided to take a break for a while. After a year, we decided to try again through a different clinic, so we asked the Lindbergh Clinic to transfer our embryos down here. I don't know if you're familiar with the process, but my eggs were fertilised with the donor's sperm in vitro, then once the embryos had formed, the strongest ones were frozen and kept in storage. There were eleven of them in my case. This method avoids having to repeat the treatment that stimulates the ovaries to produce more eggs. Because no matter what the experts say, it can cause uterine and ovarian cancer.'

Alexis felt the urge to take a deep breath. She found this kind of relentless determination to have children highly unsettling. She couldn't wrap her head around it. Was simply living with someone really that unfulfilling?

'So anyway, we asked for our embryos to be transferred,' Paola continued. 'But the people at the Lindbergh seemed to be dragging their heels, and after several attempts to find out what was going on we were finally told that the container carrying our embryos was damaged in transit and that our embryos had been lost.'

Paola closed her eyes and exhaled with a long, shuddering sigh.

Emily stared at her coffee, turning the cup around the saucer, oblivious to the shrill grating of the porcelain. The sound of Paola's voice drew her back to her senses.

'You can't imagine how devastated I was – and furious. The donor we had chosen was no longer available and making that decision had been even harder than enduring the treatments. Do you realise, we had to choose the biological father of our child just from some details on a piece of paper? And try to find someone who looked like my husband based only on a photo of the donor when he was a child, or sometimes even just a baby. The whole thing was excruciating, especially for my husband. Of course, I wanted to take my frustration out on the clinic. I know that wouldn't have resolved anything, but I suppose I wanted to set an example and offload all that anger. But my husband was dead against it. As far as he was concerned, making our private drama public knowledge was out of the question. He was concerned about how others would see us – afraid of their pity, I suppose. He wanted to live up to the image of the man his coach, teammates and fans saw. That was when Louise Lindbergh first contacted me, in the spring of 2012. She wanted to hear my side of the story. I told her what I really thought: that their clinic's reluctance to explain what had happened was an attempt to hide something. I never actually believed that our embryos had been damaged in transit. I thought they had made a mistake and were trying to nip a scandal in the bud.'

'When and how many times were you in contact with Louise Lindbergh?' Emily asked.

'We spoke three times on the phone.'

'And what was her take on the incident?'

'The first time, she just asked me a few questions. I was quite unpleasant with her on the phone, actually. I was expecting a sincere apology and some discussion, but there wasn't. Believe it or not, I hung up on her. The second time, she told me she wasn't calling in an official capacity on behalf of the Lindbergh Clinic. She said she just wanted to know what had happened. So I stated the facts and told her about my suspicions. The third and last time, she asked me some in-depth questions about the quality of my eggs, the donor's sperm and the embryos. So I sent her all the details. I might not be a doctor, but let me tell you, after all these year of MAR treatments, you become something of an expert.'

'What happened after the third phone call?'

'I never heard from her again.'

'Did you try to contact her?'

Paola glanced at her lawyer for a second, then lowered her gaze. 'No. Montse advised me not to.'

'What was the name of the clinic where you were going to pursue your treatment?'

'La Virgen del Pilar, of all places.'

Emily and Alexis frowned in puzzlement. They had never heard that name before, but Paola seemed to think it would mean something to them.

'But we ended up not going with them in the end,' Paola went on. 'I went into a depression after that incident in 2012, and we decided to stop trying. We only started again at the beginning of this year, here in Madrid. And it worked the first time, *gracias a Dios*. When I think about La Virgen del Pilar, it sends shivers down my spine.'

'Why? What happened?'

Paola and Montse exchanged a look of bewilderment.

The lawyer tilted her head to one side, so that her curls kissed her shoulder. 'I don't understand. Did you not hear about it?'

Thursday, 17 May 2012

The music is back in my mornings, and Nino has found his smile again. I wake up eager and hungry to open my eyes, the way I did when I became a grandmother twenty years ago.

Today, I get to his place at 6.58 pm. I make it to the front door just in time to see his housekeeper leaving.

Nearly three months ago, after I saw him on the news, I blended into the crowd of journalists that had set up camp on his doorstep. Nino drove me here the next day. He bathed me and dressed me and dropped me off at the corner of the avenue. In front of this bus shelter. I waited all afternoon for him to step outside, the image of the saggy, bloated man he had now become filling my mind and his hoarse moans ringing in my ears. That evening, when Nino came back to pick me up, I didn't want to go home. I stayed in the bus shelter, reflecting on his face. The face of my suffering, my drowning too.

Then at one in the morning, he walked right past me with his dog. The dog ignored me. It barely even turned its snout to sniff at the bench. It obviously wasn't a good guard dog, because it should have growled. Because the only thing I could think of was killing its master.

That was on 23 February. Every night after that, I came back to sit on that bench. And I waited until he walked past me with Athos. Every night, the dog lingered a little more. And after two weeks, he no longer flashed me a tense, fleeting, apologetic smile when he pulled at Athos's lead. But he did stop, and we exchanged a few words. I recognised that look of his beneath his drooping eyelids. And his voice, weathered as it was by old age. He thought I was waiting for the night bus. There was nothing wrong with that. I insinuated that I worked for an old lady in the neighbourhood. There was nothing wrong with that either. Perhaps I was the only person who wasn't quizzing him about the accusations hanging over his head, the ones his lawyer was trying so hard to dispel. He talked to me about his wife. His daughter. His dog. I listened to him, the smell of his breath and the memory of his hands grasping my hips never far from my mind.

A few days ago, he came by without his dog. Athos was with his wife, he explained. But he still had to get out for his night-time walk. Otherwise, he wouldn't be able to sleep. Or perhaps he needed to see me.

Now, the lights in the grand townhouse start dancing from one room to another. I check the time: it's already five to one. The hours have flown by without me realising, yet I haven't moved a muscle.

Every night it's the same choreography: the kitchen on the first floor, the reception rooms one after the other, the hallway, the ground-floor entrance, then a weaker light from a smaller window, perhaps the bathroom. Next, he opens the front door. If his dog were there, it would be pulling him out the door, scrabbling at the pavement with its paws, tongue hanging out and panting in excitement. I'm already sitting in the bus shelter at the corner of the avenue. This is the way he always walks to the park. I'm waiting for him.

Tonight, I'm going to join him on his walk. To see what it feels like to stand at his level. Stronger and less vulnerable.

Murillo Café, Calle Ruiz de Alarcón, Madrid
Friday, 9 December 2016, 5.00 pm

EMILY AND ALEXIS had easily found a seat on the terrace at the Murillo, which was deserted by the usual locals and tourists, who were probably put off by the chill in the air. Coming from Sweden though, they had not hesitated for a second and were now basking in the glow of the Spanish sun that always made everything better.

They ordered two coffees while they waited for Bergström to call them. A young woman passed by the café, and her gaze lingered on Emily and Alexis as she walked into the building next door. Alexis wondered what had caught her eye. How had she interpreted what she saw: two friends enjoying a coffee; a couple on holiday? People's perceptions were often so different from the truth, she pondered. We all see the world through our own lens, which is shaped by our past and our upbringing, our desires and our fears. That was precisely what had happened earlier, at Paola Cuevas's apartment. The young woman was brimming with life from the three hearts beating inside her, but all Alexis could see was the monumental belly, and the self-sacrifice required to give life to another being, who would spell the end of the couple's relationship as they knew it.

Emily, meanwhile, had been struggling with the memory of the child she lost, the baby who died in her arms. Alexis knew about Emily's personal drama, but this was the first time she had seen her friend suffering. The profiler had emerged from her thoughts only twice during their meeting with Paola Cuevas, managing to put her professional hat on briefly, but the pain had clearly proven to be too much and she had retreated into herself again.

The shrill ringtone of the iPad made them both jump. The faces of Bergström and Olofsson soon joined them on the café terrace.

'Isn't it cold there?' Olofsson asked, between two gulps of water.

'It's a lot warmer than where you call home,' Alexis teased.

'Let me remind you, Sweden's your home now too.'

'So?' the commissioner interjected.

Emily summed up the revelations Paola Cuevas had shared with them, from the supposed loss of the tank containing her embryos to her conversations with Louise.

'Louise must have suspected the clinic was trafficking embryos, eggs or even sperm,' Bergström thought out loud.

'She resigned, though, so what are we supposed to make of that?' Olofsson asked, opening a Tupperware container. 'Does that mean her parents or her brother were behind it all, and she decided to step away instead of blowing the whistle?' The detective pulled out a hardboiled egg and ate half of it in a single bite.

'That's not all,' Alexis cut in. 'The Lindbergh Clinic had ties to a MAR clinic in Madrid by the name of La Virgen del Pilar. Paola Cuevas was to report to that clinic if there was the slightest problem with her treatment. As it happens, in February 2012, Dr Carlos Burgos, the head of that clinic, was accused of fertilising patients' eggs with his own sperm.'

'Sheesh! What a freaking nut job!' Olofsson blurted through a mouthful of yolk and egg white.

'Have you contacted the clinic? Or did it close down?'

Emily nodded. 'Yes, it was shut down, and Carlos Burgos is dead. Natural causes. He was eighty-two years old.'

'More than eighty candles? Weren't his swimmers past their sell-by date?' Olofsson blurted.

'Perhaps he'd been storing them for years.'

'Oh, give it a rest, you're going to make me puke.'

'Right,' the commissioner interjected. 'I'm going to get in touch with the Spanish police to find out more information about that clinic. The Virgen del ... what was it?'

'La Virgen del Pilar.'

Bergström made a note of the name in his pocketbook.

'And it was Dr Carlos Burgos, you said?'

Emily nodded.

'Alexis, why don't you come back to Falkenberg? I'm going to fly down to join Emily in Madrid.'

'Why?' Alexis protested, sitting up straight.

'If I'm not mistaken, you're getting married eight days from now, are you not?'

'My thoughts exactly. I still have a week left.'

Bergström rolled his eyes and shook his head in resignation. 'All right, then. Are you going to find a hotel, or should we book one for you?'

'I've already sorted it,' Alexis said.

'No news about the Norwegian number or the other Spanish one?' Emily asked.

'Unfortunately not. They were both pay-as-you-go numbers. The Norwegian number is still disconnected, and I haven't had a call back from the Spanish one. I left another message this morning. Right then … *Suerte!* Bergström chirped, before ending their videoconference.

Alexis sighed. The hardest part was yet to come: having to tell her mother she was staying in Madrid for a few more days.

The Principal Hotel, Madrid
Friday, 9 December 2016, 8.00 pm

ALEXIS WEDGED THE PHONE between her cheek and shoulder and scanned the room-service menu.

'How was your day, Maman?'

'Yes, yes, all fine,' Mado piped, a bit too cheerily.

'What's that, Maman?'

'Just a second,' her mother mumbled. 'I'm going up to my room.'

Alexis could hear her slippers clumping up the stairs, the hinges creaking open, then the door closing with a click.

'Alexis, my little sweet pea. You know you can tell me anything. You know I'll understand. You know I'll never judge you.'

Alexis closed her eyes and sat down on the bed.

'It's all right if you want to change your mind,' her mother continued.

'Maman! That's not—'

'Will you just listen to me for a second? Who do you think you are? You're not listening. Do you think it's normal … no, wait: what would you say to a friend … no, your sister? What would you say to Inès if, a week before her wedding, right before the family flies in from halfway across the world to get the party started, she were to swan off to a meeting in Whocareswhere-on-Sea, leaving everyone just standing there like lemons, including her husband-to-be?'

'Well, I know what Freud would say: she doesn't really want to get married. But every couple is different, Maman—'

'Oh, don't go generalising on me now, Alexis! Your sister, Xavier and the little ones just got here, and you're nowhere in sight. No, because you're swanning off five minutes before Stellan slips the ring on your finger. Come on, you've got Sigmund written all over your face!'

Mado came up for breath for a moment.

'Listen, nothing's carved in stone. You're entitled to change your mind.'

'But I don't want to change my mind, Maman,' Alexis protested. 'I just have a life beyond my role as a wife-to-be, do you see?'

'All right, relax,' her mother conceded. 'Don't you at least want to talk to Stellan about it again?'

'We've spoken a few times today already, Maman.'

'That's why I said again.'

'I don't see why you're dwelling on this so much. Is there something you're not telling me? Do you think he's not well?'

'He's just a bit worried, Alexis. He's afraid you're going to the outback.'

'To back out, you mean.'

'Back out, yes. It's written all over his face. Can't you just reassure him? It breaks my heart to look at him … Alexis?'

Alexis had lifted the phone away from her ear. She had a call waiting. From a private number. She hesitated for a second and took the call anyway. Then she swore to herself when she realised she hadn't told her mother.

As soon as she heard who was calling, Alexis hurried out of her room and ran down the corridor to Emily's.

At last, they were going to find some answers.

La Virgen de los Desamparados Orphanage, Madrid
Saturday, 22 November 1952

GORDI SQUEEZED LAUNA'S HAND. Tightly.

The medic sat behind his desk and looked at them in turn before coughing into his fist.

'Sister Rosario asked me to give you both a check-up.'

He smiled at them. Gordi could see the sadness in his eyes.

'She told me you'd hurt yourselves playing in the courtyard, is that right?'

Gordi looked at Launa. She lowered her eyes. Gordi tried to imagine that smile melting away the lump of pain that was stuck inside her belly.

'I'm a bit like God,' the medic continued, coughing again. 'I'll listen to everything you tell me, and I'll keep any secrets you confide in me to myself.'

Gordi tugged at Launa's hand. Perhaps God had heard their prayers in the end, and he had sent someone to save them…

'Anything you tell me here, in this room, will stay between us,' he insisted.

Launa lifted her gaze and looked at the medic. He was still smiling. Gordi realised she had never seen a man smile before. He was the first.

'Can you at least tell me where it hurts?'

Neither of them dared say a word. Gordi squeezed Launa's hand tighter still.

The medic cleared his throat and coughed into the back of his hand.

'Maybe you can tell me how you hurt yourselves, then?'

Father Murillo's voice. His warm breath on the back of her neck. In her ear. His clammy hands…

Gordi willed Launa to smile. *Come on,* she thought, *you can make it all better.* But Father Murillo's hands smothered any hint of a smile. Gordi's heart started beating so hard, she had to open her mouth wide to summon up what little air was left deep down in her lungs.

'Or perhaps you can tell me *who* hurt you?'

'Father Murillo,' Gordi suddenly blurted.

Launa turned to her friend with a look of horror.

'It was him. Father Murillo,' Gordi asserted bravely. 'And we're not the only ones he has hurt.'

Chocolatería San Ginés, Madrid
Saturday, 10 December 2016, 10 am

ALEXIS AND EMILY STEPPED OUT of the hotel and strolled a few hundred metres down the Calle de Alcalá. They crossed the vast stone expanse of the Puerta del Sol and kept going until they reached the Chocolatería San Ginés. The esteemed chocolate shop was a hole in the wall tucked away down a rabbit warren of alleys steeped in years of history: its nickname 'l'Escondida' – the hideaway – was well earned.

That morning, Madrid was again basking in the warm, golden light of the sun, which helped take the edge of the brisk chill that had descended on the city.

They could smell the chocolate shop before they saw it. A heady scent of fried dough and sugar, reminiscent of summer funfairs, drifted through the surrounding backstreets. All that was missing was the sound of children's gleeful footsteps and cries of joy.

Emily and Alexis went straight to the back of the café area, passing a group of men crowded around two tables who were in the middle of a heated discussion about the prime minister, Mariano Rajoy. Laughter abounded and hands slapped heartily on the white, marble bistro tables, lending a rhythm to their exchange.

The previous evening, the person whose call had cut short Alexis's conversation with her mother was one Vicente Guardiola, a journalist with *El País*. Apparently he had information for them about Dr Burgos and his clinic, and wanted to meet them the next morning. When Alexis asked how he had got her number, he said they'd cover all that later – in a patronising air that didn't bode well.

One of the men stood up from the group and strolled towards the back of the café, continuing the repartee over his shoulder as he tucked his white shirt into his black pleated trousers and smoothed his artfully trimmed beard, getting ready to serve them, Alexis presumed.

Alexis scanned the menu, suspecting that Emily would turn her nose up at the house speciality – *churros con chocolate* – that she yearned to order for herself. She decided she would just order a coffee instead.

'Alexis Castells? Vicente Guardiola.' The man Alexis had mistaken for a waiter introduced himself.

Perplexed, she stood up and they shook hands. The journalist turned to Emily, who was now also on her feet.

'This is Emily Roy,' Alexis said.

'What's the Yard doing poking its nose into this business, I wonder?' Guardiola said in English, with a smirk and firm shake of the hand that Emily had extended.

'I see we're already comparing penis size, Señor Guardiola,' she quipped, returning his smile.

His mouth gaped open, freezing his face in surprise. '*Touché*, Ms Roy,' he conceded, looking Emily in the eye with a series of resigned nods of his head. He grabbed a chair from the next table and took a seat between them.

'Eh, Vicente?!' a waiter hollered from behind the counter at the other end of the café.

Without turning around, the journalist raised his left hand and extended three fingers.

'So, all roads lead to Sweden, it seems – via the Yard,' he said, pushing the paper-napkin holder into the middle of the table. 'Your commissioner got in touch with our CID officers, because he was fishing for information about Burgos and his clinic. That's how I got your number, Alexis: he gave it to the CID officers because your Spanish is apparently better than your intrepid profiler's.' He winked at Emily. 'And that same commissioner, Lennart Bergström, if you'll forgive any mispronunciation of his name, also left me a couple of messages. Now assuming I've done my homework properly, his calls must have had something to do with the murders of the people who ran the Lindbergh Clinic.'

'One of the three victims was found in possession of your telephone number—'

'Well, you certainly don't beat around the bush, do you, Emily? Yes, I was in touch with Louise Lindbergh. Can you at least tell me a bit more about her death?'

'We don't know anything more than your Scandinavian counterparts, Vicente.'

Flashing a cocky, flamboyant smile, he held Emily's gaze again with the kind of probing look that encroaches on your personal space so much it feels like skin contact.

After a fruitless standoff with a deadpan Emily that lasted a good minute, he laughed and said, 'You're a force to be reckoned with, aren't you?'

At that very moment, a waiter breezed up to their table and slapped three cups of chocolate as thick as cream and a mountain of churros on an oval platter on the cold marble, as well as a bottle of water and three glasses to wash it all down.

'At the end of 2011 I published a series of articles in *El País* about medically assisted reproduction and, more specifically, in vitro fertilisation,' Guardiola began, pouring them each a glass of water. 'I raised a flag about a few things, including the conditions surrounding the selection of sperm donors and the handling of their personal information. That was what I originally set out to do. But as I investigated, I inadvertently struck gold. It turned out that the big boss of La Virgen del Pilar clinic, that *saco de mierda* Carlos Burgos, was not only using his own sperm to impregnate his patients, but unbeknown to them he was also using top-quality eggs and embryos sourced from strangers, all to boost his clinic's success rate.'

Vicente Guardiola dipped a sugar-coated churro into his cup and took a big bite, dripping with chocolate.

'Louise first reached out to me at the end of January 2012, because she had read my articles,' he continued, munching the last of his churro. 'She told me that, officially, La Virgen del Pilar was supplying the Lindbergh Clinic with sperm from donors with Mediterranean, South American and North African profiles. But Louise insinuated that the two clinics were trafficking embryos. She suspected that certain embryos that had been put into storage and forgotten, and others that should have been destroyed, were being used in patients whose own embryos had slim chances of surviving, all against their knowledge. She didn't know who was implicated, but she had her suspicions; which she refused to share with me, unfortunately.'

'What do you mean, "forgotten"?' Alexis asked, swallowing a mouthful of hot chocolate and savouring the rich, sugary goodness that coated her tongue and palate.

Guardiola reached for a minuscule paper napkin and wiped his lips. 'During a cycle of in vitro fertilisation, several eggs are fertilised. One, maybe two, of those that turn into embryos are implanted into the patient's uterus two to six days after they form. The others are then frozen and put into storage in anticipation of a later pregnancy, should the patient want another child. Clinics then bill patients every six months for keeping their embryos in storage. Often, after one or two pregnancies, patients decide they no longer need those embryos and the clinic supposedly destroys them. In fact, more often than not, they completely forget about the embryos and the direct debit keeps coming out of patients' accounts every six months, lost in the sea of other household expenses. Meanwhile, all this raw material is just sitting at the bottom of a freezer in the MAR clinic, waiting to be exploited.'

Alexis rinsed her mouth with a sip of water. That seemed to fit with Paola Cuevas's story about her embryos supposedly being lost in transit. Perhaps the clinic had used them to impregnate other women?

'And as for that filthy *gilipollas*, Burgos, I'm still investigating his death.'

Emily frowned. She opened her mouth to say something, but Guardiola beat her to it.

'That's right, Little Miss Profiler, I saved you the best for last,' he teased, with more than a little suggestive arching of his eyebrows. 'Burgos, the filthy old pervert, didn't die of natural causes.'

Guardiola licked his chocolate-covered fingers.

'I think now's a good time for us to measure our penises, wouldn't you say, Emily?'

La Virgen de los Desamparados Orphanage, Madrid
Wednesday, 3 December 1952

GORDI CLOSED THE DOOR of the infirmary behind her.

It had taken her a while, but she had found a way. It hadn't been easy, because it meant playing along. Getting snared in the trap. In the end though, it was so simple, she was appalled she hadn't thought of it before. She would look at the map of Spain on the wall, choose a town or city, and escape there. She would plan and erect buildings, plant forests, sit in a *churrería* and eat to her heart's content, or go into a shop and buy a hat or some sweets. She would only return to the real world when the pleats of her skirt were lowered back over her thighs. When she heard the barking of his cough, the rustling of creased cloth as he tucked his shirt back into his trousers, the growling of his zipper teeth closing up again. They were the only sounds that filled the suffocating silence, when the grip of the shame and suffering felt even tighter than the fear.

Gordi straightened her blouse and went to join the others in the courtyard. She listened as Reme told her and Dulce how the new girl had been forced to eat tadpoles because she had been caught drinking from a puddle. But she had other things on her mind besides the new girl's misadventures. She was thinking about Launa and Lados, who had gone into the infirmary as she had left.

They had started calling the medic 'Tos', because he coughed all the time. And Tos had the appetite of an ogre, as it turned out. Of course he did: after all, he was an ogre. An ogre who whispered in the ear of God, just like Father Murillo.

Chocolatería San Ginés, Madrid
Saturday, 10 December 2016, 11.00 am

VICENTE GUARDIOLA DUCKED BEHIND the counter and emerged with a laptop and a fresh bottle of water. He paused for a moment beside the group of men who were still chatting away around the tables at the front of the *chocolatería*. A game of dominoes was now in full swing. Tiles crashed down like cymbals against the marble table, provoking cheers of encouragement, groans of defeat, guffaws of laughter and friendly slaps on the back. It was a jovial but ear-splitting cacophony.

'*Hombre!* Good move,' Guardiola boomed to the man who played the last tile.

'*Es que le estoy matando, tío!*' the man replied, puffing out his chest and throwing his arms wide open, as if to prove he really was 'killing it'.

Guardiola dealt the man a few healthy pats on the back as he made his way over to rejoin Emily and Alexis.

'Burgos did not die as peaceful a death as the media have portrayed,' the journalist said, opening his laptop. 'It's remarkable how the whole thing has been kept under wraps. That dirty bastard must have known a thing or two that the powers that be wanted him to take to his grave. Whenever something big like this happens, it's like a red rag to a bull for the swarms of shit-stirrers like me. So you'd have expected all the skeletons in the old man's closet to be dug up and paraded in public, wouldn't you? But nothing at all came to light. If it hadn't been for my CID contact, I'd never have known.

Even now, I haven't published anything about it. And whoever did him in still hasn't been caught. For what it's worth, whoever that was deserves a pat on the back. I've spent the last four years combing through his patient lists – his potential victims, essentially – trying to track down whoever got rid of the old creep. It's a mammoth task. You can't imagine how many women that nut job must have inseminated in all his years of practice.'

'Surely his victims must have banded together and formed support groups, though?' Alexis wondered out loud. 'Did no one agree to help you?'

'Most of them have refused to undergo a DNA test. I suppose they think sweeping this whole thing under the carpet will make them forget about it. Whereas the truth is, they're always going to keep tripping over it.'

Guardiola paused to open a file on his laptop that appeared to be double password-protected.

'Whoever killed Burgos must have done it in blind rage,' he said, turning the screen towards Alexis. 'You'll have to translate it for your girlfriend.'

'Is that the autopsy report?' Emily cut in.

'Yes it is, Ms Roy,' the journalist replied, taking a sip of water.

Alexis quickly scrolled through the document. She turned to Emily suddenly before zeroing in on the screen again.

'Carlos Burgos suffered multiple stab wounds,' she translated robotically. 'His mouth and tongue were slashed to shreds. And his tongue was almost completely cut out.'

Emily inched towards the screen, as if by seeing it close up she would somehow be able to read Spanish.

'Well, I think that answers the question that was on the tip of my tongue earlier,' Guardiola ventured. 'The Lindberghs were killed the same way as that sleazy bastard Burgos, weren't they?'

The Principal Hotel, Madrid
Saturday, 10 December 2016, 10.00 pm

ALEXIS TOSSED TEA BAGS into the first two mugs, added a spoonful of instant coffee into the third, and filled them all with boiling water. She set two of them down on the narrow desk where Emily and Guardiola were hard at work, before taking a careful sip of her tea, cupping her hands around the mug.

Once they had skimmed through Burgos's autopsy report, they had decided to continue their research at the hotel, where it would be quieter. They set up in Emily's room and started translating the investigation reports and witness statements surrounding the death of Dr Carlos Burgos.

Burgos had been knocked out, then stabbed multiple times in the chest. His lips had been slashed to ribbons and his tongue nearly hacked out of his mouth. It was the same modus operandi as they had seen in the killings of Kerstin, Louise and Göran Lindbergh. The wounds had been inflicted with less precision, however, and the killer's movements seemed to have been more haphazard and improvised. It had taken two blows to render Burgos unconscious: one to his left temple and the other to the crown of his head, with an object the killer had found at the scene. It was a small marble sculpture depicting a pregnant woman – poetic justice, as Guardiola put it. Afterwards, the killer had put the bloodied sculpture back on the mantelpiece.

The six knife wounds to the abdomen were not very deep – some were only superficial – and the tongue had not been fully removed.

According to the medical examiner, the killer must have made multiple attempts to remove the tongue, which would explain the lacerations on the lips. The killer had ended up slicing the face open from one corner of the mouth to the hollow of the cheek to reach the tongue.

This new information told them two things: first, that the killing of Dr Burgos was connected to the murder of Aliénor's family; and second, that there were probably more victims, since the perpetrator's technique had become more refined between killing Burgos in 2012 and the Lindberghs in 2016.

They were pursuing three angles of investigation: digging into Burgos's past, combing through his clinic's patient files, and searching for other murder cases with similar hallmarks to the killer's.

When Emily had called Bergström to tell him about their meeting with Vicente Guardiola and the information he'd given them, she had asked the commissioner to get in touch with his contact in the Spanish national police to request access to the investigation reports and hopefully uncover the missing links in this chain of murders. Even though Emily was sure the old doctor was their 'victim zero' and that everything had started with him, they were still taking the precaution of extending their search back to 2007, five years before Burgos was killed.

Guardiola's mobile rang. He picked up the call without taking his eyes off the laptop screen. After a few strings of *sí*, *vale* and *gracias*, he hung up.

'Good news, *chicas*,' he smiled. 'I've been given the green light to access the central police database. But I have to go right now.'

Emily and Alexis both sprang to their feet, pulled on their coats and grabbed their bags.

Guardiola chuckled and shook his head. '*Joder* … Bloody hell, there are only two of you, but I feel like there's an army standing in my way. You're not going to take no for an answer, are you?'

Emily couldn't help but smile.

'You're a dark horse, Little Miss Profiler,' he conceded, a half-smile spreading to the corners of his lips as he buttoned up his jacket. 'Why do I get the feeling I've been relegated to the backseat like a little kid? Not that long ago we were comparing penis sizes, and now I feel like I should be begging you to go easy on my family jewels.'

The journalist hailed a cab, and they drove around the other side of the park to the El Retiro district police station, a three-storey building with red bars over the windows.

A man in a dark suit and a tie that throttled his flabby neck was waiting for them outside, smoking a cigarillo.

'*Dos chicas? Joder, tío, que salud tienes,*' he whispered in Guardiola's ear with a knowing wink, clearly impressed at his friend's ability to attract two such fine specimens of the female sex.

'*Qué tal, Pepe?* Good to see you too,' the journalist replied, giving the man a hearty pat on the back.

Pepe stubbed out his cigarillo underfoot, then offered Emily and Alexis a brief handshake before inviting them all to follow him into the station. They zig-zagged their way through a maze of deserted desks and chairs to an immaculate workstation in the middle of the open-plan office.

Pepe draped his suit jacket over the back of the chair. '*Hasta ahora, guapo* – I'll be back later,' he grinned to his friend, scratching his protruding stomach with nicotine-yellowed nails. He sidled off with a fresh box of cigarillos in hand, leaving them to it.

Guardiola pulled up two other chairs, and the three of them sat down at the computer.

The journalist clicked a mouse button to deactivate the screen-saver. Then on the login screen, he typed 'JoséPerezVicente', followed by a password that appeared only as a series of asterisks. A new page opened with a prompt for two access codes. He typed one from memory, then he looked on the underside of the keyboard and entered a series of six letters and numbers he saw scrawled on a Post-It note.

'So we're starting in 2007, are we?' he asked, as a search window opened on the screen in front of them.

.   Emily nodded.

'Let's get this show on the road, *chicas*,' he said, his fingers already racing across the keyboard.

IT HAD BEEN YEARS since Alexis had pulled an all-nighter. The last time, she must have still been in her twenties.

At 5.30 that morning, Pepe had poked his head in to tell them there was half an hour left before they would have to leave the station. Alexis couldn't believe what time it was when she checked her phone. It was strange how quickly the hours had flown by, and how awake, alert and focused her body and mind had remained, oblivious to the night.

The fatigue had knocked her out in the taxi on the way back to the hotel. Once she was back in her room, she had barely bothered to take off her coat and shoes before lying down, pulling the quilted bedspread over her and falling fast asleep.

Barely twenty minutes earlier, she had been fast asleep, when Emily called to tell her they had a videoconference with Falkenberg at 10.30. She had jumped straight into the shower and had only just joined Emily in her room, when a close-up of Olofsson's face filled the laptop screen.

When the detective stepped back from the screen to sit down, Bergström, Aliénor and Mona appeared in the background, sitting by the whiteboard at the end of the conference room table.

Alexis was surprised to see Aliénor. Surely she had no place being here as they picked her family drama to pieces.

'*Hej hej*,' Olofsson chirped. 'Tell me, how are Cagney and Lacey doing? Jeez, Alexis! What's this I'm seeing, death by sangria?'

Alexis winced. She had thought she looked surprisingly peppy, in spite of the lack of sleep. Apparently the light over the bathroom mirror was more forgiving than Olofsson's critical eye.

'A contact of Vicente's gave us access to the main police database. We've spent all night in the neighbourhood police station, trying to track down cases similar to the murder of Carlos Burgos and the…' Alexis left the words hanging. She didn't have the heart to finish her sentence, with Aliénor looking at her.

'Møller gave Aliénor the green light to be here,' the commissioner explained, obviously noticing Alexis's discomfort. 'We're in the process of combing through all the family's emails – they each had several email accounts – as well as their phone records from 2011, 2012 and 2013, to check whether any of them were in contact with Burgos or his clinic. Aliénor was keen to roll up her sleeves. How many unsolved cases like this did you find in the system?'

'Twenty-six cases where the victims were stabbed and/or had their tongue slashed or cut out,' Emily said. 'We'll be going through all of those this afternoon. Guardiola should be here in the next hour or so to help us.'

'Hmm. I can't help but notice that unlike you, Em, Alexis here is on first-name terms with Guardiola … I wonder if that means you've succumbed to his Mediterranean charms, Alexis?' Olofsson teased.

'Well, I have to admit, Vicente's certainly easy on the eye,' she replied.

'One hell of a red-hot hunk, you mean!' Olofsson said. 'We did our homework about the guy and came across one or two photos … Makes me think of Julio, wouldn't you agree?'

'Julio who?' Aliénor asked.

'What do you mean, Julio who? Julio Iglesias, for eff's sake!'

'Personally, I think he looks more like Joaquín Cortés,' Alexis chimed in.

'Ooh, I couldn't agree more!' Mona suddenly piped up, her cheeks flushing as she immediately regretted her spontaneous outburst.

'Who's Joaquín Cortés?' Aliénor asked.

'A Flamenco dancer. Sensuality incarnate,' Alexis sighed dreamily.

'No news about the Norwegian number?' Emily swiftly changed the subject.

Bergström shook his head and held his face wearily in his hands.

'We'll call you back tomorrow morning,' Emily said, before disconnecting the Skype chat without further ceremony. Not wasting any time, she plugged a USB stick into her laptop and opened the first police report.

Alexis got up and put the kettle on. 'So?' she asked, stretching.

Emily raised her eyebrows questioningly and shook her head.

'Vicente. Is he a more of a Julio Iglesias or a Joaquín Cortés?'

Emily's phone rang. 'Joaquín Cortes,' she replied with an elusive smile before picking up.

The sound of the kettle purring to life covered the few hushed words Emily exchanged.

She ended the call and stared at the screen in her hand for a second before turning to Alexis.

'Pepe called Carlos Burgos's daughter this morning to let her know there had been a development in the investigation into her father's murder. She's agreed to meet with us at her place. We're expected at one this afternoon.'

60 Avenida de Menéndez Pelayo, Madrid
Sunday, 11 December 2016, 1.00 pm

FRANCISCA BURGOS WAS WAITING in the doorway, her face partly in shadow. She stepped aside to usher Emily and Alexis over the threshold, and closed the door behind them. Her warm, welcoming smile faded as soon as the handshakes were over.

'I'm sorry, I hadn't realised how dark it was in here,' she apologised in Spanish, pushing a switch below the intercom by the front door.

A dim glow radiated from the ceiling light and wall sconces, revealing walls chequered with framed black-and-white photographs, remnants of grandeur put on display to showcase the Burgoses' social standing. To show visitors who they knew, and therefore who they were.

'Come this way.' She led them into a drawing room with tall windows framed by heavy olive-green drapes.

'I'm afraid I don't speak English, but your colleague said you speak Spanish?' she ventured, smoothing her cream suit.

'Yes, of course, Señora Burgos,' Alexis smiled.

Francisca Burgos motioned for Emily and Alexis to sit on the sofa as she took a seat in a grand Voltaire armchair upholstered the same faded green as the curtains. She sat on the edge of her seat with her back straight – her pose the hallmark of a proper upbringing.

'Did you both sign the confidentiality agreement?' She glanced first at Emily, then Alexis.

Alexis nodded and pulled out the documents Pepe had emailed to her, which they had printed at the hotel's business centre earlier that morning and signed before setting out.

Francisca Burgos read the papers thoroughly before folding them and placing them on the chair cushion behind her. She allowed herself to sigh, massaging one liver-spotted hand with the other.

'I understand you have some information about my … my father's death.'

Emily had written some questions for Alexis to put to Dr Burgos's daughter – or rather, she'd listed the information she wanted to find out.

Alexis was used to meeting with victims' families as part of her research for her true-crime books. Over the years she had honed her own standard list of questions, and she would adapt it depending on who she was talking to and their emotional state. What Emily was asking was very different from her usual spiel, however.

'It appears that similar murders have been committed abroad—'

'So similar that you think it's the same killer?' Francisca Burgos cut in.

'Yes.'

'Who are the victims?'

'The owner of a medically assisted reproduction clinic, and his family.'

'And his family…' she echoed, pulling at the joints of her bony fingers.

'Did your parents have a dog?' Alexis segued.

'Yes. Athos.'

'Where was he on the night of the murder?'

'At the care home, with my mother. She was admitted there the year before my father was killed. She had Alzheimer's. The care home was wonderful. They had a pet therapy program, which was supposed to help the residents relax and rekindle memories for them. We used to take Athos to see Mamá every day. Then one day, Athos didn't want to leave when it was time to go home.' An impish smile crept across her time-weathered face.

'He just barked and barked at anyone who tried to put him on his lead, and he wouldn't let anyone other than Mamá touch him. So we left him there for the night. But…' She paused and looked inquisitively at Alexis. 'There was no mention of Athos in the investigation. So why … I mean, how did you…?'

'Your father was embroiled in a scandal that effectively stopped him from setting foot outside his own front door.'

Francisca's expression stiffened. She straightened her posture even further and tightened her grip on the upholstered armrests of the chair.

'The journalists had set up camp on his doorstep, and he went for weeks without seeing the light of day. He would never have opened his door to a stranger in the middle of the night,' Alexis continued.

'No, he certainly wouldn't have. Are you trying to say he might have opened up to someone he knew?'

'Do you have a suspect in mind, Señora Burgos?'

'No. But your reasoning sounds a lot like an accusation to me.'

'Not at all. According to your statement, you were at home all night with your husband, weren't you?'

Francisca Burgos gave a curt nod.

'Other than you and his housekeeper, I don't think your father would have opened the door to anyone at one in the morning, and you and she both had keys to his home at that time, did you not?'

She nodded again.

'So, if you had come to visit him in the middle of the night, you would surely have found him upstairs in the living quarters, not downstairs by the door.'

Alexis paused to let that sink in.

'Which brings me back to why he went out that night, around midnight.'

Francisca Burgos blinked, and a wrinkle appeared across her chin.

'I'm not judging, Señora Burgos. My colleague analysed the crime scene based on the police report and photographs to establish what we call a profile of the victim: your father. That profile helps us to understand the sequence of events and the circumstances of the crime, and therefore the criminal.'

Francisca Burgos visibly relaxed. Her face softened, and her hands let go of the armrests and seemed to find some peace on her thighs, palms wide open.

Alexis silently breathed a sigh of relief. Labelling Dr Burgos a victim had eased the tension in the air and given her some room to manoeuvre.

'So, to wrap up my colleague's reasoning, if your father was in the habit of going out at such an odd hour, Emily figured it must be a logical time for him to take his dog for a walk. And he was so used to going out at that time, he had to do so, even if his faithful friend wasn't there—'

'Fourteen years,' Francisca Burgos interjected philosophically. 'For fourteen years, Papá took Athos for a walk every single night…' She rummaged in her jacket pocket and pulled out a cigarette case and a lighter. Then she opened the case with one hand, plucked out a cigarette with the other, and snapped the case shut.

'Perhaps that's why Mamá developed Alzheimer's … So she wouldn't see my father's – her husband's – fall from grace. And that dirty, ugly death.'

She lit the cigarette, her mouth hollowing around the filter as she inhaled a long, greedy drag.

'It was the housekeeper who found his body, wasn't it?' asked Alexis.

'Yes….'

'She phoned you before she called for help, and you got there about ten minutes before the police; is that correct?'

'Are you going to ask me to walk you through the scene step by step? To see if I remember the slightest little spot of blood on my father's suit, is that it?' Francisca waved a dismissive hand through the cloud of smoke in front of her face. 'Or if I can recall how his mouth was sliced open from cheek to cheek? Or how his tongue was cut to shreds and hanging out of his mouth like a dog's?'

'No, Señora Burgos. I'd just like to know whether you touched your father's body before the police arrived.'

Francisca picked up a bowl from the coffee table and emptied it of pot pourri, then she stubbed out her cigarette in it.

'I … I made him look decent.'

She drew a circle in the ash at the bottom of the bowl, then left her cigarette end right in the middle.

'His trousers and underpants were pulled down around his knees.'

The look on Nino's face is the hardest thing for me to deal with.

Because it usually mirrors my anguish. But tonight it is blank and expressionless. I'm not shaken up, and I'm not scared. Even though I should be.

Burgos is dead.

He invited me in for a nightcap after our walk. Just an old man and an old woman having a drink, he said. Imagine that.

I felt no panic when I saw his body lying on the floor in the middle of the hallway. No satisfaction, either. The only thing that crossed my mind was that he wouldn't be going on and on about his dog anymore. Or his wife. Or his daughter. And with a bit of luck, he wouldn't be panting in my ear anymore either. That would be a lot harder to do without a tongue, anyway.

I walk into the kitchen to pour myself a beer. I can feel Nino's eyes burning a hole in my back.

There are some things we can't share, my sweet Nino.

I can't tell you, for example, that I felt a burning desire to take a knife to the part of him that had hurt me the most. But when I pulled his pants down, I couldn't bring myself to touch him. Maybe it's because his penis wasn't the way I remembered it. It was miserable and flaccid. His pubic hair was all white now, but the scar lurking beneath was still the same.

I take a sip of my frothy bubbles.

I can't shake the image of that shrivelled little thing from my mind. I shudder to think how many lives, how many women that wrinkled lump of flesh destroyed.

Isn't it funny, when you stop to think about it, how quickly you can go from wanting to sate your desire at someone else's expense to pleading for your own life?

EMILY TOYED WITH the little black box in the inside pocket of her jacket as she hastened her pace. She lifted her knees higher and lengthened her stride, pushing the pain higher, her lungs burning from the cold air and her muscles consumed by the effort.

An hour earlier, she had received a message from Aliénor with the family photos she had asked her for. Aliénor had mentioned that the funeral was going to be on 22 December. Twenty days after they died; three days before Christmas.

The Swedish took time to bury their dead. Just long enough to relive the loss and suffering, and dwell on the grief and sorrow. Just long enough to summon up the tears of absence and emptiness one more time. The waiting was like losing the person all over again, just as you were starting to come to terms with the fact that they were gone and learning to embrace the memory of them.

Emily saw the hotel as she rounded the corner and slowed to a walk for the last few metres, taking the time to calm her breath and collect her thoughts.

As soon as she was back in her room, she extricated the little black box from her pocket, opened it and turned her thoughts to Aliénor's family. She lingered on Louise for a moment. Then she thought about Carlos Burgos.

Emily undressed, dripping pearls of sweat onto the black parquet floor, and stepped into the shower.

After their conversation with Francisca Burgos, Guardiola had joined them at the hotel to go through the twenty-six case files they had pulled from the police records the night before. They had soon narrowed the list down to six cases of interest and reached out to the families of the victims. Three of them had already returned their calls.

Emily directed the stream of icy water onto her calves, then moved it up to her thighs.

Based on her initial observations from the Lindbergh crime scene, Kerstin was the key victim. But where did Carlos Burgos fit into the puzzle? His murder made sense as a mirror image of Göran Lindbergh's: two heads of MAR clinics, both killed in a similar fashion. And if Burgos's family had been there that night? Would the killer have eliminated them too, like the Lindberghs? Although how would this theory explain the fact that the killer had inflicted the least damage on Göran's body? Had the killer somehow thought that Kerstin was the brains behind the clinic? Maybe the murders were all about her, not Göran. But could Göran have been inseminating patients with his own sperm, like Burgos? They couldn't ignore the role of Louise either; she had to be the one who had uncovered the connection between the two clinics. Perhaps she had been killed because she had chosen to protect her family rather than blowing the whistle on the clinic's shady practices. Could she have been killed because she had, however unwittingly, stumbled across the identity of Burgos's killer? In that case, could she have been the main target, as the extent of the wounds inflicted by the killer would seem to suggest?

Emily stepped out of the shower and climbed back into bed, her body still damp.

Guardiola slid a warm hand between her thighs. She was ready. More than ready. He twisted her damp hair away from her shoulders, onto the pillow, exposing more skin. He licked a few droplets of water from the nape of her neck. And paused to smile. Emily had moaned more making love than she had spoken the whole time they had worked together, he mused. She urged him back to her with her eyes. Then she turned her gaze away to the bedside table, where her mobile was ringing. It wasn't even six yet. She wriggled free from Vicente's embrace to grab the handset. He released her from his arms, flaunting his desire, waiting for her to come back for more.

It was Bergström calling. Emily sat up cross-legged on the bed. She pressed the green button and listened to what the commissioner had to say, his calm voice belying the urgency of his call, then she hung up. She got dressed without the slightest glance at Guardiola, and left the room.

La Virgen de los Desamparados Orphanage, Madrid
Wednesday, 4 March 1953

SPRING WASN'T FAR AWAY now. There wasn't such a chill in the air anymore and the scent of flowers had started to drift in on the breeze. They no longer needed to do their morning exercises to warm up for chanting 'Cara al Sol'. Father Murillo had instigated those exercises over the winter, after several of the girls had succumbed to the cold and collapsed. He had got a bit carried away, however, and was making them run and jump on the spot to the point of exhaustion. They were too out of breath to sing Franco's praises though, so they all ended up wheezing and spluttering their way through his song.

Gordi had overheard a hushed conversation between a group of older girls before they went off to work in the factory. They were talking about the execution of their parents, saying that the Church existed to serve the Devil. She and Launa had another theory, though: the Church *was* the Devil. But the man on the cross didn't know it. He didn't know that the men who claimed to be His servants had changed sides. That they killed and raped with passion and conviction. With their faith, even.

As they neared the end of the courtyard, well away from Father Murillo and Sister Fernanda, Gordi slowed to a walk to nurse the stitch in her side. Launa and Lados were still running just in front of her; Reme and Dulce were a bit further ahead.

It struck Gordi how she was always the one who ended up on her own. She was the third wheel who always rolled along between the two sisters, and Reme and Dulce. But whenever she had to spend time with Tos or with Father Murillo, she preferred to be alone and was glad she didn't have to see the mirror image of her suffering the way Launa and Lados did. Gordi wondered whether she would find herself begging for death to take her away, like Lados had done once: she had snuck into the infirmary and spent all night huddled up to a girl who was dying, hoping the Grim Reaper would come for her too.

All of a sudden, Lados collapsed, her legs flopping like ribbons beneath her. Gordi rushed to her friend's side. Launa was already wrenching her little sister's arms away from her belly, trying to find the source of the pain.

'That's enough. On your feet, right now!' Father Murillo thundered up to them, his leather-belt whip trailing over the shoulder of his cassock.

He grabbed Lados by the arm and hauled her to her feet. She groaned and immediately bent double from the pain, before crumpling to the ground once more.

'That's enough, I said. Stand up!'

Lados huddled tight in the foetal position, scraping her hip and shoulder against the gravel. With a crack of leather, Father Murillo whipped her loins. Her body arched, recoiling from the impact, then immediately curled up in a ball again – the way Launa's had that night in the showers, Gordi thought.

Sister Fernanda rallied all the girls, and they instinctively huddled around in a circle. She pulled Launa away from her sister and made her stand in the front row. To make sure she had a close-up view.

Father Murillo raised his arm again and whipped the belts down on Lados's back. The crack of leather on skin was so loud, it smothered her cry.

Without warning, Launa ran up to the priest. She grabbed the belts from his hand and yanked them towards her with astonishing strength, pulling Father Murillo off balance. He landed on his knees and moaned in pain as the gravel dug into his flesh, then he swore. A glint of triumph flashed in Launa's eyes – a precarious, fleeting glimmer of freedom for them all to relish.

But Sister Fernanda was only two strides away. She snatched the belt-whip from Launa's grip and dealt her a vicious lash to the back of the neck as Father Murillo struggled back to his feet. Then she whipped her again between her shoulder blades. Launa was thrown to the ground, but she got right back up again. She turned around and opened her arms wide to form a cross, howling like a wild animal with her mouth wide open as she thrust her chest forwards to take the blows she knew were coming.

Relentlessly the nun whipped Launa's breasts, belly and thighs, every blow harder than the last. In a blind rage, she kept raising her arm and cracking it down again, until Launa finally crumpled to the ground beside her sister.

Launa was struggling to keep her eyes open, gritting her teeth to resist every crack of the whip. With every blow, she choked back the pain, echoing Lados's tears. The sound of the leather whistling through the air and cracking against Launa's skin rang out like a chorus.

Gordi noticed that Dulce was standing just in front of her, squeezing Reme's hand. A stream of urine flowed down her leg, splashing her shoe.

Then all of a sudden, Launa fell silent. But the chorus continued. Out of tune. All that remained to be heard was the sharp crack of the whip and the sound of Launa's inanimate body crunching against the gravel in time to every blow.

The Principal Hotel, Madrid
Monday, 12 December 2016, 7.00 am

EMILY AND ALEXIS WERE SITTING side by side at the narrow desk in Alexis's room, eyes glued to the laptop screen in front of them.

The camera in the interview room at Falkenberg Police Station was trained on an empty seat. They heard a door creak open, then the sound of a chair scraping over the floor. A woman in an overcoat and woollen hat walked into the room and sat down. It took them a moment to recognise her.

'This is Kommissionär Lennart Bergström speaking,' the commissioner said, for the benefit of the recording. 'Today is Monday, the twelfth of December 2016, and it is now two minutes past seven in the morning. Interview with Signe Skår conducted in English, with Ms Skår's permission.'

The acting managing director of the Lindbergh Clinic had none of her previous authority and panache. Her puffy eyes flitted from one wall to the other before honing in on her interviewer.

'Ms Skår, do you recognise the Norwegian mobile number 00 47 452 34 777?'

'Yes. That's my number,' she said, taking off her hat and smoothing down her short hair with her fingers.

'Why do you have a Norwegian number?'

'I bought a pay-as-you-go mobile when I was visiting family in Ålesund … in 2012.' After delivering her answer, she fell quiet.

Bergström held the silence for a few moments before he went on.

'According to your colleague Léopold Lindbergh's phone records, he called you on average around six times a day that year.'

Signe lowered her gaze and nodded.

'Léopold Lindbergh told us that was when you started to see each other.'

She pursed her lips, then the corners of her mouth fell. 'That's right,' she mumbled to the commissioner with a look of hesitation.

'Are you still … together?'

'Yes.'

She exhaled a long, shuddering sigh. 'But we didn't want Léopold's family to find out. Göran and Kerstin wouldn't have … I don't think they would have approved.'

'What about your husband?'

'We've been separated for more than a year. He doesn't know, either.'

'And Louise? Did she know?'

Signe Skår scrunched her eyes closed, as if she were wincing in pain. She shook her head. 'I don't think anyone knew about us.'

'But you used the same phone to contact Louise too, Signe.'

She stiffened, staring wide-eyed at Bergström with her mouth agape.

'The number you called Louise at was also for a pay-as-you-go phone.'

Signe closed her eyes. She kept them tightly shut for a good minute while she pursed and twisted her lips, as if she were lost for words. When she opened them again, she buried her gaze in the table.

'In January 2012, Louise came to see me in my office. She was preparing some marketing materials for the spring conferences and trade shows, and had been crunching the numbers for 2011. She couldn't understand how there could have been such a dramatic improvement in the quality of some of our patients' eggs and embryos. She sent about half a dozen files over to me, and we arranged to discuss them the next day.'

Signe paused and drew an imaginary line on the table with her eyes.

'My role as clinical director involves meeting with patients the first time they come into the clinic,' she continued. 'Then I establish a protocol tailored to their specific case; in other words, whatever tests are needed to determine the proper treatment. After that, if need be, I oversee the clinical decisions, but I don't monitor individual patients.'

She moistened her lips.

'That night, as promised, I went through the files Louise had sent me, and I saw what she meant. Nothing in the clinical protocol could have explained such an upswing. There was no doubt about that, and no margin for error whatsoever.'

She inhaled deeply and held her breath for a few seconds before releasing the air.

'To put it simply, we keep meticulous notes and label everything painstakingly, and there is no possible way that we could have fertilised the wrong egg or implanted the wrong embryo by mistake. And these results would suggest that several people had made the same mistake more than once. That was just not possible. Clearly, the trust of these patients had been deliberately breached. Basically, they were not carrying, or had not given birth to, their own child, but to someone's else's.'

'Did you confide in Léopold about this?'

'No, no … I didn't know whether he was somehow involved. I couldn't take the risk…'

Signe clasped her hands together and stared at the empty wall.

'And so, you met with Louise the next day,' Bergström prompted.

She nodded. 'I told her the truth: that I suspected the clinic must be involved in trafficking eggs and embryos. So we decided to examine those files more closely to see where the eggs and embryos could have come from. That was when we decided it would be safer to use unregistered mobiles to communicate with each other.'

She clicked her tongue against the roof of her mouth, as if she might be thirsty.

'It turned out to be a long, painstaking process. We didn't want to arouse any suspicion ourselves, so we had to be extremely careful at the clinic about consulting patient files and anything to do with egg and embryo traceability.'

She glanced up at the commissioner briefly before returning her gaze to the table.

'We ended up discovering that our clinic was working in partnership, so to speak, with the clinic in Madrid: La Virgen del Pilar.'

Signe Skår paused for a moment and swallowed before she carried on.

'Here's an example to give you an idea of how the arrangement worked. This patient – let's call her Patient X – is on her fourth cycle of IVF, and it fails. She decides to take a break for three cycles, so about three months; then she comes back to see us again. It's rare for patients to change clinics, because they don't want to have to go through all the preliminary tests again, not to mention pay for it all. At that point, the Lindbergh Clinic contacts La Virgen del Pilar to place an order. Patient X is blonde with blue eyes, and her husband or sperm donor also has fair hair and blue eyes. They share the same blood group too, A+. So Patient X needs an embryo from two parents with the same genetic profile. The clinic in Madrid then searches in its bank of unused embryos – embryos that patients have either kept for several years after having children or that were supposed to be destroyed but weren't – for two top-quality specimens to implant in Patient X's uterus to ensure her the best possible chances of a successful pregnancy. And obviously, that arrangement worked in the opposite direction too.'

She rubbed her eyes with her fingertips.

'So Louise and I went to see Göran. At their home, in Falkenberg. And we confronted him with what we had found.'

Signe sighed.

'He admitted it straight away – what they were doing at the clinic. He told us that yes, he had instigated this "exchange", as he put it. He insisted that it wasn't trafficking, as we had so vulgarly labelled it, and that it had nothing to do with the success rates of his clinic, or its reputation, and even less to do with the financial repercussions of its popularity. He maintained that it was all about the sense of completeness that came from motherhood and parenthood.'

She closed her eyes and shook her head frantically.

'Louise was furious. She flew completely off the handle. She was yelling and screaming, and she grabbed her father … She had her hands around his neck like this…'

Signe tensed her fingers into a claw shape.

'Göran didn't try to fight her off. He waited until she calmed down. Then he said he understood that she was angry. He told her he was sorry that she didn't understand his reasoning and couldn't see things the way he did. Louise did calm down in the end. And the three of us sat there in silence. You know the kind of silence that sets in after something catastrophic has happened?'

Alexis knew what that silence was like. It was desolate, and only shock and grief drifted like tumbleweeds across the landscape as you contemplated what you had lost.

Signe ran her tongue over her lips again. She was so desperate for water now, the contours of her mouth looked chapped. But Bergström clearly didn't want to interrupt her.

'Louise resigned right after. And she went to work for SKF, in Denmark. She cut off all contact with her parents. Well, she still came to family gatherings from time to time and played her role as a sister and daughter, but only for Aliénor's sake.'

'Did Kerstin know what was going on?'

'Of course she knew what was going on. Those two were like conjoined twins. Göran could have never embarked on a project of that scale without talking to Kerstin, or without her suspecting it.'

'What about you; how did you react?'

'Me?' She exhaled with a long sigh that almost turned into a laugh of despair. 'I … I could only think about Léopold. About his name being dragged through the mud. About the clinic he had given his heart and soul to, and all the happy families we were going to have to shatter by telling the parents the child they had cherished for months or years was not their own. I decided to keep my mouth shut in the end, but I did ask Göran to stop the trafficking. It was one thing to find out about something like that after the fact, but another thing entirely to turn a blind eye and condone it while it was still going on. Then La Virgen del Pilar was shut down, and that resolved a lot of things.'

'There was a scandal that led to that clinic being closed—'

'Yes, I know,' she interrupted. 'Dr Burgos was fertilising patients' eggs with his own sperm. I know what you're going to ask me, and I don't have the answer. The truth is, I don't know whether Göran was doing the same thing. He told me he wasn't, but I only have his word for it.'

'How many families were affected, Signe, by this trafficking at the Lindbergh Clinic?'

Signe Skår swallowed and picked at the white film that had now formed at the corners of her lips.

'A hundred and eighty-seven. One hundred and eighty-seven families since 2001.'

Coca, Spain
Monday, 12 December 2016, 12.00 pm

'SO, THIS SIGNE SCAR … Scor … *Joder*, I can't believe these Scandinavian names!' Guardiola muttered from the backseat of the hire car.

'Well, if that isn't the pot calling the kettle black!' Alexis teased. 'Is it really any better to give people names that translate to Pillar, Remedy and Loneliness?'

'At least our names don't get caught in your throat! So, you're telling me this Sig-ne didn't say anything? She didn't alert the authorities? And she just kept on working for that man, alongside him? *Joder* … The police must be tearing the place apart now, eh? I suppose your commissioner and his team must have their hands full with that?'

'No. It's all in the Gothenburg police's hands. That's where the Lindbergh Clinic is.'

Emily turned into a gravel driveway, crunching the car tyres and raising a cloud of dust in their wake. She parked in front of a quaint whitewashed house with windows framed in red brick.

Pedro Santos had lost his wife two years earlier. Beatriz Nuñez – who went by her maiden name, as per the Spanish tradition – had been found at home, stabbed to death with her tongue cut out. Hers was one of the six cold cases they had identified in the main police database. Beatriz Nuñez, Carlos Burgos and the Lindberghs could feasibly have been killed by the same person.

An elderly gentleman opened the door to them. With his earnest face and carefully combed-back white hair, there was a haughty, dignified air about him.

'*Sí?*'

'*Buenos días. Señor Santos?*' Alexis asked.

'*Buenos días.*'

'I'm Alexis Castells, and these are my colleagues Emily Roy and Vicente Guardiola,' she continued in Spanish. 'Thank you for agreeing to see us. I'm sorry, we're a bit early.'

The elderly gent frowned.

'We spoke on the telephone yesterday, about your late wife,' Alexis prompted, flashing her best smile. 'You suggested we come by today. At half past twelve. To talk about Beatriz.'

'I know what my wife's called!'

His face hardened. He retreated a step and turned his back on them. 'Vallez!' he called, into the house.

'*Sí, Pedro,*' came a female voice in response, muffled by the sounds of doors opening and closing.

'Come, come! And bring the book, will you?'

'*Sí, Pedro, sí!*'

A determined click-clacking of hurried steps across the tiled floor drew nearer, announcing the arrival of a petite woman dressed all in black. Her apron was covered in flour.

'Vallez?' Alexis hesitantly asked.

'*Sí, bueno…* Pedro here always calls me by my last name.'

'We spoke to Señor Santos on the telephone yesterday. We're working for the police in Sweden in collaboration with the Spanish police—'

'Yes, yes, I remember. I saw that in the book.'

She opened the little notebook she was carrying and flipped through a few pages.

'See, Pedro, there it is,' she pointed. '"Meet with Castells twelve-thirty Monday the twelfth." That's what you wrote.'

The elderly gent looked at them with a mix of surprise and confusion.

'*Sí,* there it is, look.'

He peered at the notebook. 'Oh, yes, so it is. I'm sorry ... if you'll excuse me, I'm going to watch TV now.'

'Come in, come in,' Señora Vallez beckoned to them.

'Would you like a little *cafecito*, Pedro?'

'*Sí, Vallez, gracias.* Coffee sounds good.'

'All right, I'll bring you one. Go up and rest, and I'll bring it to you.'

He strode off swiftly down the hall and went upstairs.

Vallez ushered them into a small room with a three-seater sofa nestled behind a round table. It was covered with a tablecloth that draped down and kissed the floor.

'Please sit there,' she insisted, motioning to the sofa. 'I prefer the armchair anyway. Would you all like a coffee? I've just made empanadas. I'll bring some through.'

She turned and disappeared without waiting for their reply.

Vicente and Alexis sat down on the sofa and promptly pulled the tablecloth over their legs. Emily sat beside Alexis, with a curious sideways glance at her legs.

'It's called a *mesa camilla*, Emily,' Guardiola explained, clearly amused. 'There's a heater under the table. The tablecloth acts like a blanket to keep your bum nice and warm so you don't turn into a stalagmite while you're eating.'

With unusual obedience, Emily followed suit and lifted the tablecloth over her knees too.

Señora Vallez came back into the room, carrying a tray with a pot of coffee and four cups and a plate laden with golden-brown pastries. *Mmm*, thought Alexis, as the aroma stimulated her appetite.

'She doesn't speak Spanish, does she?' said Señora Vallez, nodding her chin towards Emily.

'No, but I do understand more than enough,' Emily replied in a shaky Hispanic tone.

'Oh, well, the way you were looking at me so ... intensely, I wasn't sure you could understand what I was saying.'

Emily smiled.

'So you've driven up from Madrid, have you? How long did that take?' Señora Vallez continued as she poured the coffee.

'About an hour and a half,' Guardiola replied, helping himself to an empanada.

Vallez picked up one of the coffees, added milk and two sugars, and gave it a stir.

'*Dios, Señora Vallez, divinas!*' Guardiola exclaimed, with his mouth full. 'These are exquisite.'

'*A que sí?* They are, aren't they?' she smiled proudly, settling into her wingback armchair. 'So, what's happening? Have you caught whoever did that to Beatriz?'

'Excuse me, Señora Vallez, but are you related to Pedro or Beatriz?' Alexis said, trying to steer the interview back on track.

She burst out laughing and slapped her hands on her thighs. 'You're going to think I'm the one who's out of my mind!'

'Not with empanadas like that,' Guardiola winked.

'Oh, isn't he a charmer! Watch out, you two,' she tutted, with a cautionary wave of her index finger, before reaching for an empanada of her own and taking a hearty bite.

It's a bit late for that, Alexis thought. Emily had already succumbed to Guardiola's charms. Of course, she hadn't said anything to Alexis, but she hadn't tried to hide it either. Guardiola had emerged from Emily's room earlier, freshly showered. Maybe she and Jack – Detective Chief Superintendent Jack Pearce, her colleague and superior at Scotland Yard – weren't together anymore ... Although he was coming with her to the wedding...

'I've been looking after Pedro, Beatriz's husband, since she died,' Señora Vallez explained, once she had finished her mouthful of empanada. 'Alzheimer's, that's what the doctors are saying he's got.' She shrugged and frowned dubiously. 'Good heavens, it broke his heart to lose Beatriz, and the head can't work properly without the heart, can it? Oh, and did he ever love his Beatriz! *Bababa!* Like a man, of course ... by which, I mean he loved himself more, but he really did love her to bits.'

She took a sip of coffee before continuing.

'Beatriz was my sister. Well, my soul sister, I suppose. We grew up together.'

Creases spread across Señora Vallez's face. She pulled the table-cloth over her legs and swept the crumbs to the middle of the table.

'It was Pedro who found her. Upstairs, right outside their bedroom door. Hanging on to the banister with one hand. As if she didn't want to go. After that, losing his mind was the last thing Pedro needed … You know what state she was in, don't you? Of course you do, of course … Can you imagine what kind of person could ever inflict that on someone? Evil incarnate, I tell you. Whoever killed Beatriz really spent a long time making a mess of her.'

She shook her head and swept more crumbs away with the back of her hand.

'Our sweet Beatriz … whatever did she do to deserve so much hate? She would have been one of those little old ladies who never bothered a soul. You know, the kind who'll just sit in an armchair and be content to look at her grandchildren and great-grandchildren living their lives all around her.'

Emily glanced at Alexis.

Alexis gulped. 'Señora Vallez, I'm afraid I have something unpleasant to ask you.'

'*Sí guapa*, I thought you might. Otherwise you wouldn't be here, would you, my pretty?'

'Would you happen to know, when Pedro found his wife, whether he … put her clothes back on?'

'*Dios mío* … Good heavens, she wasn't … no, she wasn't … was she?'

'No, no, she wasn't … sexually assaulted, no,' Alexis was quick to clarify. 'But her buttocks and private parts were burned.'

Señora Vallez started to shake from head to toe. She clasped her hands on the table, digging her nails into her flesh in an attempt to pull herself together.

'With a candle … They burned her with a candle, didn't they?' she stuttered.

La Virgen de los Desamparados Orphanage, Madrid
Monday, 30 March 1953

AFTER LAUNA'S DEATH, they never saw Father Murillo or Sister Fernanda again. Another nun was brought in to fill her shoes: Sister Nieves. She was nowhere near as young or cruel as her predecessor.

They never saw Lados again, either. Well, she was still physically there, but in every other way she wasn't. She had not said a single word since her sister's body had been carried away.

Lados had stayed in the infirmary for three weeks, then they had sent her back to the dormitory because they needed the bed for a girl who was ill. They would be keeping Lados there, in the dormitory with the other girls, until there was a place for her in the psychiatric hospital, at least that was what Sister Nieves had told them.

Dulce had asked the older girls what they knew about that kind of hospital. They told her it was the kind of hospital Lados would never leave. Or rather, if she ever did, it would be feet first. In those places, the older girls said, the doctors gave the patients injections to make them woozy. Horse tranquillisers.

'I don't think she needs to be tranquillised,' Dulce said, holding Lados's hand. 'She's enough of a vegetable already.'

'Don't talk about her like that!' Gordi intervened.

'As if she can hear us. You can see she's not there, otherwise she'd say something. To us, at least. Not to the others. But she'd say something to us.'

Dulce planted a kiss in the palm of Lados's hand.

'The other girl, the tall one, I can't remember her number, she told me they might put electricity in her head too.'

'Electricity?'

'Yes. She said they'd put a straitjacket on her – a kind of coat that ties your arms in knots and stops you from moving – and strap her down on a bed and plug things into her head, then turn the electricity on.'

'What for?' Reme asked.

'Probably to get a reaction from her. But apparently it can have the opposite effect and end up completely frying the brain.'

'Well, if they plug electricity into her, it's going to burn her hair and her head anyway, isn't it?'

'That's for sure.'

Gordi combed her fingers through Lados's hair and arranged it neatly on either side of her shoulders. Then she leaned closer and whispered in her ear.

'Come on, Lados, it's time for you to wake up. You have to come to your senses. Your sister didn't die for nothing, did she?'

Coca, Spain, home of Pedro Santos
Monday, 12 December 2016, 1.30 pm

SEÑORA VALLEZ WAS STARING at the wall above her visitors' heads.

'The piss-pants attic,' she suddenly blurted. 'That's where they used to punish Beatriz. The nuns used to snatch her away from us and frogmarch her up to the pissy-pants attic. And lock her up for hours at a time.'

She looked down at the tablecloth and absentmindedly swept away a few more imaginary crumbs.

'Beatriz would often wet the bed. When she dreamed about her mother. It was always the same nightmare. The same sounds, the same shadows. Her mother pleading for her life. The two men laughing. The harsh insults. The muffled screams. Followed by two gunshots. And a terrible, terrible thump. The sound of her mother's body crumpling to the ground. Early in the morning, that witch of a woman, Sister Fernanda, used to come sniffing around our beds with her whip. She had made it herself by braiding strips of leather together, the way Father Murillo taught her to. Every time she came to inspect Beatriz's bed, she tightened her grip on the whip, like a soldier cocking his gun, because as soon as she set eyes on Beatriz's soiled sheets, she would lay into her like there was no tomorrow. She used to whip her thighs so hard and revel in the sick pleasure of it ... like someone deprived of the pleasures of the flesh. Then she would make us all hurl insults at Beatriz. We'd have to chant things like "pissy pants" and "filthy wench" time after time, until our cries were as hurtful as the blows those monsters inflicted on her. Then that twisted witch would march her off with the other pissy-pants girls. First to a storeroom, by the attic, where she would burn their privates with stinging nettles, before having a go at their buttocks … with a candle. Then she would lock them up in the attic. Without any water or light, and no toilet, of course.'

A heavy silence set in. A necessary pause for breath.

'Was it a boarding school?' Guardiola asked.

'An orphanage. La Virgen de los Desamparados, in Madrid. There were five of us. Five friends. We were inseparable. Like the fingers on your hand.'

The corners of her lips curled upwards with the hint of a smile.

'Five. Dulce, Gordi, Launa and Lados – two sisters who were born ten months apart but were as close as twins, and both as pretty as a penny. And then there was me, Reme.'

'And Beatriz?'

'We called her Dulce.'

'Do you know what became of these women?'

'Gordi, I have no idea, but Launa was beaten to death, and Lados ended up in the psychiatric hospital.' Reme Vallez closed her eyes. 'Oh, the suffering … there was so much suffering…'

'Señora Vallez, do the names Kerstin, Göran or Louise Lindbergh mean anything to you?' Emily asked in her shaky Spanish. 'Or perhaps Kerstin Persson – Kerstin's maiden name?'

Reme shook her head. 'What kind of names are those?'

'They're Swedish.'

'Swedish? No, we didn't know anyone Swedish.'

Emily came over and crouched down beside Reme's chair. She placed her phone on the table and scrolled through three photos of the Lindberghs.

'Never seen them before,' she said.

'Does the name Carlos Burgos mean anything to you?' the profiler continued.

'No…'

Emily showed her the photo of Dr Burgos.

'No, no, I don't know him.'

The profiler tapped away at the phone again. Reme Vallez peered at the screen.

'What about this man, do you recognise him?'

Reme grabbed hold of the armrests of her chair and swallowed painfully. 'Him, yes … I know who he is.'

Friday, 1 June 2012

Something has changed … between Nino and me.

Our synergy.

He doesn't have to choose, think or plan for the two of us anymore.

He smiles in the morning when I squeeze his orange juice and make his toast. He sits at the breakfast table and looks at me, eyes sparkling with pride, like a parent watching his child take her first steps.

With everything I do now, he lauds my newfound freedom. Not his, no, but mine. That's the way my Nino loves me. More than he loves himself.

But even though he's found a certain sense of serenity again, he's still on his guard; I can feel it. I can see the worry and the fear written all over his smile. All those years he struggled to get me out of bed in the morning, as if he were raising me from the grave – you can't just erase those overnight.

Burgos's death broke the vicious circle. Tragic as it was, it had to be done. It was like the gangrene metaphor. You have to cut off the infected limb to save your life. He was the monster within me. The parasite eating me from the inside out. The man who was supposed to be a guardian angel. Who soon fell from grace.

I was thinking about that this morning when I was making coffee. I have to tell the others. The others he possessed. The others he destroyed, like he did me.

Oh yes, at last they'll be able to rejoice, to enjoy a new lease of life.

A new lease of life.

Or just life, full stop.

REME VALLEZ POINTED at the screen of Emily's phone.

'It's Tos … it's him,' she murmured tentatively.

Alexis and Guardiola gathered around Reme's chair and stared at the black-and-white photo of the twenty-something man posing for the camera next to a racing car.

'Who was Tos, Señora Vallez?' Alexis asked, without looking up from the photograph.

The medic at La Virgen de los Desamparados … at our orphanage.

'Where did you get that photo?' Guardiola asked, turning to face Emily.

'From Francisca Burgos's house.'

'It's one of the framed photos in the hallway,' Alexis said as she peered at the screen.

'Is that … Carlos Burgos?' Guardiola asked.

'It's him,' Emily replied, zooming the photo out to its original size. *Carlos, Monaco, 1953*, read the shiny plaque at the bottom of the frame.

'*Joder*, what the hell is going on here?' Guardiola shook his head, glancing at Emily and Alexis in turn.

Emily took her phone back. She fiddled with the screen for a second, then placed the phone back on the table. This time, the photo on the screen showed a young girl who must have been eight or nine, maybe ten years old, dressed in a green pleated skirt and white woolly jumper, standing in front of a Christmas tree.

'Do you know who this is, Reme?'

Señora Vallez smiled. It was a gentle smile, filled with sadness.

'*Sí ... sí...*' She dabbed away a tear with her finger, then wiped her cheek with the back of her hand. 'It's Launa ... one of the two sisters I was telling you about. Launa's the one who was killed by the nun in the orphanage. May your soul rest in peace, my sweet Launa...'

'Who is it?' Alexis asked, arching her eyebrows.

'Kerstin Lindbergh,' Emily replied, pocketing her mobile.

GUARDIOLA PRESSED THE DOORBELL and waited.

Childlike laughter and grown-up shrieking echoed behind the door, then a *farandole* of eager steps pattered closer. Slowly the door inched open to reveal a mop of brown curls, not very far off the ground, with dark eyes that peered out curiously at Emily, Guardiola and Alexis.

'*Mamá!*' the child turned and cried down the hallway. 'Three people are here, but it's not the Three Wise Men!'

'Are you sure?'

'Yes, I am. Two of them are girls. And none of them have dark skin. Look!'

The child opened the door all the way, and they saw a woman of around forty in a wheelchair. Guardiola leaned down to give her a hug.

'Adri!' a male voice called from inside the apartment. 'When's the little *hombre*'s Christmas concert again?'

'Next Tuesday! Come in, come in,' the woman said, wheeling her chair back.

Guardiola closed the door behind him.

'What are your names?' the young boy asked, climbing onto his mother's lap.

'I'm Vicente. We've met before, but you were too little to remember. This is Emily and Alexis. And you, what's your name?'

'If we've met before, then you should remember.'

'I remember, but my friends here haven't met you before.'

'Can I tell them, mummy?'

'Yes, you can, sweet pea. I've known Vicente for a very long time.'

'My name's Pablo. What do you do for a job?'

'I'm a journalist. Emily is a police officer and Alexis is a writer.'

Pablo stared at Alexis in amazement. 'Wow! Do you write books? Like *The Little Prince*?'

Alexis smiled. 'No, my books are very different.'

'So you don't write about aeroplanes. Or asteroids.'

'No.'

'Your books are just for grown-ups, then?'

'I'm afraid so.'

'Because there are people in there without any clothes on?'

Alexis looked to his mother in desperation, who gave her an amused smile that made it clear she wouldn't be coming to her rescue.

'No, because there aren't any baobab trees, sheep or asteroids.'

'And there aren't any boa constrictors eating elephants either?'

'Come on, my little prince,' his mother interjected, 'why don't you go and tell *Papá* it's time for him to run you a bath?'

Pablo jumped down, kissed the palm of his mother's hand and ran off down the hallway.

'Come on, why don't we go to my office?' Adri suggested, wheeling her chair to the left and sliding a pair of double doors open.

She motioned for them to go in first, and then closed the door behind her.

'Careful where you put your feet,' she said, gliding around behind her desk and switching on her computer. 'Apparently it hurts like hell if you step on a Lego brick. What did you say you were looking for?'

'We need to access the register for an orphanage by the name of La Virgen de los Desamparados,' Guardiola explained. 'We need to track down three names. Three women. It opened in—'

'In Madrid? Have a seat. I don't know how long this is going to take. So you might as well make yourselves comfortable.'

'That's a mum thing, if ever I saw one. Being able to hold two conversations at once. Yes, in Madrid, Adri.'

'See, you're not so bad at that yourself, eh Vicente?' she teased, still tapping away at the computer keyboard. 'Just think what a great mum you'd make.'

Alexis gathered a pile of children's books that were scattered all over the sofa, put them on the side table and sat down. Emily and Guardiola remained standing.

'Right then, what information do you have for me to work with?'

'Year of birth…'

'Don't you have the year they started there?'

'Yes, I do, if you'll let me finish.'

'Go on, then.'

'1951.'

'That's the year they were born?'

'No, the year they started there.'

'You wouldn't have the name of a class or a registration number, by any chance?'

'How about you let me give you what I do have first, eh Adri?'

'Oh, *Dios mio*, here we go! Listen to you stressing because you're not the one at the helm, eh? All right then, Guardiola, you be the man – lead the way…'

'Aw, jeez, give it a rest with all that feminist stuff, you know it really—'

'Come on, spit it out. I don't want to spend all night in here. I'd far rather be with my husband.'

'I'm trying, believe it or not, but you won't let me get a word in edgeways! Right. Anyway. We're trying to establish the identity of three women, nicknamed Gordi, Launa and Lados, who arrived at the orphanage in 1951. Launa and Lados were sisters who were born ten months apart. Launa might have been declared dead in 1953 or recorded as having left the orphanage at that time. In her second life in Sweden, her name was first Kerstin Persson, then Lindbergh, by marriage. In 1951, these three were part of the same cohort of girls as Remedios Vallez Belís and Beatriz Nuñez Bartolomeu, who were born in 1942 and left the orphanage in 1960.'

Adri whistled through her teeth as she took notes on her computer. 'You're not making it easy for me, are you? Have you never heard about the lost children of Francoism and the law of 4 December 1941, which basically allowed the state to change the names of orphaned kids and ship them off who knows where for adoption?' she muttered. 'When are we ever going to stop mopping up all the blood Franco spilled? And that damned pact of silence – the left and the right pouring layer after layer of concrete over the bodies, burying all those war crimes. They should have been digging them up. How else will we see justice? How else can we repair our country, our history, our heritage? We never had our Nuremberg trials here. Franco died shaking Juan Carlos by the hand. *The king is dead. Long live the king...*'

Adri fell quiet and kept on working, absorbed in her screen, fingers tapping away at the keyboard intermittently.

'So, what's Vicente here told you about me?' she asked Emily after a few moments of silence, without looking up from her computer.

'Not much,' replied Emily, who was standing right next to her. 'But he did insinuate quite a bit.'

'Well, let me start by dispelling the first myth: I'm not a hacker—'

'Of course you're a hacker,' Guardiola said. 'A hacker who just happens to also be a civil servant.'

'Yes, and that's what we call an archivist. Someone who's been working for the national archives for the last twelve years. Who knows where to find anything and everything? And which documentation resources to search—'

'And for private clients too, from the comfort of your own home, without moving your arse from behind your computer. So that makes you a hacker.'

'I wish I could move my arse, Guardiola.'

'Oh give it a rest, will you, or these two femmes fatales here are going to slap me. They don't know you're kidding.'

'I'm not kidding, though. 'I'd love to be able to bike Pablo to school. And go shake my booty on the dance floor.'

'Nobody says "shake my booty" anymore. And you've always hated cycling.'

'What else?'

'Oh, I don't know, Adri.'

'I'm talking to your friend Emily.'

Emily flashed her a knowing smile. Adri returned it.

'You're very observant, aren't you? My husband doesn't know. It was a long time ago, and one hop in the sack with Guardiola was more than enough for me. Ah!' she cried. 'Here we are!'

She raised her arms in triumph.

'So … I have two sisters here. The first one is Cristina … Cristina Labajos Macías. According to the record, she left the orphanage on the sixth of March 1953 … and this is what she looked like,' she said, with a click of her mouse.

Guardiola, Emily and Alexis crowded around the screen to see the black-and-white snapshot. They saw a child in a pale dress and knee-high socks with light-brown hair drawn back into a ponytail, standing beside a fireplace.

Emily took out her phone, found the photo of Aliénor's mother as a child and held it up to the computer screen. Cristina Labajos Macías – Launa – was Kerstin Lindbergh.

'Perfect. Fantastic!' Adri enthused, already clicking on the second photo. 'And that means this must be Lados. Enriqueta Labajos Macías. She was the younger sister, so that's probably where the nickname came from. *La dos* – number two. After *La una* – number one.'

This young girl was wearing a dark blouse over a pleated skirt.

'Woooo…' Adri whistled. 'She was a real beauty, wasn't she? Even more than her sister, and she set the bar high. Do you know who this Lados is, then?'

'No,' Emily and Alexis both replied.

'OK, never mind … we're in for some fun and games now. All I can see are the girls' names and the year they arrived, then the date they either left or died. I do have Remedios Vallez Belís and Beatriz Nuñez Bartolomeu here – see.' She pointed to two of the lines on the register. 'But for this Gordi – which must surely be a nickname too, presumably because she was on the larger side – *gorda* means fat – for her, we'll have to comb through the whole list. And there are hundreds of names on here. I'm going to print it out so we can all roll up our sleeves. And you're sure you don't have any more information about this Gordi, other than the fact she arrived at the orphanage in 1951?'

'No, that's all we have to go on,' Guardiola replied, reaching for the pages that had just come out of the printer.

'May I?' Emily asked, pointing to a child's blackboard hanging low on the wall.

'Of course,' Adri replied. 'Be my guest.'

Emily kneeled down and chalked up the names and dates of birth of Gerda Vankard, the Lindberghs' live-in housekeeper; Signe Skår, the clinical director of the Lindbergh Clinic; Esther Månsson, the mother of Louise's boyfriend, Albin; Francisca Burgos, the fertility doctor's daughter; and Carina Isaksson, the Lindberghs' neighbour – and Göran's mistress.

Alexis raised her eyebrows in surprise. 'Do you think that—'

'I don't know.'

'So you're casting the net wide.'

Emily nodded and took the sheets of paper from Guardiola's outstretched hand.

'Who are all those women?' the journalist asked.

'Women who are connected to the investigation—'

'Whose age might match the girls we're looking for, if I see what you're saying,' he finished. 'With a bit of luck, anyway…'

Emily shuffled over to join them in scanning through the pages, sitting on the floor with her back against the sofa.

For the next hour or so, their search was interrupted only by young Pablo, who poked his head in to kiss his mother goodnight before he went to bed and brought them a bottle of Fanta and four glasses to keep them going.

Emily had just swallowed a mouthful of the sugary drink when a name on the list caught her eye.

The slightest furrow crossed her brow. She knew she had seen that name somewhere before. But where? Emily closed her eyes and repeated the name to herself a few times to set her memory in motion. It started to work and the information came to her one snippet at a time, and eventually she had pieced it all together in her mind.

'I've found something,' she said calmly as she stood up.

Alexis and Guardiola leapt to their feet.

'Very impressive, even for a profiler,' Adri whistled. 'We've barely been at it two hours. Well, for Guardiola's sake, I can only hope you're not that quick at everything,' she winked.

THERE WAS A GENEROUS WELCOME waiting for Alexis, Bergström and Emily, courtesy of Alexis's mother. Even Emily didn't manage to wriggle free from her warm embrace.

Beside Mado stood a smiling woman of around forty with rosy cheeks and piercing blue eyes like Alexis's.

Alexis flung her arms wide and gave the woman a big hug with a sigh of contentment. 'My sister, Inès,' she said to her friends and colleagues, reluctantly releasing her embrace.

Inès timidly shook Emily's hand and greeted Bergström with a similar reserve.

'You must be exhausted, you poor souls. Why don't you have a bite to eat?' Mado Castells suggested, already rolling up her sleeves at the kitchen island.

They dumped their coats and boots in the hallway and all went through to the kitchen together.

Alexis couldn't help but smile. Her mother had commandeered Stellan's house. She was swanning around as if she had always lived there, extending the warmest of welcomes to visitors, clutching them to her bosom, and, most importantly, filling their bellies outrageously full.

'I put a pot of coffee on,' Alexis's father announced.

'Who'd like some *petits fours*?' Mado asked, licking her lips. She started to pull dishes out of the kitchen cupboards without bothering to wait for a reply, she and her beloved husband Bert beavering away with all the energy and enthusiasm of two servers less than half their age.

'Mmm, aren't my *petits fours* just exquisite, Bert?' she gushed, arranging a plate of them for their guests. 'Why don't you go on through to the living room? Make yourselves comfortable. Your father and I are going to go for a little walk, *ma chérie*, before it gets dark. I missed the window again yesterday, and I feel like I've been cooped up in a cave all day long. This darkness is just horrible. We don't know what time we're supposed to eat or go to bed anymore. We're all out of sync, aren't we, Bert?'

Mado exchanged a smile with Emily, then swept a trail of crumbs off the worktop with the back of her hand.

'You spent a part of your childhood living at La Virgen de los Desamparados, the orphanage in Madrid, didn't you, Mado?' Emily suddenly said.

Mado stared at Emily, then averted her eyes, casting out over the dark, grey sea.

Alexis felt her mother's pain ricochet through her body. Emily had warned her. She had suggested she stay behind at the hotel or the police station and come and join them later, once all the questions were over. She had warned her in Adri's house, the very moment she realised it was Mado's name she had recognised on the register. The same name she had seen on Alexis and Stellan's wedding invitation months earlier:

Magdalena Morales Ramos and Norbert Castells Aparici, together with Henning Eklund, cordially invite you to join them in celebration of the marriage of their children, Alexis and Stellan...

Norbert Castells placed a gentle hand on his wife's back. Mado shuddered and turned to him. She tried to read the look on his face for a second, then opened her hands and contemplated the sticky sponge-cake crumbs all over her fingers.

'Yes,' Norbert answered for his wife, squeezing her hand. 'Mado did spend part of her childhood in that orphanage.'

'They used to call you Gordi, didn't they?'

Mado closed her eyes and turned her cheek, as if she were shying away from the blinding sun. Norbert nodded, sheltering Mado with his whole body.

'Do you want to sit down, Mado?' Emily asked.

Norbert shook his head at her.

Alexis flushed as she looked at her mother. She had never seemed so vulnerable before. Mado was faltering now like a lantern flame in the wind. There was nothing of the woman she knew in the haunted look in her eyes, only fragments of the child she had once been. Remnants of Gordi, the girl she hadn't breathed a word about all these years. Mado the warrior now clung to her husband like a withered old woman clutching her cane, lending him her voice, surrendering every ounce of herself into his arms, as if she could melt into him so he could speak her thoughts and words.

Alexis suddenly felt the urge to join them, to wrap her arms around her mother and help carry her through her suffering. But she sensed that there was no place for her in that embrace. Her parents were tormented by a past she knew nothing about. Mado barely had the strength to exhume her memories, let alone bring her daughter into the effort.

Tears pearled on Mado's eyelashes. She blinked them away, sending them running down her cheeks. It struck Alexis that she had seen her mother cry with joy many times, but she had always protected her daughter from her sorrow.

'I'm sorry, *mes chéries*. I'm so sorry…' Mado said to her daughters, through silent tears, as if she could read their minds.

'Oh, Maman…'

'And you're getting married in just a few days, as well … Oh, heavens … If only I'd known … I'm so, so sorry, my darling…'

'Oh, there's no need for that, Maman. You don't always have to worry about us and everyone else, you know.'

Alexis rested her hand on the kitchen counter, palm facing up, ready to clasp her mother's. But the pain and shame seemed to make

Mado keep her distance. Instead Norbert gently squeezed her hand three times, the way he always would when she was a child. A silent *I love you*. Then he pulled his hand away and held Mado again.

'Are you sure you don't want to sit down, Mado?' Emily insisted.

'No, no.' Her voice was just a whisper, but her tone was firm.

Norbert released his embrace, but held his wife with his gaze, ready to dive in again and save her if she showed the slightest sign of going under.

'You were one of a group of five young girls at the orphanage, weren't you?' Emily continued, aware she was skating on thin ice. 'Reme, Dulce, the sisters Launa and Lados, and you, Gordi, correct?'

Mado nodded.

'I think Alexis told you about Kerstin Lindbergh, who was killed with her husband and daughter here in Falkenberg, didn't she?'

Mado looked up at the profiler with a barely perceptible arch of her eyebrows, her arms suspended in mid-air like a puppet waiting for the next pull of the strings.

'Yes, she did mention it. Aliénor's family, wasn't it? Ah, the poor girl. Why do you ask?'

'It turns out that you knew Kerstin Lindbergh a long time ago. You called her Launa back then.'

Mado's jaw dropped. She took a step backwards.

'No, no ... Launa died. She died there. Right before our eyes.'

'She didn't die, Mado. She was transferred to another orphanage. Do you remember Dulce?'

'Yes,' she whispered.

'She was killed the same way Kerstin was. But in Spain, three years ago.'

Mado's eyes darted around the room, scrabbling for memories.

'Does the name Carlos Burgos mean anything to you?'

'No,' she replied, shaking her head.

'I understand you called him Tos,' Emily said, showing Mado her phone with the photo of a young Carlos Burgos.

Mado turned as white as a sheet. She clenched her teeth, and her face turned to stone. Steeling her gaze, she crossed her arms over her belly and nodded, averting her eyes from the image on the screen.

'He was the medic at the orphanage, I believe?' Emily continued.

'Do my daughters really have to be here?'

Silently pleading with Emily through a veil of tears, she then turned suddenly to Bergström, as if asking him the same question.

'No, of course not, Mado,' Bergström replied.

Emily looked up and gave Mado a smile filled with infinite tenderness. Alexis could feel its warmth too, and she started to shed silent tears like her mother.

Inès clasped Alexis's hand in hers, clutching her tight.

'But I think Alexis and Inès need to be here by your side, Mado. So they can be close to you, and comprehend what's happened. They know now. And you know your daughters: if anyone can understand, it's them.'

Mado swallowed and nodded.

Emily gave her the same smile; it shone like a late-summer day, filled with gentle, warming light, but tinged with a hint of melancholy.

'Did Tos abuse you, Mado?' she asked softly.

It took Mado a moment to swallow back her tears, her lips fluttering as if her heart was in her mouth.

'Yes,' she replied, hanging on to the kitchen island. 'He abused me. All five of us. And others. But he especially liked to spend time with Launa and Lados. Just the three of them. Together.' She breathed a deep sigh of release.

'Were you abused by other men or women, Mado?'

'Father Murillo…'

Her lips started to shake.

'Most of the time, we used to wish we could just curl up and die. We would go to sleep at night praying not to wake up in the morning. One night, Lados snuck into the infirmary and got into bed next to one of the dying girls, hoping whatever she had would rub off on her and take her away as well.'

Alexis wondered how her mother had managed to conceal the abuse and all the grief she had suffered. Where had she kept it hidden away? Behind how many smiles? Alexis could have seen it if she had known what to look for. She could have found it lurking behind her mother's rapacious love, her anxious inquisitions, her unreasonable outbursts.

'Did the five of you share a secret, Mado? A tragedy you all witnessed, perhaps? I'm not talking about neglect, or sexual abuse either, but rather an isolated incident.'

'Only Launa's death ... well, we thought she had died, but now you're telling me she didn't...'

'Do you think you could tell me what happened, Mado?'

Mado ran her tongue over her rough lips. 'It was in the morning. When we had to sing 'Cara al Sol' in reverence to *El Caudillo*. We used to do some exercises first, then we would start to sing. But Lados just couldn't put one foot in front of the other to run that morning. She was bleeding, and she had such terrible pains in her tummy – from all those horrors Tos and Father Murillo made her suffer.'

She released a deep, throaty sigh, almost like a cough, as if suddenly winded by a frigid blast of air.

'So Father Murillo started to beat her. He had his own leather whip, made of three belts braided together, like Sister Fernanda's, but he would beat us with the end that had the buckles too, the sick monster. Launa butted in to stand up for her sister ... the way she always did. She would always put herself between Lados and anyone else. She yanked the whip out of Father Murillo's hands and made him lose his balance, and he fell to the ground. Ah, that brief moment, that fleeting moment, was the greatest triumph I'd ever felt. The shortest, but the sweetest.'

Mado twisted her mouth in disgust.

'Then Sister Fernanda, the witch, started laying into Launa with such hate ... such fire in her eyes ... it's like she was possessed, that woman. She was young, not even twenty, but she was fierce. So much hate and resentment...'

Mado closed her eyes and shook her head.

'Sister Fernanda kept going until Launa stopped screaming. Then Launa suddenly went quiet, just like that. As if they had stolen her voice. One second she was screaming her head off, and the next … nothing. Only the sound of the leather slicing into her skin. And her body, swaying to the side with every blow.'

A primal sound escaped from Mado's lips, something between a sigh and a moan, as she turned her gaze out to sea once more.

Emily waited patiently for a few seconds before easing her back. 'Who told you she was dead, Mado? Father Murillo? Sister Fernanda?'

'No one told us she was dead. No one told us anything. The next day we saw a coffin leaving the orphanage. A little coffin. We all thought she was in that box. "That box" – that's what Lados called it. We never saw Father Murillo or Sister Fernanda again after that day.'

'Do you know what happened to them?'

Mado shook her head.

'And Lados?'

'She lost it completely when her sister died. There was less than a year between them, but Launa had been carrying her sister's pain as well as her own. They sent Lados to a psychiatric hospital a few weeks later. We never saw her again, either.'

'What about Reme and Dulce?'

'We stayed together for a few more months, then I went off to live with my aunt, and we never saw each other again. My aunt had fled to Belgium at the beginning of the civil war and was only able to return to Spain in 1953. It took her months to track me down. She was actually trying to find my mother and my father. But I was the only one left. Do you know what happened to Reme? And Lados?'

'Lados, we don't know, but Reme lives near Madrid.'

Mado nodded wearily, her face devoid of all expression.

Emily motioned to the commissioner. She had no other questions.

'Norbert, we're putting the house under police protection,' Bergström said. 'Stellan's going to be home soon, but if there's anything whatsoever, no matter what, you call me, all right?'

Alexis's father nodded.

'What about Tos?' Mado suddenly blurted. 'Is he still alive?'

'No, he was killed, Mado. Murdered.'

'The same way as Launa and Dulce?'

'Yes.'

Mado's face creased into a broad, sour smile, streaked with tears.

Norbert wrapped his arms around his wife. 'You have the right to be happy about that, Mado. It's all right, *mi cielo*, you can be happy now.'

OLOFSSON CLINKED THREE FALCONS onto the conference-room table and took a swig of his own beer before he sat down.

Being at work make the first drop taste even sweeter. Especially in this room, where they had pored over so many dead bodies, the walls were dripping with blood, sweat and tears. To Olofsson, the beer tasted so good. It was better than a flute of champagne. Even though it was supposed to be chic and sophisticated, he wasn't a fan of the bubbles. Like a woman who was hot to trot, they were too flirty for him, the way they fizzed and popped at his tongue. There was no colour to the stuff either, no real substance or character. But beer … ah, hand him a nice cold beer and he'd be happy just holding the glass. Beer filled the mouth with pure, honest goodness. Beer was the genuine article. There was nothing pretentious about it.

Emily and Bergström were sitting so still, they almost looked like statues, drinking in silence. Mona hadn't touched the bottle in front of her. She seemed to be listening to the hollow sound of her colleagues' lips embracing and releasing the bottle necks.

Olofsson leaned back on two legs in his chair, flirting with the fine balance between the vertical and the horizontal. That was just the way he liked to be, teetering on the edge of control. He knew that as soon as they set foot inside the door to the station, Mona was his no more. There was none of the hunger in her eyes, none of the burning desire, none of the insatiable appetite for him that had filled him with more joy than he had ever imagined possible. Like last night:

her, eyes closed, writhing with pleasure amid the rumpled sheets on the bed. Him, standing at the end of the bed grasping her by the hips, revelling in every ripple of ecstasy that shuddered through the curves and hollows of her body, captivated by the changing texture of her skin as it responded to his touch. He had been attuned to every vibration, every tremor as the tension built up and up. Savouring every note of their symphony, the throaty sighs, the rustling sheets, the muffled tones of bodies rubbing together, teasing, revealing more and more of themselves to one another.

Bloody hell, Mona had really cast a spell on him. Olofsson leaned forwards and guided the front legs of his chair back to the floor with the gentlest of landings.

Taking another mouthful of blonde nectar, he turned to Emily and Bergström, who were both still adrift in their own silence.

'How did Alexis take it?' he asked.

'She's still reeling,' Bergström replied, staring into space.

'I bet she is. Can you imagine, finding out that your mum was beaten and raped as a child? Poor Alexis, it must have knocked her for six. Family secrets are like ticking time bombs ... So is the wedding off, then?'

'What makes you think the wedding would be off, Kristian? Don't you think they have even more of a reason to celebrate their union now? To lay the past to rest. And celebrate what Mado's managed to make of her life in spite of all her trauma.'

'What do you mean, what she's made of her life?'

'Her family, Olofsson.' Bergström rested his bottle on his knee for a second, leaving a wet circle on his jeans.

'So,' the commissioner went on, 'on the one hand, we have three murders connected to La Virgen de los Desamparados orphanage: Beatriz Nuñez – nicknamed "Dulce" – and Kerstin Lindbergh – nick-named "Launa" – who were residents, and Carlos Burgos, who was the medic. Two victims and one tormentor – *their* tormentor. That makes it challenging to identify a motive, to say the least. Killing the paedophile, that makes sense; but his victims too? Not to mention the fact that the deaths of Göran and Louise Lindbergh seem to be more connected to the Lindbergh Clinic and the embryo-trafficking scandal it was involved in.'

'The scandal Dr Burgos's clinic was embroiled in, don't forget,' Olofsson added. 'When you think that Göran Lindbergh was doing dirty deals with the paedophile who abused his wife ... that's just nuts, completely nuts.'

Emily pointed to the whiteboard. 'There are five murders in all,' she began. 'Two in Madrid: Carlos Burgos in 2012 and Beatriz Nuñez in 2013; then three here now in Falkenberg, three years later: Kerstin, Göran and Louise Lindbergh. So, the case begins in 2012 with the scandal implicating Dr Burgos's clinic. And the event that triggered this series of murders...'

Emily left her sentence hanging, pausing in reflection as if another light bulb had just flashed above her head.

Beer in hand, she stood and moved over to the whiteboard. She peered closely at the photo of Carlos Burgos, then her gaze moved to the image of Kerstin Lindbergh/Cristina Labajos Macías as a child. Young Launa.

'No, we have six murders,' she corrected, without turning away from the photos on the wall. 'Because Kerstin Lindbergh essentially died twice.'

She paused again, this time turning to examine the photo of Kerstin's sister, Enriqueta – 'Lados'. The two sisters had struck the same pose: arms crossed over their stomachs, grasping their clothing at the waist, hands balled into fists and wrinkling the material. Building a barrier to protect themselves from the outside world.

'The triggering event was actually Kerstin Lindbergh's first death, in 1953,' Emily continued. 'The day she – or Launa, I should say – was presumed to have died.'

Chairs scraped against the floor as the bodies in the room shifted position.

'Nearly sixty years before Burgos's murder,' Olofsson recapped. 'When you put it that way, it changes everything.'

Mona inched forwards to the edge of her seat, weighing up her thoughts. 'What if … I wonder if these could be political crimes…' she timidly ventured. 'Well I mean, crimes that had something to do with Franco.'

'Good point, but why kill them now, forty years after *El Caudillo*'s death?' the commissioner countered.

'And why kill the victims as well as their tormentor? It just doesn't make sense,' Olofsson added.

Mona retreated, lowering her eyes.

'It makes sense to the killer,' Emily corrected, with another sip of her beer, turning back to the mosaic of photos on the whiteboard.

'What the hell is this mess?' Olofsson shook his head, reaching across the table for a fresh bottle of Falcon. 'A good old-fashioned case of revenge, do you think? Or maybe we're dealing with a nut job who's started to collect human tongues?'

Emily kept her thoughts to herself.

'What about Kerstin's sister, Lados? What happened to her?' Olofsson asked, with a swig of beer.

'She died in the psychiatric hospital in 1955.'

Olofsson leaned back in his chair again and whistled. 'What a shit show … Who do we still have in our sights as a suspect, then?'

Emily shot the detective a glance.

'Before we can think about the *who*, we have to figure out the *why*,' she replied. 'Then the *who* will slot right into place.'

Skrea Strand, Falkenberg, home of the Lindberghs
Tuesday, 13 December 2016, 8.00 pm

EMILY RAN ALONG the sea's edge with a measured stride, her breath the only sound breaking the snowy silence as her headlamp forged a path through the darkness. But despite the silence, she felt as if the chaos around her was deafening.

The blustery wind that had buffeted the plane that morning when she and Alexis had landed at the airport in Gothenburg had subsided. But the air was still biting cold, chilling Emily's muscles to the bone and numbing the skin of her face so it felt like a mask.

Something was eluding her.

She had been working on cases involving sociopathic serial killers for so long, she understood that they saw their crimes through a lens of fantasy, one that made things clear for them alone. But Emily knew how to crack the code and bring things into focus. She was a master of her craft who knew how to tailor her methods and hone her strategy based on a profile she pieced together bit by bit, as she gathered information from the crime scene, the bodies, and the victims' own profiles. The more she learned about the murders, the clearer the killer's face and personality became in her mind, until she had a portrait to present to her colleagues.

With this case, though, Emily found herself on the trail of a serial killer who had a motive – for the first crime, at least: Burgos's murder was revenge, she was sure of it. But killing Burgos – that initial act of revenge – had then somehow acted as a stressor, causing another trauma in the killer's past to resurface, triggering the psychopathic behaviour that had led to the other murders. Emily was sure that the perpetrator was a sociopath and would have killed sooner or later anyway. The revenge aspect and the personal history had simply served as a psychological pretext – a catalyst for the killings.

Emily knew there was a logic to this case, a path she had to map out that would link everything together and lead her to the killer. It might seem as if that was an easy thing to do, because she had now identified the triggering factor. But somehow it wasn't. Emily's closeness to Aliénor was blurring her vision. She had to peel away a layer of emotion before she could think straight. She kept opening her little black box to put Aliénor in there, and every time she found she had to spend much longer than usual before she could close it and focus on the case. Aliénor was almost like a child to Emily. And that was surely why her thoughts were clouded. Aliénor had tugged at her heart strings … as a mother. A mother who felt battered and bruised, frustrated and unfulfilled.

When Emily had called Aliénor earlier, she had been picking out funeral outfits. Aliénor's voice had sounded strained and high-pitched, but she hadn't shared a word of pain or anguish. In the quiet pauses in their conversation, Emily had heard voices buzzing away in the distant background, snippets of conversations imbued with the gentle melody of the Swedish language, sentences that flowed like ripples on the tide. Léopold, Albin, Carina and Gerda were just about to leave, Aliénor had explained. Gerda had wanted to make dinner for them all before she went back to see her partner in Varberg.

Emily quickened her pace, but the cold seemed to bite deep with her every effort. She embraced the pain, allowing it to occupy her mind for a moment before turning her focus back to her breathing.

The story of the killer's struggle had begun with the presumed death of Kerstin Lindbergh/Launa in 1953, an event that had traumatised the killer and influenced their every action since. The only person who would have been so deeply affected by such an emotional and psychological trauma was her sister: Lados. If she had found out that Launa was still alive, it would have come as such a shock, the grief and the surprise could easily have given way to anger and it might have been enough to push her over the edge. And driven her to kill. But back in the orphanage, Lados had been so devastated by witnessing the death of the sister with whom she had been so close, not to mention dependent on, it was no wonder she had been sent to the psychiatric hospital. Electric-shock treatment was commonplace at the time, Guardiola and Adri had explained, and patients frequently died as a result. And Lados had been one of them. According to official records, she had died in 1955, her body buried in the civil cemetery in Madrid.

In one swift movement, Emily wiped away the beads of sweat that were dripping into her eyes.

What was she missing?

Perhaps she was approaching the whole case from the wrong angle. Perhaps what had triggered these crimes wasn't Launa's presumed death, but the disappearance of her tormentors: Father Murillo and Sister Fernanda.

Emily slowed to a brisk walk. She could see the Lindberghs' home rising from the fields across the dunes, just steps away from the beach. She hadn't realised she had run so far. It was as if her feet had by themselves brought her so close to Aliénor.

Emily pulled her phone out of her pocket to call her. The screen was filled with missed-call alerts. With so many thoughts running through her mind, she hadn't heard the phone ringing or felt it vibrating. She stopped in her tracks, her chest still heaving from her run. It was Guardiola. He had tried to call her twelve times in the space of two minutes and texted her to call him back as quickly as possible. In all caps, with exclamation marks.

Guardiola's name flashed across her screen again. Emily picked up right away.

She listened to the journalist's first two sentences, then set off again at a sprint, this time towards the Lindberghs' house, phone still glued to her ear as Guardiola filled her in about his latest discovery.

He had also left a message for Bergström at the station, and for Alexis on her mobile. To save precious seconds, Emily bounded her way over a border of pebbles and slipped, reaching a hand out to break her fall. She heard the smash as her phone screen hit the rock. But still she kept going, willing her legs to carry her faster, further, moonwalking for a split second as she struggled to gain traction between two pebbles, her broken phone still in hand. Emily coughed to release the fire that was blocking her lungs and slowing her down.

Finally, she had made it to the Lindberghs'; there was only their snow-filled garden left to cross. She literally couldn't run a step further. She had to take big, striding steps, lifting her knees waist high to make any headway through the compact snow. Spitting and her chest heaving with her hoarse breaths, she kept putting one foot in front of the other. Eventually she made it to the top of the garden and quickened her pace, now she didn't have the snow to contend with. There were lights on in every room on the ground floor. They must have seen her coming. Heard her, even. But she was not going to be too late. She was sure of it. There was no way she was going to be too late. They weren't going to take Aliénor away from her. She wouldn't let them. Emily skirted the house to the right – the spiral staircase on the left would slow her down.

As she sprinted the final metres to the porch, she recognised the only car parked in the driveway.

Taking a deep breath, she pushed the door handle, trying to collect her thoughts and determine the best strategy to take once she was inside the building.

The door opened, but only a sliver, as if there was something blocking the entrance. Emily swallowed and ran her rough tongue over her dry, weather-chapped lips. She braced her shoulder against the door and gave it a shove, managing to open it just far enough to slip inside the hallway.

Emily saw her immediately. First her feet, with her boots still on, then her body slumped against the door, legs akimbo and arms dangling, with the backs of her hands braced awkwardly against the floor. Her head was lolling to one side, towards the door opening, as if she had turned in greeting, except for the fact her wide, childlike eyes were closed. Then Emily forced herself to look at what she had refused to register: the line of blood wrapped around her throat like a scarf, trailing all the way down to her waist.

'Aliénor!' she heard herself scream. 'Aliénor!'

Skrea Strand, Falkenberg, home of the Lindberghs
Friday, 2 December 2016, 9.00 pm

KERSTIN LINDBERGH WAS SITTING cross-legged. The floor in the cellar was as cold as an ice cube.

She needed to have a good cry. Let it all out. Scream at the top of her lungs. Before taking refuge down here, she had thrown up her entire meal.

She didn't know how to tackle this problem, or even where to begin. Let alone how to fix it. She had no idea. She didn't want to dredge anything up about La Virgen de los Desamparados. She hadn't breathed a word about that godforsaken place since she had been carted out of there on a stretcher, away from her sister, Lados. She hadn't even shed a tear over Lados. It was as if … as if closing the gates to that hell behind her had meant she'd had to turn her back on her sister. Break the bond between them. She had almost died to save her. But in the end she had saved her own skin and left her sister alone with the monsters.

She heard Göran walk across the kitchen, open the door to the cellar and hurry down the stairs.

He crouched before her and rested his hands on his knees.

She couldn't bear to look him in the eye. She was ashamed. Ashamed of her lies. Ashamed that she had betrayed him. And she was scared. Scared to death. That he would walk out on her and leave her all alone. Alone with her demons.

'You're scaring me, *min älskling*…' he began, as if echoing her thoughts. 'Good grief, whatever is going on?'

Kerstin closed her eyes. She didn't know how to tell him. How to even begin to explain that chapter of her life. How to share that with him now, more than sixty years after the fact. He knew nothing of that Kerstin. Of that *Cristina*. Still, those terrible years in the orphanage had shaped her into the woman – the wife and the mother – she had become.

She clenched her teeth. Ground them together. She should never have had children. Because exactly what she feared would happen had. With every step her children took, she could see her own footprints. More so with the girls than with Léopold. That was why she had distanced herself so much, so she wouldn't pass on her own fears to them, smother them with her own anxiety and damage them. But now she could see she had grown too distant from her children. And she had clung to Göran the way her sister had clung to her. She had only given him space in the most intimate part of their life together. Because she could never satisfy him. She just couldn't. She had never stopped seeing Tos and Father Murillo between her legs. Never. Even when their children had been conceived. There was no escaping what those two monsters had planted in her. What they had broken. All she had ever managed to do was bury those memories at the very bottom of her being.

'I'm sorry … I'm so, so sorry,' she murmured, staring at the stone floor. Tears streaked down her face. She reached for her husband's hand and planted a kiss in his palm, tears pooling in the hollow as if it were a chalice.

'Kerstin, what's going on?' he implored, his face aching with concern.

Kerstin sniffed, her lips still pressing into her husband's hand. Göran. Her husband. It had been so easy to live in his shadow.

But now she had to tell him. She had to confess that her life hadn't begun in Denmark, as she had told him, but long before then. She had to tell him about the time she spent inside. In the orphanages. About La Virgen de los Desamparados. About the cruelty of the priests and the nuns. The abuse. The neglect. The violence. The rapes. Those fateful cracks of Sister Fernanda's whip that had ultimately saved her from that hell. About her recovery in the infirmary. And about her adoption. But most importantly, more than anything else, she had to tell him about her sister. Lados.

'Talk to me, Kerstin. I'm right here. Talk to me, please.'

Always the same echo between them. The words that went unsaid amid the silence.

'You're scaring me, Kerstin. You have no idea how much you're scaring me, *min älskling…*'

She wished she could suspend time. Just for a few seconds, so she could still hold back the monster. Hide it. Tame it, somehow.

Kerstin raised her head and faced the truth. She no longer had a choice in the matter. The time had come for her to open up and release her inner demons.

EMILY COULD HEAR HERSELF crying Aliénor's name.

There was a muffled voice coming from somewhere on the left, towards the kitchen.

Emily abandoned Mona's limp body and sprinted across the hall, her heart pounding so hard, it felt like it had burst out of her chest and was beating at her temples.

The kitchen was empty; the table set for six.

Still she could hear the same muffled voice.

There was only one other door to try: the one to the cellar. Emily pulled it open and descended into the darkness. Only the bottom two steps of the staircase were bathed in light. As her eyes adjusted, her mind wandered to the candles on the table and the number of place settings.

Enriqueta – Lados – wasn't buried in the civil cemetery in Madrid. That was why Guardiola had been trying so desperately to reach Emily. Kerstin's sister was alive. Guardiola had managed to track her down the way Emily had suggested, by searching for the names and dates of birth of the other women who had cropped up during the investigation. Lados – or Enriqueta as she was then – had left the psychiatric hospital in 1955, as they had discovered, but not in a coffin. She had been released under the name Esther González Sibella, not Enriqueta Labajos Macías, and sent to another orphanage in southern Spain.

Everything was starting to make sense now.

'Which one should we crack open, then, Louise?'

Creeping her way down the staircase, Emily saw him the moment she heard his voice. Albin had his back to her and was perusing the bottles on the wine rack, one hand grasped firmly around Aliénor's, the other holding a kitchen knife.

'It's important we choose the right wine to go with the meal, my darling. Let's just keep our cool, shall we? We'll just tell her that now it's my turn. She'll understand: she's my mother. Don't leave me, will you? Hold me tight, Louise. Tighter … Tighter than that. I want to feel you close to me. I need you to be there when I talk to Mum. I don't want to hold *her* hand anymore, do you see? I don't want to be killing for her anymore. The worst thing was afterwards, you know. The tongues … the tongues she made me cut out so they'd finally stop talking to her. Burgos had been whispering in her ear for so long. She wanted me to shut him up. She's my mother, I had to do what she said, didn't I? But every time I touch you, Louise, all I can see are my fingers spreading their mouths open wide. And I can sense my mother right there, looking over my shoulder … like she's making sure I do my homework.'

Albin wiped tears from his cheeks, oblivious to how much Aliénor was shaking.

'I know you won't betray me. Not you, I'm sure of it. You're not like that. You're loyal like me, aren't you, my sweet Louise? *You* would have tried to find me, wouldn't you, if we'd been separated like them? I know you would have. You're not Kerstin. That's what I'm going to say to Mum. That you're different from Kerstin. And I'm going to tell her that I love her and that I'll always take care of her, but I don't want to … fix things for her anymore. If I tell her that over dinner tonight, in front of you, and her sister, her brother-in-law and your brother, she won't dare to make a scene. She'll be disappointed in me, she'll be angry with me, of course. But it won't be the end of the world. We'll get through it, you and me. Did you know that cousins can marry each other in Spain? What would Mum say about that, do you think? Maybe you and I should go away, just the two of us.'

Emily froze on the bottom step. Aliénor's eyes widened as she saw her. Instinctively, she pulled away, but he yanked her back towards him.

'Albin?' Emily cut in.

He whirled around, the look of surprise on his face turning straight to anger.

Emily tilted her head to one side and flashed a beaming smile.

'Everyone's up there waiting for you, Albin. For you, Louise and the wine. We'd like to make a start on dinner. Don't you want to? I understand that you might need some time, just the two of you, for you to, er, connect, because you're flying off to Russia tomorrow, but the starters are getting cold, you see…'

Albin burst out laughing. 'Oh, sorry, yes … What do you think about this sweet wine, Louise?' he asked Aliénor, showing her a bottle of white.

'Yes, lovely,' she blurted, her eyes locked on Emily.

'Perfect. Is Mum upstairs?' he asked, letting go of Aliénor's hand to slide the bottle out of the rack.

Aliénor froze. Her jaw started to quake. Then her hands. She clasped them tightly together.

'Yes, Albin, she's waiting for you,' Emily carried on, still smiling sweetly.

'Isn't she upset?'

'No, not at all. Just tired. Are you two coming upstairs?'

Right then, a thundering crash rang out overhead, followed by a hail of hammering sounds.

Emily heard her name being called, then Aliénor's. She recognised the sound of Bergström's voice. And heard a roar that must have been Olofsson's as he saw Mona lying in the hallway.

Albin turned towards the stairs.

Emily seized her opportunity and shoved Aliénor to the floor. She grabbed Albin's right arm and twisted it behind his back, trying to make him drop the knife. He groaned and slammed the bottle into her ribs with a loud crack. Emily yelped and let go of Albin's arm.

He pulled the knife towards him, before thrusting it out to the side, slashing Aliénor in the calf. She screamed. Emily shrieked and rugby-tackled Albin, jabbing her head right into his solar plexus, sending him crashing into the rack of bottles and slumping to the floor.

Looking around to make sure Aliénor was all right, Emily heard the blade clatter against the stone. She crouched down and fumbled around the floor for the knife, or a shard of broken glass from one of the bottles, trying to keep Albin at bay with a jab of her elbow, then a swift kick. He lashed out with a punch just below her breast, right where he had hit her with the bottle. Then he wrapped his arm around her throat, pulling her into in a headlock.

Emily yanked at his elbow to free her throat, her legs scrabbling in thin air, then suddenly Albin screamed and let go of her, his arm hanging limply in front of his chest. Struggling to catch her breath, Emily shoved him away and whirled around. The knife was firmly planted between Albin's shoulder blades, with Aliénor's trembling hands slowly releasing their grip around the handle. Emily grabbed Albin's arms and secured them behind his back, her eyes still trained on Aliénor as Albin slumped to the floor.

Footsteps thundered down the stairs. Voices barked orders. Arms carried an unconscious and bleeding Albin Månsson up the stairs. But all Emily could see was Aliénor. She was wavering, and she was wounded, but she was alive.

I should go back and fetch Albin. Make him get into the car and come home with me, to Gothenburg. But I know I won't do it. Because he's my Nino, and he's going to sort all this out the way he sorted everything else out. And wiping the slate clean is perhaps the best way forward.

I've been waiting expectantly for too long, dwelling on the past. The two of us can't go back to embracing ghosts. Not anymore. Not after Burgos. Not after Dulce. Not now that we've clawed our way out of the chasm that swallowed us up for twenty years.

As soon as we sat down to dinner, Albin caught on that something wasn't right. He could sense the atmosphere. Our eyes met when he came back up from the cellar with Louise, two bottles in hand. He could see my distress behind the veil of decorum.

We left their place earlier than planned, on the pretence of Nino's trip to Russia. When he got behind the wheel, he nodded and closed his eyes. I told him in one sentence.

Kerstin is my sister, Nino.

He turned to me, and for a moment I drifted away in his gaze. Then I floated back to the here and now, in the car. His mouth gaped open, as if he were screaming loud enough to wake the dead. But the silence in the car was deafening.

That wasn't what he was expecting, my Nino. He thought that it was Göran I had recognised. That he had been another of my tormentors. He buried his face in my bosom. I can't remember the last time he needed me, my Nino. I didn't think I could remember how to be a mother. For a moment I hesitated, then I placed my hands on the nape of his neck, not really sure what he wanted me to do. He was dripping with sweat.

Kerstin is my sister. The words echoed around my mind.

She was the one who opened the door to me, that night. We recognised each other in a heartbeat.

Oh … that moment … the moment I finally felt complete again, for the first time since we were separated at La Virgen de los Desamparados. I wanted to throw my arms around her, hug her tight, kiss her, smell her, breathe every bit of her in. But she held out a hand for me to shake. Like a stranger. Telling me now was not the time. That we had to think about our children. Our children who loved each other. Even though they weren't allowed to.

The only words we said about it were in the kitchen after dinner, when I was helping her clear the table. She just said to me, 'Mañana, Lados.' Tomorrow. Let's talk about it tomorrow. *But there was no more Lados, no more Launa. I was no longer her shadow. She was no longer my light. I spat in her face. She wiped it away with the back of her hand and went back into the dining room without the slightest glance over her shoulder.*

Launa. The sister I had told Nino about with so much pain and regret; she was alive and had never come looking for me. She should have moved heaven and earth to find me. But she abandoned me to our tormentors. My Launa, my sister, the other half of me, the very essence of my existence, had erased me completely from her life.

I closed my eyes to let the truth sink in. The pain seeped its way in, like a weight bearing down on my chest, slowly crushing me.

All of this should have come to an end with Burgos. Not Dulce; I was never expecting it to come to that with her. Dulce was one of our five. One of us.

I remember how Dulce served me coffee and sat down across from me. Her arms crossed over her old-lady apron. Marking a boundary. I told her about my descent into hell. I told her about Burgos. I could see the fear in her eyes, when I told her Nino and I had killed Tos. That we'd done it for all of us. She told me I was crazy, calling me a criminal, yelling at me that it wasn't right to kill for so little.

'For so little? How can you have forgotten, Dulce?' I cried.

Her withered body sparked to life, pulsing with an unbridled fury. Her eyes were full of horror and she was gesticulating wildly, spitting her moralising venom at me. Then she picked up the telephone to call the police. The police! To report us, me and my Nino! And she said I was the crazy one?

Albin was left with no choice. She had to be stopped as well.

And to rub that 'so little' in her face, to remind her what a filthy pissy-pants she used to be, I burned her, just like Sister Fernanda did.

I know, I know. I'm the one who drove my Albin here. Who put the knife in his hands. I armed him with my hate and my suffering throughout all my years of autarchy. And I clung to him like a parasite. Until Louise came along. Maybe that's why he managed to create some distance between us. Because Louise was a little part of me.

And so I opened the car door for my Nino. For him to go and restore peace. I told him to get his things from the boot of the car, but to leave his mobile with me, and go back inside. He was to wait an hour and a half, time for me to get back to his place in Gothenburg with his mobile and build him an alibi, to answer the questions we were sure to be asked.

He didn't protest. All of a sudden he was just as docile and loyal as he used to be, before Louise changed him. I could tell that he had understood – my Nino had understood that Louise would only end up repeating the same thing as her mother had. One day, she would just abandon him, the way Launa had abandoned me.

This had to come to an end. It really did. No matter what the cost.

We had to get rid of Launa and the man who harboured her secret. Göran was the one who had insisted his wife forget about her past, I was sure of it. He was the one who made her turn her back on her sister, her roots, the blood running through her veins. He shaped her into the woman he wanted her to be. Not the woman she really was. He took her away from me.

Yes, this really had to come to an end. For us to be rid of this chapter of our life. Sever this limb. Once and for all.

It had to come to an end.

No matter what the cost.

NORBERT CASTELLS TURNED HIS GAZE away from Alexis and Stellan, and looked at his wife. That night, she too had only had eyes for their daughter and son-in-law, and the newlywed joy they were spreading all around them. Mado smiled with a newfound serenity. Or rather, a sense of ease and freedom Bert had never seen in her before.

He reached for her hand, but she pulled away. She opened her purse and took out a piece of paper, which she carefully unfolded, smoothing out the kinks, and handed to him.

Not really understanding, Bert took the letter from his wife and read it, his eyes flitting between Mado's face and the words she had so carefully written on the page.

Seeing our Alexis hold her husband's hand makes me think of holding yours, my sweet Bert. Do you remember the first time you held my hand, when you took me to the pictures? You were so determined, as if you were taking me way further than the street corner. In the hollow of your palm, Bert, I felt the pull of the ocean. It was like you were taking me out to sea. My feet were firmly on the ground, but my heart started to sway like a boat on the swell.

You scooped me up and sailed away with me to another world, Bert, because when I found you, I found myself.

You're the one who showed me how to love my own skin. The skin I used to wear like a coat, a shell, a cross to bear. I had to share this body with all those who tainted and mistreated me. Revealing this body to another's eyes was like seeing them all, all over again. Their feigned smiles and affection, then their guilty pleasure that turned to anger and rage. It was like feeling the ravages of their desire, the damage they had done.

This body was a temple of pain and shame.

But not with you. You, my sweet Bert, you uplifted every moment. You made the time feel shorter and the joy never-ending. And you went on to inhabit this body with me, Bert, this body I wanted nothing of. You made it more than a temple; you made it a vessel.

When I found you, my sweet Bert, I found myself.

At first, I needed to take refuge in your gaze even to breathe, then I taught myself to turn the shades of grey into colours. Even in your absence, you were by my side. I knew I could wrap my arms around you as I wrote, feel your sighs caressing me, listen to my heart fluttering when I called your name.

With you, I savoured every taste love had to give.

That's what made our daughters, my sweet Bert. They are the echo of your love, your patience and your loyalty.

Look at our lovely Alexis now, Bert. Look how radiant she is. We made her.

It was hell before you, Bert, but you gave me the kiss of life.

Flask Walk, Hampstead, London, home of Emily Roy
Saturday, 24 December 2016, 8.00 pm

EMILY FILLED TWO STEMMED GLASSES with a California red, and another with pear cider. She thought about Alexis, and how she wouldn't approve of her choice of New World over Old. She placed a chunk of Stilton and a cheese knife on a slate, and fanned out a handful of *pepparkakor*, the traditional Swedish Christmas ginger snaps, on a plate. Emily carried all these treats through to the living room on a tray.

Aliénor was relaxing at one end of the sofa, legs tucked under her, one arm draped over the back, the other propped against the armrest, captivated by the flames and white-hot chunks of coal in the compact fireplace. Jack was sitting in the armchair, resting his long legs on the coffee table. Emily handed the glass of cider to Aliénor and a glass of the red to Jack, then she carried her own wine over to the window.

Gordi, Dulce, Reme, Launa, Lados. In her mind's eye, Emily could see all their faces. First Mado, and the look of emptiness in her eyes when the truth came pouring out at Stellan's house. Then Reme and Dulce, soul sisters until death parted them. And finally, Launa and Lados. Their lives had each been a mirror of the other. The two sisters had followed one another without knowing it, from their native Spain to Sweden. They had spent decades living just a few hundred kilometres apart, both married to Swedes. It was as if they had been trying, without being aware they were doing it, to rebuild the broken bond between them. So many times their paths might have crossed.

And Gordi – Mado – had also ended up following in their footsteps, making her way to Sweden to see her daughter get married, without ever suspecting for a moment who she would find there.

Emily took a sip of her California red. The past had a way of almost catching up with people, she thought. Almost. Because the past could point the way to the present, but it was up to us to pave that way.

The police had found Esther at Albin's place, calmly eating her dinner at the table. She knew they were coming for her, and she had prepared bags for her and her son.

Esther and her Nino. It was hard for people to give more than they had received in life, Emily mused. When the odds were stacked against them, some people, like Mado, managed to make something of their lives. But many others could only dance with despair or flirt with madness as their suffering slowly ate away at their very existence. What could they ever hope to pass on to their children?

Flask Walk was resplendent in the shimmering lights her neighbours had strung up. Emily could hear singing coming through the wall from the maisonette next door. And the sounds of children laughing and crying with joy. She closed her eyes. And listened to this music she had never known. She thought about the Hugo poem, 'When the Child Appears'. Her own child had been snatched away from her before she could hear the sweet sound of his laughter. Emily exhaled the pain out of her chest. Swirled the wine around in her glass.

They had got back from Falkenberg the day before and hadn't had the heart to think about celebrating Christmas, let alone preparing a special meal. They just needed to be together and enjoy the silence. A silence filled with the presence of those who mattered the most. A silence as soothing as a warm embrace, which could only be filled with familiarity, love and trust.

Each in their own way, they contemplated their pain and their grief, opening their arms to those who were no longer there, picking a memory and fleshing it out until it hurt, bringing their absent ones back to the brink of life, where they could still smell their scent, hear their laugh and feel their lips on their cheek.

Emily sensed the caress of Jack's gaze on the nape of her neck, the gentle brush of his kiss on her skin. She turned around. In his eyes, she could see that he knew. He knew that she had strayed from him for a moment. But he also understood that her escapades with others were only bends in the road. And he loved finding her again, here with him, amid this silence. With them. Because the growing roots and branches of this new tree were all her doing. The new tree she had planted. Their new family tree.

Old Siset said to me
On the porch at dawn
While we waited for the sun
And watched the carts roll by

Siset, can't you see the stake
We're all tied up to?
If we never untie these knots
We will never be free!

If we all pull, then it will fall
It can't hold fast much longer
It will fall, yes, it will fall
It's rotten enough already

If you pull hard like that
And I pull hard like this
It will fall, yes, it will fall
And we will all be free

Excerpt from the song 'L'Estaca' (1968) by Lluís Llach,
Catalan singer and leading figure in the resistance
movement against the Franco regime.

Translated by David Warriner

Acknowledgements

WRITING *BLOOD SONG* brought memories of *Block 46* flooding back for me. Both novels emerged post-pregnancy, but this time there was double the trouble! As my grandmother would have said, I had my hands full, to say the least! Without the love and support of my Viking of a husband, none of this would have happened.

I want to say a huge thank-you to all of you readers and avid crime fiction fans for your messages that have given me goosebumps and tears of joy. Knowing that you were hungry for more was a huge motivation for me to write *Blood Song*, so there is a little part of you in every one of these pages.

Blood Song is a book about sisters, more than anything else. And so, I would like to dedicate these pages to my little sister, Elsa. She and my sons are my *raison d'être*. They motivate me and fill my heart with their joy and zest for life every growing day. Here's a little anecdote: when Elsa first read the manuscript, she asked me, 'should I be worried that you're dedicating a novel called *Blood Song* to me?!?'

There are sisters we grow up with, and sisters life brings our way later. Eva Muñoz, our fabulous Eva, is one of those sisters. She took us under her wing like a guardian angel, and a Catalan guardian angel at that, taking us by the hand and whirling us into a dance. Without you, my sweet Eva, *Blood Song* would not be *Blood Song*, because you were the one who told me all about the terrifying Francoist orphanages and prisons for women; you were the one who started the research we could not bring ourselves to turn a blind eye to. My sweet Eva, I owe the very essence of this book to you – and more.

As always, my parents, my tribe, *Papa* and *Maman* Lagunas have stood behind me, like an army all their own. Thank you, '*Paman*', for all your edits, readings, re-re-readings and babysitting, not to mention your encouragement and your big bouquets of love. Thank you also, my mother-in-law Britt, for your never-ending support.

Huge thanks to you too, Alexandra, for being so genuine and bringing so much strength, determination and joy my way.

Not to make anyone jealous, I would like to thank three of my simply exceptional publishers: My precious Lilas Seewald, whom you all know as my 'writing fairy godmother', who paved the way for me as an author and continues to guide me forwards from the heart with just as much passion and determination; the phenomenal force of nature that is Karen Sullivan, *Mrs Orenda Books*, to whom I owe so much of the Roy & Castells series' success, with a special mention for my beloved Anne, editor extraordinaire West, the Sullivan brothers, and of course Max, as well as the fabulous extended Team Orenda family; and finally, Gianni La Corte, a man of great passion with a true love for literature, who together with his wife Serena and family carries the Italian publishing house La Corte Editore.

Thank you with all my heart to my amazing English translator, David Warriner, whose talent has carried my voice across the Atlantic as well as the Channel. It doesn't hurt that he loves smelly cheese as much as I do!

To the team at Bragelonne, Stéphane, Yolande, Guillaume, Raoul, Alain, Leslie and Fanny, to name just a few of you, many, many thanks for believing in me and my stories, back then and still now.

Many thanks to the great Maxim Jakubowski for his unconditional support.

Tusen Takk to my fabulous fellow writer Thomas Enger, who took me by the hand with Scandinavian patience and walked me down the path to meet Nino and Esther when I felt too overwhelmed by the birth of my army of mini-Vikings to start writing again.

Sincerest thanks to Elisabet Guillot of the L'Étoile d'Asperger association, who helped me paint and strip our dear Aliénor by answering even my most embarrassing questions with admirable openness, honesty and spirit.

Huge thanks to the Catalan journalists Montse Armengou and Ricard Belis for their incredible investigative work into the children's homes under Franco's rule, which truly formed the cornerstone of my research for this book.

Many thanks also to Vincent Garcia for the CD of Spanish music that is so close to my heart and gave me Lluís Llach's voice for the closing lyrics to *Blood Song*.

When I was writing this book, I lost two of my very dear loved ones: my grandmother, who had a lot of Mado Castells in her, and Georges Alexis, the man who gave his name to my heroine. As well as acknowledging them in these lines, I wish I could hold them in my arms and hug them just a little bit tighter.

One more thing about the essence of *Blood Song*. This is a book that sits very close to home, even more than *Block 46*. First of all, because it talks about the Spanish people and their struggles, whose blood pulses through my own veins. My maternal grandfather was Catalan by birth and Valencian at heart, and my paternal grandfather fought in the International Brigades to try and save the Spanish Republic before being deported to the Buchenwald Nazi concentration camp – whose story I told in *Block 46*.

Blood Song also resonates a lot with me and my husband, because we are among those parents to whom Mother Nature denied children. Our three precious boys came to us only after a great many struggles, but what a joy it is now to have fought and won the battle. Many, many thanks to you, my darling Mattias, for agreeing to share and talk about this journey of ours that fills me with so much pride. Our journey has taught me that happiness truly lies not in the extraordinary, but in our day-to-day life.

London, 14 May 2019